Shoot
the
Moon

Shoot
the
Moon

A Novel

ISA ARSÉN

G. P. PUTNAM'S SONS
NEW YORK

PUTNAM
— EST. 1838 —
G. P. PUTNAM'S SONS
Publishers Since 1838
An imprint of Penguin Random House LLC
penguinrandomhouse.com

Hardcover ISBN: 9780593543887
Ebook ISBN: 9780593543900

Library of Congress Control Number: 2023943871

Printed in the United States of America
1st Printing

Interior art: Space imagery © Chikovnaya / Shutterstock

BOOK DESIGN BY ALISON CNOCKAERT

To my mother, for always welcoming me back into orbit.

It is no good trying to stop knowledge from going forward. Whatever Nature has in store for mankind, unpleasant as it may be, men must accept, for ignorance is never better than knowledge.

—LAURA FERMI (FROM *ATOMS IN THE FAMILY: MY LIFE WITH ENRICO FERMI*)

Shoot
the
Moon

Prologue

---✦---

1966—THE MANNED SPACECRAFT CENTER, DR. ALLEN GIBBS'S EMPTY OFFICE
Houston, Texas

I blew a piston of smoke through the open window and took another draw on its heels, my eyes fixed on the waxing moon hanging high above. The sill dug softly into my elbows as I drank the fresh air.

I was lucky the door had been unlocked, and luckier still the random room I'd chosen had a window. Beyond the door I'd shut tight behind me, the office-wide Christmas party carried on with a crush of seasonal noise and bluster I hadn't been doused in since I was a kid. My parents were the only ones of their friends who had gone and had a child amid the heaving groundswell of the 1940s. Having a daughter bouncing around like a free agent didn't deter Mother from throwing her Christmas party in excess every year. With the other lab men and their wives on leave from Los Alamos for only a precious handful of days, for one night a year our house was a tiny nucleus of normalcy warmed to bursting by laughter, spiced wine, and the popping of paper crackers I had helped make at the kitchen table the week prior.

I couldn't remember much from my childhood, but I could remember those parties.

I had one vivid memory left of my father. I turned it over in my head as I stared up at the moon, out at the sky, along the endless stars like batter flung against the scooped-out bowl of the night. As the only kid at the Christmas parties, I'd gotten good at entertaining myself. After enough stolen sips of amaretto made my lips pucker, tasting nothing like I had hoped, I sought curiosities beyond the bar cart or record cabinet.

I got great at eavesdropping.

I remembered standing just outside the kitchen archway while Daddy and four friends chipped ice from the freezer into their glasses and talked about a rare vacation one of them had managed to take to a dude ranch farther north.

When I peeked around the corner, I saw Daddy was smiling. His smiles were rare and precious to me, like the annual appearance of Mother's spiced rum cake. He was leaning languidly on a friend's shoulder, all of them dotted with little blue pins on their lapels, as though they'd been marked with bingo blotters, and he pointed at one of the other men. He swayed a little where he stood.

If they're going to drop another, he had announced, *I'd better be far away from here. That's all I'll say about that. You know what I mean.*

The others had chuckled and patted his shoulders and cheeks as they continued making their drinks. For the rest of that night, until I got tired and Daddy carried me carefully to my bedroom, the smell of his aftershave strong on his collar, an incessant itch of apprehension had buzzed under my skin.

The single moment was as clear to me in Dr. Gibbs's window as it had been when I was seven years old. I leaned forward onto the windowsill again, sticking my head out to breathe the light December air of our solitary stretch of Houston. The respite from humidity at this time of year dug me even deeper into those childhood thoughts of parties long past, the shapes and colors of them in the desert like vibrant movement through frosted glass.

New Mexico was nothing but a dream from here.

The door swung open behind me. A brief shout of the chatter outside underscored by Connie Francis wailing about "Baby's First Christmas" tugged me around and quieted again as whoever came in after me pulled the door shut.

"Occupied," I blurted.

The intruder looked far from offended. His tipsy smile beamed, and a thick pair of Buddy Holly glasses framed eyes that could have been sharp in their viridian shimmer if not for whatever battalion of cocktails swirled in his belly. His tie was loosened at his neck, his sport coat sleeves rucked up messily to his elbows, and he sauntered over to lean on the windowsill beside me as though I had invited him.

He waved an easy hand. "This isn't the restroom."

His hair was a sandy blond, still smoothly combed and parted despite his dishevelment. From so near, I could smell the faint touch of a woodsy cologne overpowered by sweet vermouth. The man snickered as his face brightened with mischief—he glanced over his shoulder and shot me a conspiratorial look as if we were already friends. "Although this is Gibbs's office, might as well be a shithouse."

The long taffy-pull of his voice was native to these parts of Texas, all honey-sticky vowels and back-of-the-tongue purl. My interloper fixed me a smile just sideways enough to be charming.

"I'm bothering you," he said plainly, like it was some sort of achievement.

I gave a tight shrug. "Not really."

My cigarette had one last draw in it before I stubbed it out on the sill. I dropped it into the full ashtray to my right. Mine was the only one with a rind of lipstick on its filter.

I fussed with the lay of my collar and smoothed my skirt, wishing I was still alone so I could tug at the band of my left nylon, which had worked itself askew. I held in a tight sigh. "Are you escaping, too?" I asked the man, looking at him in my periphery.

He glanced back at the door and shrugged. "Needed some air, and Gibbs won't ever shut the hell up about winning the straw-draw for the office with the window. So. Figured I knew where to try first."

I peered at the dark sky again. I glanced back at the stranger to find he had followed my gaze with a dreamy look on his face. The lines of his cheeks had softened. He had a proud mouth, a handsome set to his jaw . . . I forced myself to quit watching him and fixed my eyes back up at the moon, that heavy gaze of one pearly eye.

"Ain't she something?" the man murmured. I swallowed a bundle of nerves and tucked a lock of hair behind my ear. It curled in on itself, tickling the heel of my jaw. I ignored the shiver along my back.

"Must be some reason everyone wants to be first to land."

The man turned to me with a sideways grin. "Gimme some of yours."

I couldn't help the spasmodic little smile that chased its way onto my face as an answer to his. "What do you mean?"

"Some of your reasons—why would *you* want to go up there?"

I found my eyes searching habitually down to his breast pocket where a name tag might be, but of course, it was a party so we had all shed our skins for the evening. "You're on Apollo," I guessed, and correctly: he puffed up with pride.

"Norman," he said as he stuck out a hand, "call me Norm. Navigator."

I took his hand in mine and shook it with a firm grip. "Anne, call me Annie. Secretary."

The man, Norm, gave me another grin that wasn't so giddy this time. A fizzing sensation prickled my mind like a brief and dazzling searchlight.

"So, Annie secretary," Norm said, "why do you want to go to the moon?"

I leaned through the window again and thought for a moment. "I suppose from up there, everything down here would feel so . . . manageable. As though I could reach out"—I stretched my hand up, pretending to pinch the moon between my thumb and middle finger—"and pluck the Earth out of the sky to keep it safe in my pocket."

Norm turned to look at me, his expression open and wondrous. He was even more handsome than I had thought at first glance. "And what makes you think Earth needs keeping safe?"

His voice was soft, as though we were sharing secrets. *The fact it's so fragile,* I wanted to say, *the fact we could crack in half at any moment—do you know* anything *about the bomb?*

But of course Norm knew about the bomb. He was a rocket man, only just the other side of that work's coin. I gave him a wry smile instead. "What makes you think it doesn't?"

Norm leaned forward and kissed me square on the mouth.

I hadn't kissed a boy since I was sixteen: poor Mickey Fields in his father's Thunderbird, whacking his knee on the gearshift when he tried to lean forward and feel me up after I told him it was okay.

This was different. This felt . . . right.

Norm held us there for a moment, our lips still. "Sorry," he breathed when he pulled back. I was left with the pleasant cloy of cherries from his drinks.

I stared at him. "It's okay."

Norm peered at me so closely, honesty eddying in those green, green eyes. "Do we know each other?" he murmured. A swooping sensation flew through my body. I ignored it.

"I don't know." My lips brushed his as he leaned into me again, as though testing whether I was just a mirage from the bottom of several Manhattans.

"I'm pretty sure I'm drunk," he said. I snorted as I tried to swallow a laugh, which made his shoulders jump against mine with his own laughter.

He came forward and kissed me again with a pitch almost like another apology. I gripped his elbow, warm solidity through his rumpled sleeves, and tried to speak back without saying anything, either: *This is good. You know what I mean.*

01:00

---*---

1948—THE APODACA HOUSE, THE BACK GARDEN
Santa Fe, New Mexico

The far corner of the garden was filling up again. Annie didn't know where the strange objects came from. She never knew where they came from, but even though they were a miscellany of staplers and paperweights and all sorts of scribbled notes, it was always exciting to find them.

The garden sat at the back of the house. The house on Apodaca was a cozy stack of adobe where the front yard spilled tidily through its creaky gate. Through the front door, the foyer opened up into three paths—left hall, center hall, right hall: a choice to be made every time Annie came home with her little hand held tightly in Mother's.

Daddy was gone most days then, gone so often that Annie was missing him more regularly than seeing him. But the day after they dropped that great big something onto a great big somewhere far across the sea, Daddy had come home and knelt down in that foyer of choices and held Annie so hard she could have sworn she felt him crying.

But Daddy didn't cry. Daddy was a grown-up. Grown-ups kept secrets, and drank drinks that tasted like matchsticks, and made sure to shut the door behind them and speak very, very softly when they argued.

Annie was very good at keeping secrets, too. She never did tell anyone else about the corner of the garden and its staplers, its paperweights, its impossible pieces of paper.

The little girl from nowhere appeared one evening when the sun was getting low and hot-heavy. Mother was in the den inside, and Annie had just picked up a typewriter eraser with the nub worn low from under the rosebushes, where she liked to hunt for treasures.

"Hello," the girl said. Annie looked up and forgot about the eraser.

She was a little shorter than Annie. She had a pair of glasses and a pretty face that looked sort of like a young version of Fran Allison from the television. Her hair was strawberry-fair, blonder than the auburn red of Annie's own, and instead of wearing it short at the chin like Annie did, the girl had hers long in two pretty braids. She wore a striped shirt and tan corduroy pants. Annie fiddled with the hem of her skirt and scuffed the toe of her saddle shoes on the white gravel.

"Good evening," she said, as mother had taught her to be polite to everyone, even strangers. "My name is Annie Fisk. I'm eight years old. What's your name?"

"I'm Diana," the girl said with a wide, toothy grin—one of the front ones was missing in a tiny gap, and Annie burned briefly with envy. "I'm eight years old, too."

With the camaraderie only a child could muster, Annie decided immediately that they must be the best of friends simply by virtue of being the same age. "Do you also live on Apodaca Street?" she asked, hopeful for a neighborhood kid who wasn't practically grown up. Diana shook her head.

"No," she said simply, and she seemed to stop herself. "I'm from far away," she said with a touch of hesitation, as if her mother had also taught her all the right ways to say things. "Just visiting."

Well, if she was just visiting, Annie would have to make her visit worthwhile. She stooped briefly to hunt around in the soil bed before holding up another trinket more interesting than the forgotten eraser: a tiny model rocket, patterned in black and white, which fit perfectly in the palm of her hand.

"Do you want to play spacemen?" Annie asked, and this time Diana nodded.

But when it felt they had only just begun, Diana stopped to look at a slim silver band on her wrist. A tiny clockface was worked into it. Annie thought of her mother's cocktail bracelet, which she saved for special occasions like her Christmas parties. This must have been a special occasion for Diana.

"I have to go," she said, and stuck out her hand; handshakes, those were also something grown-ups did. "I'll see you again soon, okay?"

Annie took Diana's hand and gave a firm shake, just the way Daddy taught her the first time she met his friends from the big lab. "You'll come back?"

"Of course I'll come back!"

Annie beamed and believed her.

An idea came in a flash—a souvenir!

Annie glanced over her shoulder to make sure Mother couldn't see them through the sliding back door into the den. She hunted into the back of the rosebush, where the biggest blossoms were safe from the breezes and birds and still had all their petals, and snipped a billowing pink rose from its stem with her fingernails.

"Here." Annie held it out to Diana in one flat hand while she wiped the green residue off on the side of her skirt. "So you remember where you found me."

Diana stepped carefully over to the end of the soil plot, where the wall turned, hiding the far side of the garden from the house. She turned once in place and gave another big grin as she gently took the rose. "See you, Annie."

Something itched at Annie's periphery. She looked away to glance at it and blinked, finding nothing.

When she turned to ask Diana if next time she might bring the playing cards she had mentioned, Diana was gone.

"Annie, dinner!"

The patio door rolled open before Annie could scramble up the garden wall and see if Diana had somehow vaulted over it and begun tearing across the neighbors' lawns already. How fast was she? Was everyone so fast where she came from?

"Annie?"

She managed to tear her attention away from the horizon and abandon the idea. "Coming, Mother!"

Annie straightened her skirt and made for the patio door with one last glance at the bushes, the hidden trinkets, the tall impasse of the garden wall.

Diana had said she would come again. Annie had a new friend, just for her, and she would be back soon.

1958—THE APODACA HOUSE, THE DRIVEWAY
Santa Fe, New Mexico

"I *measured* you," I grunted, shoving my shoulder against one last suitcase. "I know *exactly* how much room is in there; you didn't *grow* overnight, so tell me *why* you won't fit now, you *son of a—*"

"Annie?"

One final heave slid the clothing trunk home into its slot in the yellow Nash Rambler so endearingly ugly Mother all but jumped at the chance to get rid of it. I dusted my hands off on my hips and turned as I smeared a lock of hair off my forehead with the back of my hand. I pushed my glasses up my nose. "Yes?"

My mother was making her steady way down the front walk—the world paused for Helen Fisk, and it would wait as long as she bid it with her quiet, careful way.

"Here." Mother stopped beside me, eyeing the looming stack of luggage I had finally wrangled, and extended one hand without preamble. "It was your father's."

My eyebrows went up of their own volition. The red-varnished fingers of my mother's loose fist waited for me. I wordlessly opened my palm. A small weight, metallic but warmed by Mother's skin, dropped into my hand with surprising density.

"He always meant for this to be yours." Mother, face blank, plucked an invisible mote of dust from the edge of one sleeve. "It's small, but I think it suits you."

It was an upside-down teardrop-shaped lapel pin of shiny royal blue. At its center, an abstract jot of white lightning coming down from an eyeball shape cracked a yellow circle into pieces. The iris of the eye was a blue star ringed with red.

"This was Daddy's?" I looked up at Mother, frowning. Her expression was trained, but I saw a flash of sympathy pass through it.

"It's from Project Y."

I stared at her, my heart tightening in my chest. "Did—did he ever wear it?"

I turned it over to see its tiny clasp, a serial number on the back, all of it so painstakingly exact. I shouldn't have been surprised that atomic physicists could make delicate things. Their science was micro- and pico-, elements that needed to be handled with such careful attention that to split them was to transform them entirely.

Mother regarded the pin in my flat palm. "On occasion." She brushed a glossy pin curl from her temple with one graceful finger— the barest hint of gray played at her roots, well-hidden. "Mostly just when the others were wearing them, too. You know how he felt about bringing his work home with him."

Her even expression tolled familiarly deep in me. Did I? Did I truly know anything about my father?

What did you see, Annie?

Mother had looked me straight in the eye the night Daddy died and posed the question. That day was like a hole punched through reality, a sucking black vacuum that dragged the rest of my childhood into obscurity along with it. The only thing I could remember was swooning on my feet.

I don't know.

Tell me what you saw. Mother had gripped me hard by both shoulders. My eyes had welled up.

Red, I stammered, *everything was red.*

She covered her face briefly with one hand and looked dangerously close to crying—but she schooled herself and drew her hands down my arms until she had both my hands gripped hard in hers. *It was a heart attack,* she whispered.

What?

It was a heart attack, Annie.

Reality's teeth, ugly and long, caught up to me in that moment and snapped shut clean through my middle. Heavy tears broke from my lashes. *Daddy's dead?*

She held me then, kneeling and rocking and lulling me as I bawled into her shoulder in the kitchen. I remembered the oven timer ringing. Neither of us rose to turn it off for a long while.

She hadn't held me since.

Beside the hatchback, I glanced up at Mother as my throat grew tight. "Thank you." I glanced away and pinched at the inner corners of my eyes to keep the sudden, spiny tears from coming. "I—I'll wear it. It will make me think of him."

Mother nodded, her expression unreadable. "Do."

A breeze blew over from the northwest and rustled the cottonwood trees overhead. The distance between my mother and me felt infinite in that moment—she wanted me to stay here, take a typing job somewhere nearby, but we both knew the only place I would have fit in was Los Alamos. Mother would throw herself naked into the Rio Grande before she let me follow directly in Daddy's footsteps.

I didn't have any concrete plan besides getting the hell out of Dodge and seizing my education in both hands—first, a stopover in the heart of Texas to get my degree at St. Christopher the Martyr, then probably onward to Georgia after graduating. Two distant cousins of mine lived outside of Atlanta and had done rather well for themselves with a pair of handsome husbands and a brood each of apple-cheeked babies.

The very thought of marriage made my gut turn over on itself. Mother always told me I'd feel differently when I met *the right one*, as though men were an equation to be solved and would seem more appealing in my preferred vocabulary.

I liked men just fine. They were nice to look at. I just couldn't for the life of me imagine myself as a wife, with a child, with a husband who might disappear at any given moment just like Daddy had.

"You'll drive safely, won't you?" Mother nodded and said with an air of finality. I swallowed and pocketed Daddy's pin, glancing at the full-up car and the trunk tied to the luggage rack on the roof.

"Yep." I patted the side of the car like the withers of an old nag. "I filled the tank last night, and I have the route marked onto the map."

"Don't let any strangers pay for your food."

"I won't."

"And be sure you deadbolt your motel room in El Paso."

"I *will*."

Mother fixed me with a look, the same one I got just a couple years back when she'd come home early from her shift at the dry goods shop and found me and Peggy Lipton giggling on the floor in the den with a half-gone bottle of wine between us. "You're sure you have enough money?"

"I'm sure," I insisted. "When you told me to start saving, believe it or not, I listened."

Sighing lightly, Mother seemed assuaged. She mulled something over for a moment, there beside the front gate and the open trunk. "I hope you know I love you very much, Annie," she said.

She was half-frowning, and so it took a moment to register that Mother had just shown me the most affection I'd had in years. My heart stuttered, as did I: "I—love you, too."

Both of us hesitated when we stepped forward, but she folded me into a hug after a moment. I had a good three inches on her; the last time we'd hugged, she'd been taller than me. She gathered my head down into her shoulder and squeezed lightly. "I'm proud of you," she said into my hair. I couldn't help but tear up against her blouse.

I could think of nothing worth saying when she released me, so I turned quickly and hefted the trunk shut. Clearing my throat and sniffling sharply, I swiped at my lower eyelids beneath my glasses and nodded once. "I'll call. I'm sure the motel will have a phone I can use."

Mother gave me a nod and the palest touch of a smile. I would never get any sweeping acknowledgment of the heavy weight we both carried, the both of us stumbling through life after Daddy. But a smile like that might be enough. "That would be lovely," she said.

Before Mother could turn back to the house, I reached forward and hugged her again. I buried my face in her hair, the geranium scent of her powder makeup, and reveled in the memories that didn't slip through my grasp like sand: Mother teaching me how to drive, showing me how to mix a proper drink on my eighteenth birthday, instructing me how to change a tire on the Cadillac here in the front yard with her hair done up in pin curls; filling in the blank spaces of Daddy's absence in the small ways she could.

I pressed a brief kiss to the crown of her head. In the tree beside the gate, a crow muttered gayly to itself. Daylight was burning. "Drive safely," Mother replied, her voice thick, and patted my cheek once before gliding away through the gate. It latched softly behind her. The front door fell shut. A breeze swept past and gently rattled the branches above me. I settled into the driver's seat and started the engine with its tumbling growl. It was eleven hours to San Antonio, and I was determined to do it in two days. I slipped my left hand into my pocket and stroked Daddy's pin with my thumb before shifting the car into gear.

1958—THE COLLEGE AND ACADEMY OF ST. CHRISTOPHER THE MARTYR, A LECTURE HALL
San Antonio, Texas

"Reviewing the basic properties of ellipses. Firstly, they're defined by two points, two foci—"

Professor Laitz drew a wide arc that soared across the whole of the board. An ellipse came to life, stark in white, and he denoted two axes with tidy dotted lines. From the back of the lecture hall, I copied the shape judiciously onto my page of notes.

Laitz dashed two marks onto the shape, *chak chak,* quick with his chalk. "The sum of the distances between two foci, at any point on the ellipse, is constant. Secondly, the eccentricity. The flatter the ellipse, the more eccentric. For example, a circle has an eccentricity of zero, and a parabola has an eccentricity of one."

A lofty sigh floated up from beside me. I spared a glance to my right and caught sight of someone vaguely familiar—one of the two, *maybe* three, other women in all my other classes. I had noticed her in this lecture before. She never sat in the same seat twice, and never beside me until today. She caught my look with her heavy-lashed brown eyes and leaned over to me.

"Are you catching any of this?" she whispered.

I let my gaze flit to her notebook propped on the little boomerang curve of our writing desks. Where my page was riddled with detailed notes, bullet points, copies of Laitz's illustrations, hers was bursting with rambling sketches. Beneath the casual curve of her hand holding her pencil, I noticed the edge of what looked like my profile, my father's roman nose and the edge of my round glasses visible through her fingers.

I angled my head toward her ever so slightly without taking my attention away from the head of the hall. "What part are you stuck on?"

We had enough space between us and the majority of the class, the backs of their heads in slick pompadour and ducktail haircuts, that nobody would turn around and glare at our chatter—they expected it from us anyway.

Her face twitched into a wry smile. She had a mane of wavy blonde hair down to her shoulders, teased and folded in a similar style as several other girls around campus. I had seen her in our hall, with fluffy slippers on her feet and a blue bathrobe down to her knees, her calves bared as she went to and fro between her room and the showers. *Evelyn*, that was her name. I remembered seeing it on her door. Evelyn Moore.

I cleared my throat tightly and pushed away the image of Evelyn shooting me a smile the first time we passed each other in the corridor on our floor, me with my toiletries clutched tight to my chest and anxious I might accidentally let my gaze wander a little too far in the communal bathroom for any reason beyond plain observance of my hallmates.

"All of it," Evelyn whispered, her unpainted lips sly in their curvature. "Last time I heard the word 'eccentric' it was applied to a sculptor, not a planet."

Professor Laitz had drawn another set of foci around concentric sets of ellipses. I itched briefly under my left sleeve cuff and adjusted my glasses. "Well."

Angling my notes toward her, I scratched the equation Laitz was writing as part of the Hohmann transfer from one planetary orbit to another—$a=\frac{1}{2}(r1+r2)$—at the top corner of the page and circled it. "To travel from one circular orbit to another, the point at which the transfer ellipse is furthest from the sun is equal to the larger orbit value, and the point at which it's closest to the sun is equal to the smaller."

Evelyn watched me evenly. Her eyelids had a weighted quality to them, a soft gravity as though her lashes drew her gaze down, down, down toward her mascaraed bottom lid. She dressed like a Kerouac heroine, with blue jeans and a knit blouse—at striking odds with my own carefully tailored skirt, starched middy, and a smart little cardigan to go with my sensible collegiate Mary Janes. On my lapel, I had taken to wearing my father's pin for good luck as I found my footing.

My skin felt hot under Evelyn's stare but not uncomfortably so. She extended one slim finger and pointed to my note sheet, her knuckle brushing the heel of my hand. "So that's the moon?"

I nodded. "And if someone were to launch from Earth to get there," I murmured, tracing the slim edge of my ellipse with my thumb as an excuse to pull my hand away from hers and rescue myself from the way it made my pulse jitter, "this calculation would get them to land safely, instead of over- or under-shooting it. Like Sputnik, but flung out even further."

Evelyn hummed recognition to herself and nodded. "Like a sling-shot."

"Yes," I said, "exactly. A moonshot."

She smiled and propped her chin on the hand holding her pencil. "Shoot the moon," she hummed to herself, before blowing one edge of her soft bangs from her forehead with a slouch of amused defeat. "You're smart. I don't think I'm cut out for this stuff."

"No," I said, frowning and careful to keep my voice low, pointing at the page again, "you did just fine, you got it. Like a slingshot. That's exactly how it works."

Evelyn looked at me, her bright gaze searching around mine like someone digging through the overfull clutter of a cabinet drawer. I didn't look away from her. Not immediately.

When the hour was through, Laitz released us with his usual airy farewell and students both deep in their notes and nodding to bored-stiff sleep began rousing themselves to leave. As I shut my notebook, Evelyn stopped my hand flat on the cover. Her almond-shaped nails were varnished a soft, pearly pink. I hadn't repainted mine, chipped to hell after unpacking the car on my own, since I stripped them over the bathroom sink the first night I arrived here.

"Will you walk with me?" Evelyn asked over the clatter of students packing up and milling to the door. I could have no sooner refused than torn my eyes from the winsome grin she gave me.

She led the way, talking easily now that we weren't hunkered over diagrams of planetary trajectories. Evelyn had grown up farther north, close to the border of Oklahoma. Her daddy was in ranching, her mother ran their house of eight tight as a barracks, and she wanted nothing more than to be a painter.

"Why is a painter taking Astronomy 101?" I asked, our feet falling into unconscious step on the sidewalk. The September sun lanced down from the sky without a single mountain to cage it in, endless and blue and rolling with thick, white clouds.

"The paint is where my heart's at," Evelyn said, casually shaking a hand through her hair. "My mother refused to send me to school to 'draw pictures,' so I'm snagging a humanities degree. I needed a science. Space seemed fun, from the other end of the course catalog."

Fun. Space was so much more than *fun*, but I stayed quiet. Evelyn hadn't signed up for my passions when she asked me to walk with her. I chewed on the inside of my cheek for several brisk footsteps.

"You still paint on your own time?" I asked. Evelyn nodded.

"I'll come away with a teaching certificate, which I suppose is good since it might take some time 'til I have enough weight behind my name to start getting into galleries." She leaned closer without breaking her stride as though we were scheming. "But between you and me, I think I'll just end up running off to West Texas and living alone in the desert. I want to be the next Georgia O'Keeffe. She really has this whole life thing figured out, I'd say. You ever hear of her?"

My mother had O'Keeffe prints hung back home at Apodaca. She and my father had bought them from the artist herself at a place called Ghost Ranch when I was just a kid — they took a summer there after Mother told me plainly, as she so delicately put it when I asked about the prints once in high school, that *Daddy's doctor said he needed some fresh air.* Apparently, I had stayed with my aunt in Montana for two months. I couldn't remember anything about the trip.

My gut panged with the first big dose of homesickness I'd had since reaching Texas.

"I'm from New Mexico," I said, which was definition enough for Evelyn. She stopped walking and fixed me with a wondrous look.

"My daddy took me to New York in '46 to see her retrospective." A pretty blush had risen at her cheeks, and I couldn't have looked away even if those huge clouds hanging above us suddenly burst into flames. "Have you seen her stuff? There was this one piece I kept going back to the whole time we were there. She painted the daytime moon through a steer's bone. Does the sky really look like that?"

A rush of something light and limitless flitted through me, making my fingers tighten around the straps of my bookbag.

"It's like . . ." I said when I found my voice again. "It's like something just scooped out the earth and poured the sky right in after it."

Evelyn smiled sideways at me. "You a poet, Annie?"

She said my name easily, with a certain reverence I couldn't quite divine. I shook my head, my tongue more than a little dry. "Definitely not. I just like numbers."

Evelyn laughed, her head tossing prettily on her long neck. She nodded backward at the mathematics hall. "Don't sell yourself short, I'd bet you're smarter than any of the boys in that building."

I glanced at its stony heft, bold and serious against the horizon behind us. When I turned back to her, Evelyn had drawn a pack of Salems from her purse and tapped one out to hold between two fingers. She passed a second one to me.

"My father was a scientist," I explained, unprompted, as Evelyn reached out with a blue enamel lighter and sparked my cigarette to life. I took the first drag—menthol curled cool and sharp across my tongue. Everything about my new friend was jarringly fresh, the whole of her simmering under an alluring exterior. I held the flavor in my mouth until it began to burn. "I'm basically his carbon copy, to my mother's chagrin," I said as I exhaled.

Evelyn's answering chuckle around her own draw was little more than a sniff. She smoked delicately, those shimmery short fingernails holding the cigarette at the corner of her mouth. "Mothers are a trip," she said. "Mine saddled me with her middle name and then had the audacity to get uppity about it when I didn't turn out exactly like her."

"Mine did the same thing."

Evelyn tossed out a laugh in full then, a coyote's bark on crystal water. "No kidding? Mine is Florence. What's yours?"

"Helen," I said. "We could sue for damages."

When Evelyn laughed again, a hot coil of camaraderie swelled gently at the base of my throat. By the time we approached the library,

Evelyn's destination, she had already invited me to her room that weekend to listen to records.

"Bring your favorite album," she ordered over her shoulder as farewell. She turned on one heel to face me and kept walking backward as she made for the firm concrete mouth of the library. "And a bottle of wine, your pick. They're sticklers about age laws, but they'll look the other way at the place on Broadway and Burr since you're pretty."

I tried to ignore how easily she applied the word *pretty* to me—as though it made all the sense in the world. I didn't tend to look at myself in the mirror much beyond making sure I was presentable enough not to get laughed out of a classroom. The optics were a horrible seesaw: If I looked too plain, I would be little more than a mosquito whine in the ear of the men who taught my courses. If I looked too polished, none of them would take me seriously. I hated it.

But when Evelyn called me pretty, I didn't hate it.

On my way to a trigonometry lecture next, I made sure I was at least halfway across the quad again before I tipped my nose down and sniffed my collar. Evelyn's perfume had attached itself when she hugged me goodbye. She wore a scent I didn't recognize, a dry sandalwood that made me think of the desert.

She really has this whole life thing figured out, I'd say.

Daddy used to say there were lines that bound us to other people, unseen and unfelt until they pulled us together. He thought the idea of fate was silly, but those invisible threads were something he held close until he was gone.

I couldn't hold back the tentative laugh that leapt from me, books clutched to my chest and feet quick on the pavement. The Texas sun was hot on my face. I had a new friend who thought I was pretty. I was learning how to theoretically reach the moon. Perhaps I could figure out this whole *life thing*, too.

1949—CONEY ISLAND CAFÉ, A BOOTH
Albuquerque, New Mexico

One of Annie's favorite places to visit was Albuquerque, because the best ice cream in the world lived in Albuquerque.

The café clattered and hummed like the inside of a beehouse as Annie stuck another spoonful of sweet cream into her mouth. She savored it just like she was savoring the whole day. Not only was she in Albuquerque, and not only was she wearing her new white shoes with the blue frilled socks, but Daddy was with her and Mother this time.

Having Daddy for an outing on a Saturday was a rare gift. They only got to have him on clear, perfect days like this if the lab didn't need him. She was proud that Daddy was important enough to be needed, but it was nice to have him to herself.

Annie had begun to see the rarity of Daddy's free time like a lending library of his warmth. She wasn't sad when he had to work so long as someone else needed him just as much as she did, but it didn't seem like Mother always saw it that way. Annie ate another spoonful of her ice cream and watched them as Mother prodded Daddy's knee under the table.

"So, jellybean," Daddy said, his chin on his hand with a smile directed at Annie, "how's school?"

Annie shrugged. Mother gave her a pointed look, so she swallowed around her spoon. "It's good."

The corners of Mother's eyes tightened a little. "She's doing well in reading, but her mathematics leave something to be desired."

"Oh?" Daddy cocked his head and raised his eyebrows. The daylight through the diner window caught the corner of his glasses and winked at Annie. "A Fisk who doesn't like numbers?"

Annie hazarded a small smile.

Mother turned the tiny coffee spoon around in her yet-untouched coffee cup. "Her last progress report was fine," Mother said, looking into the swirl of the coffee, "but I don't know if—"

"Helen."

Daddy's voice was soft and his large, delicate hand gently touched her elbow. Annie had always thought that Daddy's hands looked like a dove's wings—long lines, delicate bones, fair and lightly freckled. Mother looked at Daddy for a moment before digging into her purse for her cigarettes. She nodded at Annie. "Tell your father about your class, Annie," she said. "He misses you."

The idea hit Annie somewhere below the gut and twisted hard. Adults didn't miss people. Annie was looking forward to not having to miss people when she got older—that sick and pitching sense of loneliness, the unending worry of it jittering around behind her teeth, Annie had always believed one grew out of missing people by at *least* high school.

Daddy's eyes were honest, all patience, when she looked straight at him. She reveled in the cold ice cream against her tongue before swallowing it down. "I like reading," Annie said, corroborative. Under one poised thumb, Mother's lighter sparked to life. "My teacher is nice, too. She has pretty hair."

"Do you have some school friends?" Daddy asked. "I knew a few of my buddies at the university *way* back when we were just ankle-biters in school together."

Annie swirled her spoon in her softening mass of ice cream. Whenever Daddy talked about *the university*, it was from the life he and Mother lived before New Mexico—back when they lived in Pittsburgh and Daddy had something called tenure, when Annie was just a baby. She shrugged. "Not really."

She could have told him about the girl in the backyard, Diana, with her gap teeth and her glasses and her sunshiny smile. Diana was like nobody Annie had ever known before, but these days Annie was growing sure Diana was imaginary. She never stuck around for very long, and Annie hesitated to tell anyone about her. Daddy always treated Annie like she was such a big girl, and big girls did not play with imaginary people. They made friends with real people.

So Annie said nothing.

Daddy sipped his fizzy drink and made a soft sound around the lip of its sweating glass. "Nobody? Not even anyone from the neighborhood?"

"The neighborhood kids are too old for her, and the family across the street are all fundies," Mother said lightly. Daddy's expression flattened and his left cheek buckled gently, as though he was chewing on the inside of it. Daddy tended to do that when he got to thinking a lot, especially when he was in one of his blue moods. But Annie hadn't seen him in a bad blue mood in a long time.

"I like being on my own," Annie said simply, a bid for peace. Even with her ice cream and Mother's coffee and Daddy's drink—the things that made them happy—the air felt stiff and sour, but Annie couldn't figure out why.

"You should try making some friends, jellybean," Daddy suggested gently, swirling his glass a little. "You might like your alone time, I know I do, but there's a difference between being alone and being lonely."

Those words were synonyms. Annie had been learning about those at school. They meant the same thing, *alone* and *lonely*, so how could there be a difference? She looked down into her ice cream cup and drew aimless shapes in what was quickly becoming soup.

"Don't play with your food, baby," Mother said on an exhale. Annie put her spoon down.

A short silence persisted before Daddy stood up with a sigh, unfolding to his full height and replacing his hat on his head. "Shall we go for a drive?"

Daddy was the best driver in the entire southwest. He steered his big red Cadillac with the confidence of someone piloting a whole rocket, and sometimes if Annie closed her eyes, she could pretend he was driving out among the stars. The desert wind tossing Annie's hair around her face could become stardust, the leftover slipstreams of meteors, and when it was just her and Daddy it felt endless.

Mother extinguished her cigarette in the little glass dish beside the napkin container on the table and hitched her purse to her elbow. She held a hand out for Annie across the table. "That sounds lovely. Say thank you, Annie."

She took Mother's hand, waved to the clerk behind the register at the counter, and squinted in the lowering angle of midday sun when Daddy held the door open with the little bell on the lintel chiming.

The whole drive up from Albuquerque, Annie drowsed easily to the tune of the engine grumbling at the pace of the highway beneath it. Sleep stole her gently, and she curled sideways along the back seat with her cheek pressed to the sun-warm leather.

Between the bands of cottony consciousness, Annie became aware of Mother and Daddy talking in hushed, reined tones. Mother had lit another cigarette, the smell of it sharp.

". . . needs you to be home more reliably," Mother said with low intensity, "and I need you here, too. I'm not going to raise her alone."

"You're not *alone*. It doesn't work like that, you think I can just take it off and hang it up like a coat? What she *needs* is for me not to bring that shit home."

Shit was Daddy's swear of choice. Annie had never heard him say anything worse than *shit* in her life.

Mother sniffed tartly. At a soft tapping sound, Annie visualized her stubbing out her cigarette in the ashtray compartment. "You've always been more comfortable hiding in that lab than you are talking to me about it."

Silence persisted then. Annie cracked her eyelids open.

"I don't—" Daddy said, and stopped himself. In the rearview mirror, Annie saw him purse his lips briefly. "I can't stand the idea of there being another one of you to leave behind, if I . . . buckle. Again."

"Jesus, Ford."

"Can you blame me for thinking it?"

"No, but—I thought we were past this part."

"Which part?" Daddy's voice was tight.

"The part where you're still thinking about it."

"I can't just quit *thinking* about it. I know *you* can, Helen, but you don't know what it's like. You don't know what any of this is like."

"Well, if you keep letting yourself dwell on it, you can't possibly be helping your case by tempting fate."

Mother sounded alarmed in the quiet way she did when something bad had already happened, like the night she found Annie trying to hide her badly bleeding thumb after helping slice carrots for dinner.

"Fate?" Daddy spat it out like a bad word, like *shit*. "Please. We've gone too far playing God; if there was ever a plan it's out the window now. We just get to stand and watch the same fucking song and dance all over again. There's no future. *None*."

"Ford."

"It's all still stirring in the Pacific, just you wait. I'm not going to bring another child into a world I don't even know how to explain anymore."

"*Stop it,*" Mother snapped. "Just because you have clearance doesn't mean your paranoia is wisdom."

The engine growled, a steady acceleration. Annie held her breath. Mother was glaring at him, angrier than Annie could remember seeing her. Maybe it was because Daddy had said . . . *that* word.

A thick silence lingered, simmering.

"Maybe it's for the best then," Mother said, her voice low and furious. "If you insist on foxholing yourself like this, then I should start counting it as some sick blessing we haven't been able to take another to term."

The car lurched as Daddy stomped the brakes and yanked the car onto the shoulder. Mother let out an instinctive gasp, and Annie's eyes flew open wide as she threw her arms out to catch herself on the front seat with her hands. She slid halfway to the ground between the cushions but sat up easily, rubbing her eyes and squinting blearily at the front seat.

"Goddamn it!" Mother shouted. She whirled around to face Annie, and shock melted into relief for the briefest moment before she shut her eyes momentarily. Her red mouth in a firm, worried line, Mother reached over and refixed the barrette in Annie's hair. "Are you alright?"

"Sorry, jellybean."

Daddy's voice was tremulous. His knuckles were white on the wheel. In the mirror, the sadness in Daddy's pale-gray stare was so bare and depthless that it made Annie's ears ring.

"I'm okay," Annie said.

Daddy flexed his hands on the wheel, the leather squeaking. "Don't be cruel to me, Helen."

"Ford, can th—"

"I understand you're upset with me," he insisted, raising his voice evenly overtop of hers, "but I can't stand knowing you can be cruel."

Mother watched him without blinking. The edges of her mouth trembled. Her chin creased softly. Annie's heart lurched.

"Can we go home?" she asked, her voice small and sleepy.

Mother glanced back at her and then again at Daddy before she nodded, blinking a lot, and shifted in her seat to stare hard out the passenger-side window. Daddy turned to give Annie a soft, bruised smile. The sadness was still there, but poorly hidden.

"Sure."

Annie did not fall asleep again the whole way home. The landscape peeled apart as the zipper of the northward road carved up through it. Daddy flicked the radio on to a twangy station when it was clear Mother had nothing left to say, and Annie continued stealing glances at him the whole way back to Apodaca.

The sadness did not leave, persistent and dark. Annie wondered if Daddy grew tired of hiding it; if it was sometimes easier to let it show at the front of his stare instead of strong-arming it to the back. Annie knew that compulsion, at least a little bit, to hide.

Daddy caught her watching once the car trundled up La Bajada Hill. The corners of his eyes creased with a reassuring smile as Annie's ears popped faintly at the altitude. At the edge of the mirror, Annie saw Mother's hand clasped ardently in Daddy's grip between them even though Mother was still looking away through the window.

✳

1949—THE APODACA HOUSE, CHRISTMAS
Santa Fe, New Mexico

The crisp lightness of wintertime met Annie's face when she slipped out into the backyard. As she eased the patio door shut behind her, the rollick of Mother's record player spinning carol after carol fell quiet.

Annie welcomed the stillness of solace from the party. Being around so many people at once had blushed her cheeks to a high burn and made her nerves jangle like bells.

A pair of Daddy's colleagues were standing at the far side of the patio. They weren't close enough to Annie's secret spot by the roses to make her uneasy, but they had spotted her coming outside. She approached them with her chin high and her shiny red shoes smart against the patio. Both of them stopped mid-sentence.

"Good evening," Annie announced with her very best posture.

The men each had a cigarette in hand. The shorter of the two had his tie loosened around his neck and his cheeks tinted lightly red from the sidelong throw of light coming from the wide sliding doors to the den.

"Well hey there, Annie," the taller one said, and Annie wished she knew his name, too. "Taking a breather?"

"It gets loud in there." Annie nodded her chin over her shoulder the way she had seen Mother do sometimes in conversation. "What do you do at the lab?" she asked.

Both men laughed. The one with the catawampus necktie was a little louder—he had a round face and broad shoulders, with a voice a touch lower than his companion's.

"Yeah, your daddy isn't allowed to tell you much, huh?" he asked. He looked at Annie with a bright pair of spirited eyes, wavery with drink.

The taller man put his free hand in his pocket and took a tight drag on his cigarette before angling toward Annie. He wasn't quite stooping, but seemed to take her into consideration as he would an adult who simply happened to be quite short. "The government says so," he clarified.

"Is it like school?" Annie asked. The shorter man laughed again, which made Annie frown. "I don't see what's so funny about school. I like school."

"'Course you do," the rumpled man said, "you're Ford Fisk's girl." He went carefully to one knee and caught his balance on the back of the porch chair beside him when he tipped slightly. Annie peered at him at eye level.

He gave her a quick little smile and took a finishing draw of his smoke. "What do you know about what we do there?" he asked, stooped sideways to grind it out.

"Archie." The tall man's voice had an edge of sternness. He gestured with his cigarette, an abstract pattern trailing along its end in the chittering nighttime. "The worst stuff is behind us," he said to Annie, "you'll see. Don't worry so much about it."

Archie was apparently the one crouched in front of Annie; he snorted to himself. He said nothing. Annie turned to the tall man and put her hands on her skinny hips. "Well, what's so bad about the lab? My daddy doesn't think it's bad at all."

"It's complicated," the tall man said. "Not really stuff a kid like you needs to be thinking about."

Unswayed, Annie's curiosity got the better of her manners. "I'm the only one in my math class who knows my multiplication tables up to the fifteens, you can tell me. What do you do there all the time?"

The tall man looked almost impressed, his mouth pinching with amusement. He sucked another mouthful from his cigarette, and Annie had a passing thought that he looked not unlike the illustration of the smoking caterpillar in the *Alice's Adventures in Wonderland* Mother had read to her.

The two men shared another inscrutable look. Archie regarded her for a moment before his expression melted into a cousin of concern. He reached up and took Annie by the shoulder. The heft of his hand was gentle. "It's all just hubris, kid: Sail too close to the rocks and the ship gets dashed, you know?"

The barest flicker of fear so subtle Annie almost didn't pick up on it fluttered through the backs of Archie's honest, shiny eyes. "What's hubris?" Annie asked, but her voice didn't have any of its prior bluster.

The door to the porch rolled open. Annie's attention vaulted back to the house. Her mother leaned out, backlit against the glow from the den. "Annie?" she called into the dark.

Archie steadied himself back up to his feet, where the tall man helped balance him with one arm before easing it close around his shoulders. "Hubris," the tall man said briskly, "is what makes Archie think he can have six highballs and still talk a lick of sense."

"Annie! There you are." Mother came over with her hair piled up in glossy curls and her lips painted red. Her emerald-green party dress made her look like a queen. Mother set her hands to Annie's arms and rubbed briskly to work the warmth back in.

"I'm so sorry, Walt, was she bothering you?" Mother corralled Annie slightly behind her. She and the tall man shared a brief look that remained foreign to Annie, not anger but still spiky in a way that certainly didn't fit at a Christmas party.

"Not at all," the tall man said, before Annie could insist she was only being curious.

"She's asking about the *lab*, Helen," Archie drawled. "Better catch her early, huh?"

Mother glanced back at Annie briefly, tight-lipped, before looking between the two men.

"Did you ever give them a call?" she asked.

"Who," the tall man asked, "the ranch?"

Archie scoffed. "Enough about the ranch, Walt." He drew his shoe along the ground lightly and stared at it. His voice dropped a little lower. "Haven't pulled any shit since the year before last. You know that."

The tall man took a tight drag of smoke and tapped the rest of his cigarette out hastily in the ashtray on the patio table. He bundled his arm a little more tightly around his companion and nodded at the house as he began to turn them away, like he was asking for privacy again. "She should get back inside. It's getting chilly out here."

"It could help," Mother said to him. "He can always talk to Ford about it." Her voice was gentle, the careful kind of measured tone she tended to use at bedtime. She looked down at Annie and gave her a rushed half-smile. "Come on. Dr. Harris is right, you'll catch cold without a coat."

A subtle rankling of betrayal burbled low in Annie's gut. She held the tall man's gaze until Mother started to steer her back toward the bright shout of the party.

Mother slid the door soundly shut behind her and fixed Annie with a look. "Why don't you go see if the ice bucket in the dining room needs refilling?" she said, in a way that made it clear the idea wasn't a suggestion.

Before she slipped back into the party, the music, the too-many-bodies, Annie stole one last glance through the sliding door at the two men on the patio—still standing with their shoulders touching, they were bent close as though they would each crumble without the support. Annie's reflection framed the sight of it, thrown back at her in a pale wash against the glass.

He can always talk to Ford about it.

Did that mean Mother knew what they did at the lab? Well, it was sort of unfair that Mother got to know and Annie didn't. But maybe that was just another line on the very long list of things grown-ups got to do, smack-dab between "smoke fancy cigarettes just for Christmas" and "stay up late enough to see what the night sky looks like when the coyotes start yipping after bedtime, instead of just hearing them and staring at the glow of moonlight against your curtains."

1955—CRISTO REY CEMETERY
Santa Fe, New Mexico

The raw summer heat worked exhaustion deep into my bones. It did not help that I was stuffed into a black dress that had grown a bit too tight since puberty yanked me onto its track. My feet were pinching in a long-untouched pair of patent flats. Walking next to me, Mother was crying beneath the wide brim of a black hat with a sagging satin bow.

I couldn't bring myself to look at her. We both had stared side by side at the abject ugliness of death, the slow descent of a simple casket that made me think of hell despite the lack of Christian wiles in our family, and now we were going home like nothing had changed.

It was agony. *Everything* had changed.

The back of my neck prickled with the tack of sweat against my stiff Peter Pan collar. All of me bristled against the strangeness of the day.

Daddy is dead. I forced it through my brain in rote repetition to wear down its spines: Daddy was dead, Daddy was dead, Daddy was dead.

"Don't do that," Mother said. She pried softly at my hand on the hem of my dress, where I had been unconsciously rubbing at the tulle beneath its fabric.

I wormed my hand out from where she tried to hold it and kept walking, speeding up a little so she was trailing a step behind me. "Sorry."

My throat felt like glass. I looked behind us down the lane at the gravestones littering the ground like tossed marbles.

The funeral had been jarringly small, not that I had any prior comparison: just me, Mother, and a rheumy pastor.

Since waking up that morning, as Mother and I got ready on opposite sides of the house, I tried uselessly again to remember anything about Daddy but came up dry; not the smell of him, not the warmth of him, not even the once-familiar shape of his crow's feet creasing with a smile. I knew they had been there, the sight almost clear in my mind's eye like muscle memory stuck on repeat. But I couldn't remember it, not really. Not in any way that mattered.

The landscape sprawled with obstinate sunniness, silent as any beautiful day in the high desert was wont to be. A deep anger took root in me at the world for persisting in the wake of my loss. I wanted to hurl rocks at the sun until it went out so the rest of the planet could feel this sudden darkness.

We were halfway home already. I had never stopped to think before how rotten it was that we lived so close to a cemetery. At home, Mother would cloister herself in her room and pen carefully worded letters to Daddy's colleagues and our far-flung relatives to let them know her husband had died. There might have been a wake if Daddy had died less suddenly, had it not felt like Mother and I were missing an entire limb between us.

The aftermath was a deceptive stillness. We circled each other carefully, each of us wary of pressing too hard at bruises we couldn't see in the other. Mother took to a manic habit of tidying the house with a militant daily rote. I mostly stayed out of her way, until my own quiet guilt got the best of me and I started bringing in the mail one morning.

You've never checked the mailbox without me asking first, Mother said. She didn't look up from the stacks of bills, estate agent correspondence, life insurance missives in a ragged pile.

You haven't asked me to help with anything else, I replied as I filled a glass of water and set it down on her side of the table. When she looked up at me, I shrugged. *Figure it's the least I can do.*

The quiet truce with my mother was different from the confounding frustration I felt toward the rest of the lab. If any of Daddy's colleagues had reached out to us, I didn't know about it. And perhaps that was Mother's aim, to keep me shielded from anything that might make me think of him, but that was the worst part in being unable to articulate how twisted up I was about the whole thing. I *wanted* to think of Daddy. I wanted to remember him.

More than anything, I just wanted to remember him.

I glanced back at Mother and found her trailing more than a few steps behind, so I stopped and waited for her to catch up. She was wearing a nice pair of pumps that made the going a little slower. I predicted that she would weather this new chapter of the world well and solemnly, like a vow of silence. I wondered if I would adjust similarly, if ever at all.

"Annie."

When she drew up beside me, Mother took both my hands in hers and absently smoothed the hem of my skirt. She mulled something over for a moment to herself, her mouth bunched up tidily. "None of this was your fault," she said with a certain trained-in steadiness. "Your father was never able to love you as much as you deserved."

I bristled. "What's that supposed to mean?"

"He struggled deeply with a lot of very . . . heavy things."

My pulse cantered up with a sharp kick of adrenaline—fear, grief, whatever it was it burned on the way up. "He split atoms for a living. Those aren't heavy at all."

Mother's expression flattened. "Anne Helen, that is *not* fair."

"None of this is fair!" I threw a hand out at the openness. The still-ness. The absolute cosmic silence. *I hate it here*, I thought for the first time with harrowing conviction.

Mother looked at me for a long, searching moment. The back of my neck kept itching.

"What?" I grunted.

"It's like only his half made it into you," Mother blurted.

I glared at her. "Good."

Mother's gaze buckled, the lines at the corners of her eyes deepen-ing in a wince. "See there, you're already well on your way to breaking my heart someday, too."

A deep and virulent hurt leapt up along the forward junction of my rib cage. "Let's speed up the process then, why don't I just get a job at Los Alamos after I graduate? D'you think they have a legacy program?"

I heard the slap reverberate shallowly down the empty street be-fore I really felt it. The stinging in my left cheek only started when I peeled my stare up to my mother's devastated expression, pinched and miserable.

"Don't you ever threaten me like that again," she said emphatically, tears building with an exhausted feebleness on her eyelids. *"Ever."*

I turned away before one of the tears could fall. Even watching Daddy's simple coffin sink into the red, cracked dirt of the cemetery not twenty minutes ago had been more bearable than seeing Mother finally shed a tear.

I nursed my stinging cheek with a flat hand and stared at my stupid, pinching shoes. My eyes welled up of their own horrible, empathetic volition, tears burbling like a storm surge, buckling my forbearance. "He loved me," I said, my voice bruised past the sob I barely held in. If I said this enough times, maybe I might someday believe it. "He loved me more than *anything*."

Mother took my hands again and kissed me fiercely between my knuckles as her thumbs ran over the ends of my fingers. She sniffled hard, a wet and utterly bereft sound. "Of course he loved you. He did. I spoke rashly. I'm sorry."

I pulled one hand free from her ardent grip and reached back between my shoulders to paw at the zipper on the back of my dress. I wrenched it down my neck just enough to free the strain of it along my shoulders. Mother made a tight sound at me. "Annie."

"It's hot," I bawled, and pawed at my cheeks with flat hands as I raked myself back together with wobbling determination. I didn't know what else to do.

Daddy would have known what to do, but he was gone.

We trudged home, weary and side by side but so very alone.

＊

1965—MRS. HALLIDAY'S SECRETARY SCHOOL
Houston, Texas

"I'm taking lunch outside today," I told my supervisor, a sturdy woman named Lynn, as we all broke from our covered typewriters for the hour. Lynn glanced outside at the sun beating hot and relentless on the field just past the parking lot.

"Don't melt," she hummed, and let me be.

I had spent three years drifting through odd jobs in Houston— switchboard operator, a speaker salesclerk, hotel concierge, and finally librarian, which at least was quiet.

I either needed to bite the bullet of my ambition and really use my diploma and my head full of numbers, or just keep floating and guessing palely at what came next.

Returning to New Mexico was out of the question. The place where both my parents had died, the place that could so easily let fifteen years of my memory slip away into a confounding black box of its own making, could never be home to me again.

So I dusted off my pipe dream and made for NASA.

I found a walk-up rental on the bus line that went all the way to the

Manned Space Center, even though I had a car—a contingency plan if the hatchback ever quit starting.

A smallish place with a narrow foyer that led directly into a cramped den, I made it cozy with some careful decorating. The kitchen and my rickety two-seater Formica table was to the right, and a slim hallway with one closet and the sink set into either wall of it opened up into the bathroom and my bedroom past it. Rent was affordable, as there was nothing to do for miles past the tiny fistful of buildings on my corner. But the place kept me dry, warm, and safe, so I liked it just fine.

At night, I would lie awake and stare at the ceiling or out at the moon as a distant feeling of familiarity hummed between and across the small gaps of my body like the leviathan frequencies of planets in orbit, coming from nowhere and everywhere at once.

I'd found Mrs. Halliday's Secretary School in a newspaper ad while taking lunch at a café across from the library, where I had picked up a handful of hours to keep my ends meeting while I figured out how to get myself launched toward NASA. That afternoon, I'd mailed a check as my deposit for the next round of typing courses and let the library know I wouldn't be able to come in after the first Monday in May. After all, I figured, NASA needed secretaries as much as engineers.

I had little in common with the other ladies in class. Most of them were wives or mothers or both, sharpening their skills now that their babies were getting older or wanting to supplement a husband's income. There were even a few of my coursemates who, I knew by way of whispers, were on their own now after divorce. The way you heard some of those women hiss and mutter, you would think someone had been murdered.

I was older than the women newly graduated from high school and younger than the mothers, so I floated unassociated. I didn't mind—it was one calendar year of classes and certification, and then I was free to find work where I could get it. I did wonder what Evelyn would think of me now, though. The last letter she sent me had come about a month ago. She was heading a few towns northward after a stint as a ranger at Big Bend as an excuse to get dark-sky views of the stars.

My lunch sack crackled as I rolled it open on the bench outside, baring the apple and the turkey sandwich I picked up from the deli next door each day on my way to class. The field was empty for the heat, but I'd gotten mostly used to it by now.

I bit into my sandwich. The tomatoes burst ripe as summer itself against my tongue. As I chewed, I stared far into the distance and pretended I could see through the city; out to the gulf itself in glittering deep blue. I no longer looked for mountains on the horizon.

A flash of something small and metallic suddenly erupted up into the sizzling heat-warp where the sky met the ground.

I squinted. My eyes burned to watch against the sun. The little thing whirled madly, spangling the sun on its surface as it flew in a high arc. I wished for binoculars and gripped my sandwich harder.

A trail of faint white smoke belched from its bottom, and then it was gone—the little pod disappeared.

It was either extraterrestrials or rocket tests. The idea of either one made my heart squeeze so fiercely at the edges of my lungs I almost couldn't breathe.

I looked down and hissed a low oath to myself when I found I'd squeezed my bread so hard the sandwich had begun dribbling on my skirt.

That night, when I rolled over on my side and looked out at the moon, my knees drawn up to my chest under my covers, I imagined I could see the ambling pathways of every vessel, every wink of ever-expanding matter that had crossed through the sky in a complex lattice against the dark—streaming, living, breathing with the endless pulse of the universe.

I had been working very hard lately at exhuming old memories of my father. The further I reached into my childhood, the younger I went, the easier it was to remember what he sounded like, the sort of things he might have said to me.

One had begun sticking around when I least expected it. I held it close and repeated it to myself like the only prayer I had ever thought to send up:

Think you can help figure out how to get to the moon?

02:00

---✦---

1967—THE MANNED SPACECRAFT CENTER, THE SECRETARIAL POOL
Houston, Texas

Three sounds had comforted me when I had expected them to unsettle: first was the encompassing roar of an airplane engine when we flew to Washington for Daddy's work in '47; second was the massive throb of the computer bank in the basement of the St. Christopher library as it chewed through our capstone data; and third was the fluttering of the Center's secretarial pool, our typewriter keys chattering along with the occasional hushed strain of gossip, as we transcribed launch calculations from the navigation team.

I was hired in a whirlwind after a single interview—*Can you type? Good. Double bachelor's in physics and astronomy? Handy. At least it won't be like transcribing Greek to you*—and set loose in the secretarial pool after a day of training.

I was a fast typist, one of the fastest on the massive technical models that swallowed the majority of our desks. I could tear through volumes of notes and memos in half the time it took my colleagues to transcribe the same amount. I tried not to let it get to my head. We were paid by the hour, not the word, and the other girls were sure to remind me.

"Christ, Annie, your fingers on fire?"

I spared a fraction of a glance up at Frances Greene, who was taking her cigarette break leaning against her desk beside mine. Fran was a leggy woman a few years my senior who painted her eyeliner as though her eyes would fall out without the color to keep them in place. She was one of the first hired onto the Apollo team from Gemini when they were just a tiny cabal of speculation and experimentation. She had clout, and I supposed I was some sort of lucky she liked me enough to talk to me.

"I'm working on Norm Hale's sim report," I said, my eyes glued to the chicken-scratch page at my right. Fran hummed knowingly.

"Enough to make a gal want to *set* her hands on fire, isn't it?"

I let out a snort and kept my left hand going as I reached down to the lip of my ashtray with my right to take a quick drag.

Norm's handwriting would have probably been easier to read if I didn't have any idea what his calculations meant. He scrawled as though his mind had outpaced his own hand, backtracking and scratching out and retracing every other thought he put to the page. It had taken me a full week to figure out his system, and once I had it down, it was only marginally easier—most of my time on his notes was spent determining which equation he had decided to follow. He was a genius, undeniably, but a messy one. More often than not, Norm accidentally scratched out the numbers he ended up plugging in.

Every time I saw his name at the top of the sheet, I did my best not to think about kissing him last Christmas.

"*Frances?*"

With a sigh, smoke pluming from both her nostrils, Fran kicked herself into a stand and smoothed her skirt. The space between her hem and her knees had been growing with each passing week. It didn't go unappreciated by the engineers.

"Yes, sir?" she called back over the clatter of keyboards. I glanced up to see her roll her eyes. The chief EECOM officer rounded the corner, looking sharp as ever. Of the rocket boys, it was largely agreed upon that John Aaron was one of the finest.

He gave us all a bright grin, summoning several *Morning, sirs* and *Hello, John*s. "Could I borrow you for dictation?" he asked Fran, pointing a thumb back over his shoulder.

Fran gathered up a legal pad and a heavy pen and smiled right back. "You can borrow me for just about anything."

John went pink, as intended. A titter ran through the typists. Fran disappeared down the hall behind John, her heels at a clip behind John's pace, and I set back to deciphering Norm's notes.

At the end of a simulation report, a blank space waited for the controllers to add additional hypotheses and conclusions to their notes on the results of the lander tests. In today's report, one of the crew had failed to recognize a hull pressure warning.

They'd been failing on hull pressure warnings for *weeks*.

Norman and the other boys of his station were on the ascent team, the minor nobles of mission control. He was a navigator, acting as one set of hands that made up the collective brain of whomever was behind the controls in the module: fuel, thermal, the whole nine.

I had only seen them in action once, thanks to the day I had to wait an entire afternoon just for a single signature.

Sure, sure, everything is urgent now. Wait there, sweetheart, the simulation supervisor had said over his shoulder, waving a hand at me without looking up from his transport or taking off his headset. I took a seat at the back of the suite and watched. Fuming quietly at first, I quickly fell rapt as the simulation started. From there, it felt like all of us, our work, truly did reach out for infinity. It became tangible in a way it never had been before.

That day's simulation failed: a misfired abort on a rotation gauge malfunction. The sim supe all but stabbed his pen through my clipboard with his signature, fuming and prattling into his mic about how someone needed to beat some goddamn sense into the astros' heads before the Soviets beat us to the punch.

I was enchanted.

Norm's memos didn't make me nearly as starry-eyed.

I could have just set my teeth and barreled through the triplicate copy if I didn't think of more efficient coordinate transforms every time I looked at his notes. The man reasoned as though he had a debt to pay back in planar rotation angles. I could understand it, to a certain extent. It was easy to assume the rocket would be a rigid body on launch. But I always thought back to the way Professor Laitz described the flexion that occurred under immense pressure, gravity pushing back against a massive body. A rocket would never truly be rigid at launch.

I recalled with a shiver the disaster of the first Apollo mission last month. I couldn't let a mistake slide on my watch, not with the oxygen fire so fresh in my memory.

I glanced quickly about the room to make sure nobody was hovering. Digging into my desk, I drew out a small notepad and pen and looked hard at one of Norm's calculi, as though I were simply trying to decipher the difference between a 3 and an 8. The equation leapt up at me from the page: Euler's method.

I copied down the values Norm had charted and stared for a moment. I was acutely aware of the seconds ticking by, of my typewriter's silence. Tapping the point of ink against the page several times, drumming up process and courage both, I plugged them instead into a rotation matrix.

I stared at my handiwork for a moment once it was done. It looked correct.

Clearing my throat, I put down the pen and sat back in my chair.

My fingertips tingled as though I'd just picked a lock on some unbreakable safe.

I figured the other matrices in my head. My adjustments continued smoothly. As each line of replacement spidered across the page in front of me, my fingers flying, my pulse went fizzy like it had when Norm kissed me in Gibbs's office.

He had been the perfect gentleman since, if not lending me an extra smile or two or always going out of his way to hold doors or give me right-of-way when we crossed paths in the halls—but then, he did that with all the girls. He was a charmer. Everyone liked Norman Hale.

He was the son of an army officer and a schoolteacher, I confirmed on the first workday back in January, when I found an excuse to dig ever so shallowly at his records. He would have been an outlier if his manners *weren't* so perfect.

He probably didn't even remember kissing me. My cheeks warmed to recall it—the way his wide hand had spread over my back between my blouse and my blazer, the flutter of his long lashes on my temple, the way our noses bumped when he finally pulled away before I was entirely done reveling in it.

I'm not usually so forward, he had rasped.

I don't mind, I admitted, fussing with my hair and straightening my glasses, *but I'll have you know I don't make a habit of kissing engineers.*

'Course not, you're too smart for that. Norm gave me a cockeyed smile I could still trace at the back of my mind. *I can tell.*

Well. Regardless of what Norm Hale could tell, he certainly had let the encounter lie quiet between us.

As my fingers sailed across my keys, the equations firmed up and the rest of the report fell into step as I tweaked and pushed values and symbols to match.

I let my mind wander briefly while I tugged the last sheet of paper from the typewriter. The taste of cherries from Norm's lips lingered at the back of my mind, and I thought of Evelyn Moore. I could still remember the first time she kissed me.

I peered at the end of my cigarette and took one last peck of smoke. When I ground it into my ashtray, the filter balanced straight up and down on its own for a moment.

I toppled it with a gentle flick of my fingertip and got back to work.

1958—ST. CHRISTOPHER, THE WOMEN'S DORMITORIES
San Antonio, Texas

There were so few women at St. Christopher that we suffered the acute benefit of not needing to share our rooms. They were small and shoebox-like but easy enough to make comfortable with a delicate touch: posters, trinkets, creative angles of furniture both given and found, and racks of clothing halfway to small boutiques in some cases dressed up a space in an instant.

After the first night of wine and records in Evelyn's room, it became an almost nightly fixture for us. Evelyn's room felt like an embrace—everything of hers was chic, understated, a product of her sharp eye for complementary shapes and colors with ubiquitous accents in deep blue. Posters for movies like *Strangers on a Train*, *Rebecca*, and a pouty centerspread of Dovima were tacked to the wall.

The more time I spent with her, the more I found myself daydreaming about Evelyn—the way she twisted her hair around her finger while she did her best to grasp Laitz's lectures, the way her top lip curled when she laughed, the subtle tilt to her head when I said something off-color.

I was surprised I could make such fast friends. The carefully worded progress reports my mother received from my high school teachers had contained scant evidence of any social achievements — *Annie is a joy to have in class, if not reserved. She is more than happy to be left to her own devices and causes no trouble with her fellow students.*

I'd felt what I was beginning to feel for Evelyn only a handful of times before. I could count them on one hand: Tommy Gonzales, Mickey Fields, Laura Shelley, Peggy Lipton. Tommy had stood behind me in choir with a rich baritone voice that made my knees weak, I called Mickey my boyfriend for a grand total of two giddy months before he started going steady with a girl in the glee club, Laura's breasts were the first I ever saw in person in the sophomore phys ed locker room, and I spent my first kiss on Peggy in the front seat of her mother's car the summer Peggy got her driver's license.

Peggy and I stayed close for a little while. Our secret education felt to me like an answer to every truth of the universe, but Peggy ended up engaged before we graduated a year later.

I hadn't kissed anyone since.

I knocked twice on Evelyn's door with tonight's wine bottle hidden under one arm as I glanced over my shoulder to ensure our hall mother, Ms. Wincoate, wasn't making her rounds yet. She'd rapped on the door once when Evelyn and I ended up spinning the latest Everly Brothers album a touch too loud a few weeks ago, but luckily we'd had the forethought to hide the bottle under the bed between swigs.

"There she is!"

Evelyn greeted me with a broad grin as she swung the door open. Her perfume hit me in a sweet wave. She was wearing the same slim-cut slacks she had on earlier today in Laitz's lecture hall, but she had changed into an oversized pullover that was probably a cherished hand-me-down. She looked comfortable, surrounded by her own space and standing with her balance to one hip. I wanted to wrap her up and live in that feeling.

I shuffled in, and she shut the door soundly. Proffering the bottle like a two-bit sommelier, I opened my mouth with a soppy-fake French accent just to see if I could make her laugh, then stopped.

"What?" I frowned lightly at Evelyn's vulpine smirk while my heart reached up through my nerves to have that expression fixed on me. She looked like she was going to kiss me. We were standing too close for anything else. Evelyn was going to reach out and kiss me, and—

She slipped a hand into her back pocket. Two tightly rolled cigarettes sat in her palm, their papers a faint brown and the scent on them sharp. Evelyn raised one eyebrow. "I've come into some *wealth*," she purred.

Ignoring the way my belly made a tight, inconvenient curl, I set the wine down and flopped onto the fluffy cream-colored bedcovers she kept impeccably made. "How's that?"

"One of the mop-tops in my literature course, Andy," Evelyn said, perching on the foot of the bed across from me with her face full of mischief. "He grows it himself. Lives with one of the chemistry guys, something about growing up on a farm and being 'intimately familiar with pH balance.'"

I snorted, unable to stop myself. "He was trying to pick you up."

Surprising bitterness came out in my voice. I would have scrambled to walk it back, but Evelyn was unfazed. She shrugged and smiled to herself—she wasn't dense, she had to know he'd been flirting. She tucked one of the rolls into the lower drawer of her jewelry box and held the other between her middle and index fingers like any old cigarette as she hunted for her lighter.

"Well, it didn't work for him," she said loftily, and flashed me a grin that warmed me down to my toes, "but it worked for us."

Riffling through her purse on the vanity beside her hairbrush, she found the lighter at the bottom. She cracked the window near the foot of the bed to let the smoke go out despite the brisk touch to the air, and then curled her knees up under her and flicked her thumb for flame. Evelyn drew it to light slowly—I should have been embarrassed by how closely I watched her mouth around the end of the roll. I very much wasn't.

"You ever smoke anything besides tobacco before?" Evelyn asked, exhaling after holding her breath for several moments. Her voice was dampened, as though she had put the brakes on it.

I shook my head. "Not really the scene with the crowds I ran in back home."

Evelyn raised an eyebrow as she took another pull of smoke. "Annie the square didn't have fun?"

It would have sounded mean-spirited from anyone else, but Evelyn offset it with a smile and a twinkling sparkle in her eyes. "Here," she offered, scooting closer and holding the joint out to me, "I'll show you."

Evelyn coached me through it with easy instruction, her voice steady and low. I wanted to impress her. I wanted her to tell me I was doing a good job. After two attempts that made me cough, I had it down comfortably enough that it didn't make my nose burn.

"Atta girl." Evelyn gave me a small, proud smile. I had to work to keep my tongue from falling out of my mouth with adoration.

She had to know I was interested. Didn't she? I had flashbacks to my first kiss with Peggy, that tender, clumsy thing on a bench seat, and the absolute desert of romance in my life since then scraped over me like sandpaper. I glanced down at the roll in my fingers. "When does it start working?" I asked.

Evelyn made an airy sound as the paper fizzled. She exhaled through her teeth, half-pouting and supremely content. "Soon."

I was *real* gone.

To Andy's credit, wherever he was, once our highs seeped in, they were soft as silk. Mild and buttery, the mistiness rolled up from my toes to my wrists to my neck and my brain. Soon enough I was tingling all over and lying with my head on Evelyn's leg as she stretched out on the mattress. We had smoked the roll down to nothing, the spent end discarded among plain cigarette butts in the empty lowball cup Evelyn used as an ashtray.

"Moon looks pretty tonight," Evelyn said and sighed. She stared through the window with a serene smile and heavy eyelids. I wondered if her mouth tasted like strawberries. Everything felt like *more*, swelling around and through me like the pulsing of a giant set of lungs. Whether that was the grass or the nearness of Evelyn, I couldn't quite tell.

I nodded against her thigh, my head cloudy. "Yeah." I was gazing up at her along the horizon line of her body, the sky a faraway thought, if that at all.

Evelyn reached her fingers out in a pinching motion and shut one eye, lining up the gap between her fingertips around the shape of the moon outside. "Times like this, makes me want to reach up and pluck it out of the sky to keep in my pocket. Keep it safe."

I made a soft hum of assent. "My dad said once that the moon must pity us."

"Pity?"

I shifted, resting my head up higher on Evelyn's flank. "Our appetite for meddling, I suppose. Blowing shit up. He worked on the bomb. He died a while back."

One of Evelyn's hands came down to settle lightly on the back of my head. She cradled me there. I decided it was the most graceful response I had ever received in response to Daddy's death.

I had a deep and absolute sense that Evelyn was someone who, somehow, understood the heavy box deep in my gut—filled with memories I couldn't look at, locked tight with a combination I would never crack.

I almost flinched when her fingers began to comb lazily through my hair. Almost.

"I think," Evelyn said as I shut my eyes, "the moon must look down and wonder why none of us has come to visit yet."

My heart pulled with sympathy to think of the quiet rock, spinning around us forever but never able to make contact in any way, only tossing the sun's light back at us in cold silver mimicry. I wanted to reach up and wind my fingers together with Evelyn's. "Well, some are certainly trying. You think she's lonely?"

"Maybe she doesn't quite know what she wants," Evelyn murmured, "but she knows she needs *something* from that little blue marble."

I couldn't tell anymore which of us was *she*.

Evelyn's fingers on my scalp fractured my thoughts into a comforting scatter. Any worry I had dissolved with honeyed give. I sighed, angling my head into her touch. "Maybe the moon just needs your hand in her hair."

Evelyn's chuckle made the air dance. She shifted and guided me up to lean into the layers of stacked pillows beneath us, so I could prop my head up and stare at her for as long as I wanted. "I think the moon is really high," Evelyn whispered.

I snickered. "Yeah, really high up." Evelyn rolled her big brown eyes, which made me laugh harder.

"You're a *genius*, Annie Fisk." The way she said it, the long pull across her pretty Texan accent made the sarcasm land soft on my surface. I slowly ran the tip of my tongue along my bottom lip, still grinning.

"And you're prettier than the moon," I said, the words jittering in the small space between us. Had I not been loaded, I would have been mortified.

Evelyn's pupils did an interesting thing, growing even wider than they already were. The shining black infinity prickled at the back of my neck. I watched her for what felt like an eon as I memorized the endless depth of her gaze.

"You like girls then?" Evelyn's nose was almost touching mine. Humor took me, broke me from my reverie, to think of our noses nudging together. I inched forward and did it.

"Girls, boys, no real difference," I said, crossing my eyes to see where our noses touched. "Not to me. But maybe girls more."

Evelyn regarded me evenly when I scooted back to my side of the pillows. She was the most beautiful thing I had ever seen. When I tried to open my mouth and tell her so, I couldn't make my breath work past the thunder of my pulse.

"Annie," she whispered, "do you want to go on an adventure?"

Mute, I nodded.

"It's a lot of secret-keeping." Evelyn lifted her hand to trace the shell of my ear with one fingertip and watched as I shuddered. "There are people we could tell, and people we can never tell. Like the good motels versus the shit ones. But I know the way, I'll drive. You wanna be navigator?"

When I could move my face again after the next pulse of tingling that bubbled down the underside of my skin, I reached up to touch Evelyn's hair, still soft. My thumb slid over the elegant whorls of her ear in return, and I watched Evelyn bite her lip with her gentle, perfect teeth. I swallowed and nodded again, mussing my hair sideways into the pillow and wondering distantly which of us remembered to take off my glasses. "I'm really good at reading maps," I said, for only the air we were sharing to hear.

When she kissed me, belonging bloomed across every little blood cell in my body. She was magnetic. I slid my hands up and down her arms and tangled them around her waist to draw her close, my palms itching with purpose. Somehow I ended up on my back, and then Evelyn really was driving. After she'd moved to saddle herself atop my hips, she sighed across my lips when I let my touch wander up her sweater, over the delicate lace of her brassiere.

"You ever done this before?" Evelyn asked against my mouth. She hitched up her sweatshirt and unfastened the hooks at her back. The fabric came away under my helpless hands, and she guided me to her bare skin. I swallowed.

"Only kissing."

"I'll teach you if you want." Evelyn's hands flexed over mine as I grasped softly, desperately, at the half-hidden swells of her breasts. Her nipples hardened beneath my fingers and I was dizzy with vertigo, high and sweet.

"Okay," I said. She leaned down and kissed my neck. The air tasted so sweet it burned.

She touched me like I was something precious. When I could breathe again, see with my head on straight, I mirrored her gentle, steady fingers against me with a tender presence of mind I could easily imagine her applying to one of her paintings.

Evelyn reveled in slow gentleness, a minor ache, fingers sliding and wrist twisting with fevered elegance until her legs started to tremble. She folded over her own limit with her head bowed into my shoulder and a sound like springtime breaking from her teeth.

"Annie," she gasped against my chest. She had rucked my shirt up and out of the way.

"Hey," I panted back.

"You're pretty good with a map."

"Told you so."

Evelyn huffed a chuckle against my skin and caught her breath. When she sat up again, her attention on me redoubled—the warmth of her palm, the gentle and unhurried way she kissed me whenever I dragged her mouth back to mine.

She made me see stars twice in a row.

Afterward, I laid in a pile as Evelyn lit one of her Salems. She passed me the second draw on it and let me sip a drag directly from the vee of her fingers.

I was too jellied to move in earnest for several slow molasses-minutes, all my split-apart small bones floating in the air around me. I collected myself by small rights until I was back in one shape again.

"I gotta get back across the hall," I finally croaked, my forehead resting on the round of Evelyn's naked shoulder.

"Yeah?"

"Yeah."

Evelyn smiled at me. She looked sated to her very edges, like the slow bleed of watercolor. "What do you say then—another road trip sometime?"

I swatted her bare leg. "You're paying for gas," I quipped.

Evelyn pinned me with a look of tender scrutiny in my periphery as I roved my fingertips along the inside of her knee, enchanted by touching her. "So you want to do this again?"

The trepidation in her eyes was a smear of doubt like oil on chrome. I leaned up to kiss her until I felt it melt away and nodded with our foreheads pressed together. "As soon as possible."

"Stay a little while," Evelyn hummed. She nuzzled at my temple and collected me down into her arm, holding me snug and close. "Don't need to think about 'next time' yet."

How could I deny her that, deny myself the closeness? I adored her.

I turned to my side and watched the branches of the oak outside the cracked window whisk softly over the moon, peeking out like a stare between wooden fingers. Evelyn was petting my hair again and humming a song I recognized after a moment as "Lavender Cowboy." I reached up and squinted at the little opal orb outside, imagining it pinched bright and cool between my fingers.

"Almost seems possible sometimes, huh?" Evelyn said between phrases of her rambling, off-key tune. "Holding it like that." She stubbed out the last of the cigarette and kissed me on the forehead.

I hunkered closer into her shoulder and sighed against the slender jut of her collarbone. "Yeah. Just about."

✦

1953—THE APODACA HOUSE, FORD FISK'S OFFICE
Santa Fe, New Mexico

Given that Daddy spent so much time in his office, there had to be something interesting inside.

Right?

Annie made sure Mother and Daddy were both occupied, the patter of their voices low from the den as they pored over something to do with the calendar, money, boring things—things that didn't hold any promise for the curiosity of a thirteen-year-old looking for something to do on a Sunday afternoon that was passing more slowly than honey drizzled on a snowbank.

Up on her toes to root at the top of the doorjamb that she was able to reach now, Annie's fingers brushed the prying tool Mother kept on the lintel above every locking door in the house. Once she got it in the handle—jimmying it up and down, testing it gently with each twist of her pinched thumb and forefinger—it was quick work. The lock sprang open and the door gave way. Annie knew to move slowly to keep it from creaking.

Inside, she shut the door again with a silent catch of the latch.

Adrenaline sparked through Annie's body. She had only ever glanced inside from the hallway before, forbidden by Mother's explicit rules to never bother Daddy or disturb the things in his office. *Those are important things*, she said once when Annie was seven years old and trying to follow Daddy inside, *government things. Not for little girls.*

The promise of secrets had lit her curiosity like a firecracker, but Annie stored her patience for the perfect opportunity to present itself. She was nothing if not a patient child, quiet and observant, and time tended to reward her.

Daddy's desk sat heavy and tall at the center of the room, sturdy teakwood with stacks of files laid across it in organized chaos. An abstract set of little sculptures, almost like toys, were arranged neatly at its edges, and two photographs flanked each side of it: one in color of the family in the garden—taken with Daddy's tripod and a timer on Annie's fourth birthday one early March, the roses in nascent bloom behind them—and the other in black-and-white, of Mother and Daddy looking younger and happier than Annie had ever seen them. Mother's wedding dress was like a princess gown, her smile pretty as a magazine model's, and Daddy was wearing a white tuxedo that made him look even taller than he was.

Annie never saw them smile like that anymore.

The bookcases stole her attention before she could fixate any longer on the snapshots. They took up the entire eastern wall of the room, rows and rows of thick books—was that what Daddy did when he shut himself away in here, did he read and read and read? Surely the secrets Mother was so cagey about weren't just books? A room full of books was heaven.

Annie couldn't help but obey the itch to reach out and run her fingertips along the spines nearest to her height: *Constitution of Atomic Nuclei and Radioactivity. Mechanica. Stars and Atoms.* All of them were arranged alphabetically, as though Daddy had a slice of the big Albuquerque library stored here.

Glancing over her shoulder at the still-shut door, Annie tipped one out just to look at the cover. *Thermodynamics*. As she pulled it from the shelf to peel it open, something fluttered to the ground and landed facedown at her feet.

She knelt to flip it over and paused. Carefully penciled writing looked up from the top-left corner of the white photo paper. *With A. Brooks & W. Harris. July 16, 1945. Before Trinity.*

Annie plucked it up from the floor and turned it over carefully in her hand as though handling a pressed rose petal. There on its other side was a monochrome photograph—a young man who was undeniably Daddy in the middle, and two strangers on his left and right, one of them beanpole-tall, the other stout as a bulldog. Daddy had his arms slung over each of their shoulders and an easy look to the way all three of them were leaning on one another, fraternal. Annie flipped it over to see their names again: *A. Brooks. W. Harris.*

She glanced at the book in her other hand and found a bold wash of red curves intersecting and running into one another across the cover. It made Annie's eyes hurt. Opening the book to an early page, she scanned the blocks of text and diagrams: *We now consider a system S which undergoes a transformation—*

"Annie?"

Nearly leaping from her skin, Annie fumbled the book and whipped around from her crouch on the floor to see Daddy standing in the doorway. She blinked quickly, tightening her jaw, the photograph still in her hand. "I was—"

She stopped herself. The lie about books and school and research for a project died on her tongue as she stared at Daddy. Annie swallowed and tried again: "What's this photograph?"

She hadn't meant to ask. She had meant to apologize. Nonetheless, she waved the photo flimsily.

Daddy came over to stoop beside Annie. He peered at the men in the picture.

"Those are my friends," he said plainly.

"From the lab?"

He nodded. "From the lab."

Daddy's brows furrowed. Part of Annie was compelled to reach out and smooth down the notch between them with her thumb. "Did they die?" she asked. Daddy shook his head.

"No. Walt still works with me. Archie was transferred to Sandia."

Annie thought for a moment about the tidy ranks of men in suits Daddy considered friends. "Have I met them before? At Christmas?"

"Probably. They're inseparable. They met overseas working with the Premier Bureau in France. I spent a lot of time with them when your mother and I first came here, they . . . helped me get oriented."

"Mrs. Adams told us a lot of men went overseas," Annie said. "Laura Shelley's uncle was killed in Japan; she brought his flag to an oral report last year."

Daddy nodded shallowly, his mind briefly far away as his eyes stared through the photo. "War is messy," he murmured. "It sticks to everything it touches. You can never wash it away."

His hand rested softly over the crown of Annie's head. Daddy took the photograph in careful fingers and turned it over, where he examined his own handwriting on the caption for a long time.

"You live in a different time now, Annie. Angry men with short fuses are more dangerous than they ever have been."

Annie's chest squeezed hard. "You're not angry, Daddy," she said, her voice tremulous. She picked up the book she had dropped and offered it out to Daddy like a peace treaty, just in case he was. "Are you?"

Daddy pulled her into a sideways hug. The book in Annie's hand dug softly into her ribs between them. "Of course not. I could never be angry at you," Daddy said into her hair.

He held her there for a long, silent moment. From higher up on the shelves, a wooden clock sheared away at the seconds.

"Let's go for a drive," Daddy announced, still holding her close. "How about that, jellybean?"

Annie nodded, which prodded the stem of her glasses into the side of her face at an angle. "Okay."

* * *

Daddy rolled down all the windows of the Cadillac and took the highway north toward Taos. Annie leaned her cheek on her hand, her elbow balancing on the sill. She watched herself in the rearview mirror, seeking Daddy's evidence in the shapes of her face slowly climbing the ladder from girlhood to adolescence—the color of his hair, the line of his nose, the serious draw of his brow in her own.

"So this friend of yours, with the uncle who served," Daddy said over the noise of the road passing and the radio buzzing pleasantly, "Laura?" His expression was open, curious when Annie glanced over at him. "You've mentioned her before. She's a friend, right?"

"Yeah. Laura Shelley. We sit together at lunch sometimes."

Laura had also given Annie her first cigarette a month ago, under the bleachers during gym class as they both pretended to have stomachaches to avoid running the track. She was one of the tallest in their class and wasn't even fazed by the boys who teased her about it. Annie liked watching her smoke.

"Well, that sounds like fun." Daddy hummed.

"Yeah. She has nice teeth."

Daddy glanced at Annie with a smile. It looked proud, a little knowing, a little enigmatic. Something about that smile made her feel seen. Safe.

Annie returned it before leaning forward, dialing up the radio volume, and sticking her head back out the window to let the air buffet her cheeks.

1958—ST. CHRISTOPHER,
PROFESSOR EDWARD LAITZ'S OFFICE
San Antonio, Texas

My first instinct on campus was to avoid office hours and let my professors have their time to themselves. But the longer I spent devouring the texts and assignments for Professor Laitz's classes, the more I found myself craving someone off of whom to bounce the curiosity that was coming to life in me. I wanted to know every single way in which the universe made itself work, the ways life stumbled into happening, the trajectory of randomness.

Laitz's office was like something out of my wildest dreams. It was crammed with books and maps and souvenirs, evidence of a pilgrim visiting the homes of astronomy in Baghdad, Bursa, Samarkand, Copenhagen. Woven rugs rested under plaster busts of gods and zodiac animals on his shelves; astrolabes and orbit models crowded the tops of file cabinets and hung from the ceiling on fishing wire.

"But see here . . ." Laitz scribbled a quick equation in the margin of the sheet where I had sketched out the rudiments of mass distortion on space-time. "Rather than approaching it from a Newtonian perspective assuming a Euclidian flat space, you could approach it instead with a *non*-Euclidian viewpoint."

He turned the paper back toward me. Professor Laitz was made of long lines, his slender limbs like a gazelle who had found his way into a university and tricked the faculty board into giving him tenure. He had dark features that sat boldly against his complexion, a thick head of hair, and a push-broom mustache. His soft mannerisms were calming—from the way he talked evenly through his thought processes like telling a bedtime story, to the way he would hold his chalk or his pen with light fingers as though waiting for the numbers to simply pull the instrument down to the page and write themselves out.

I stared at his elegant, angular diagramming and mulled over the shape of flexible reality. ". . . You would get distortion equal to—*relative* to mass," I muttered. I leaned forward and drew another diagram for him, a more dramatic curve, with $RS=2GM/c2$ scrawled above it. "Time would dilate in the space distorted by a more massive object."

Laitz examined my work. His dark eyes flicked quickly over the page, a half-smile threatening at the edge of his small, firm mouth. "Correct."

Pride and validation surged in me. I grinned, wide and heedless, before I cleared my throat. "Great. Good. Thank you, Professor. That makes a lot more sense."

Laitz leaned back in his chair and laced his fingers together over his knee as he propped one shin over the other in conversational ease. "Have you started thinking yet of a career after you're through here, Annie?"

I fussed with the hem of my wool shirtdress. "Not quite. It's still early, right?" I crossed and uncrossed my ankles under my chair, itching for a cigarette. "I think I'm still . . . figuring out which corner of physics suits me best."

Laitz nodded. "Wise. Have you considered rocket science?"

I had considered it, sure. I had been casting distant, wistful dreams onto it for a long time. But it was a man's world, through and through. I chuckled. "Hasn't everyone?"

"Not necessarily. Lots of folks are afraid of it." Laitz was smiling when I glanced back up at him. "You don't believe me," he said, amused. I chewed the edge of my lip.

"I think I'd rather work in a field where I wouldn't be laughed out of the office," I said lightly. Laitz raised his eyebrows.

"And what would that be?"

At my side, the nail of my index finger roved over the cuticle of its neighboring thumb. "I don't know. Switchboard operator, clerk some-where, maybe a university library. All I know is that I don't have the patience to be the only one who believes I'm smart enough to be in the room."

Laitz nodded again, slow and thoughtful. My face was on fire. *Fuck 'em*, Evelyn always said when I complained about the way some of my other mathematics professors addressed me, or failed to entirely even when mine was the only hand raised. *It's because they know you're smarter than them, and they can't stand it.*

I wished I had her confidence.

"If you could do anything," Laitz said, narrowing his eyes in scru-tiny, "anything at all, no holds barred, what would it be?"

I knew the answer before he even finished asking—I had known it since childhood, that strange pull in me toward a distant somewhere. "NASA," I said.

Laitz looked intrigued. "That's rocket science."

I felt my cheeks go even pinker. "I know."

Laitz thought in silence for a long moment. He leaned back in his chair and tapped his fingertips against his chin. "NASA," he repeated, halfway to himself. "Your father was a scientist, no?"

"With Los Alamos. I would love to do something . . . important, too, but . . . You know—" I made a vague gesture, sketching one hand upward and the other down. "Angling in the other direction."

"Of course." Professor Laitz leaned forward again and set his elbows on his desk. A burst of conversation approached through the open door behind me, and Laitz waited until the gaggle of students was gone again before he held up one finger and turned to pull a book from the wall full of shelves behind him.

"Read this," he said as he held it out to me. *The PGM-11 Redstone*, it read beneath an illustration of a sleek, white missile, *M. Sherman Morgan*.

"What does he cover?" I asked, turning the book over in my hands. Laitz smiled.

"*She* is a rocket scientist. This one is about missiles, but I think her work in general could be very inspiring to get your gears turning in the 'other direction.'"

My heart fluttered. With both hands on the book, I gave Laitz my most earnest smile. "Thank you, Professor."

"Take all the time you want with it," Laitz said. "And consider this an open invitation for a letter of recommendation, whenever you need it. Even if you're going in as a secretary or with logistics, clerking, whatever it is; getting your foot wedged in that door is the first step, but don't stop yourself before you can keep on walking. You're smart, Annie. Don't forget that."

My immediate instinct was to hug him. The ragged paternal gap in me glowed, but I held myself in my seat and clutched tightly to the book's spine. "That— Wow, thank you. Truly. I don't know what to say."

Laitz stood after me and put one hand in his pocket. "Say you'll get that foot in," he said with a smile.

I shook his hand and left his office with vigor spurring the soles of my feet.

In the hallway, I paused beside the staff directory and looked at the book again. I turned it over and found a photograph of Mary Sherman Morgan looking up at me. Our glasses had the same slim, rounded frames. Her hair curled sensibly, parted at an angle and piled neatly. She smiled with a sideways tip of intrigue, like she was holding in a secret. A freckle stood out on her left cheek.

I hazarded my own subtle grin down at her before tucking the book back into the crook of my elbow and striding through the cavernous halls of the physics building, into the sunshine, across campus to my advanced calculus class. I spent the entire period with my nose in the book, combing through things like fuel calculations and taking my own notes on thruster patterns and launch plans to look up in more depth later in the library. I didn't try to raise my hand once.

1954—THE APODACA HOUSE, THE BACK GARDEN
Santa Fe, New Mexico

On deep, heady summer evenings, when the mountain air grew heavy with the preempt of the next cloudburst only hours away, the purple dusk felt endless. Daddy would sit outside with a cigar and a drink if he was home at a reasonable hour, and it was a rare sort of invigorating to see him there in his favorite garden chair as Annie crossed through the den.

She sidled outside through the sliding door and pulled a second chair up beside him. Daddy smiled and blew a perfect set of smoke rings into the darkening sky. "Hey, chickadee. Good day?"

"It was fine." Annie folded her feet up under her. It was the second summer in a row she was helping Mr. Ochoa man the counter at the dry goods store on the plaza, and although the pay was just pennies here and there with a few handfuls of sweets thrown in, it was enough to spend her days running numbers far away from Mother's tendency to create chores from thin air.

The afternoon breaks at the store were her favorite part of the job, as she could walk up and down the promenade at the Palace of the

Governors and marvel at the pieces of silver and turquoise and coral laid out like intricate scales in front of the artists who came into town from their pueblos.

Between the ends of her shifts and returning home for dinner, Annie would either while away a few hours at the library or go for long, winding drives with Peggy Lipton and her mother in their new Plymouth Savoy—her daddy had old money, and her mother had lots of friends and interesting stories to share about traveling the world as a magazine model when she was younger. Either option was an escape: the sweeping annals of a good book, or the thrill of her and Peggy's hands held secretly between them in the back seat.

Annie looked sideways at Daddy when he didn't respond in kind. His profile was strong, solid as granite, and she cataloged the firm notch that seemed permanently fixed between his brows these days as he took another meditative draw on his cigar. "How about yours?" she asked.

Daddy blinked. He was doing that more often lately, the floating away to some far place—Mother had waved it off as one of his quirks when Annie hazarded to ask if she'd noticed it as well, but his mental absence was hard to ignore.

"Oh, it was fine," Daddy said, a smirk on his mouth. Annie narrowed her eyes at the taste-of-your-own-medicine serving but couldn't help smiling back.

She felt solid when Daddy was home, re-centered, as though her axis was at a very strange tilt whenever he was away.

"What did you work on today?" she wheedled. Daddy heaved a theatrical sigh.

"Numbers," he said, pretending to think hard about it, "with a touch of numbers, and after lunch it was . . . ah, what was it . . ." He fluttered his hand at his forehead, screwing his face up in mock concentration.

Annie pulled a fake face of scrutiny. "Numbers?" Daddy snapped his fingers and pointed into the air.

"That's it!" He ruffled Annie's hair and took another steadying sip of his drink. "It was all numbers."

"Doesn't sound half bad."

A small shimmer flitted through Daddy's stare at that. Annie looked away from it at the sky, where the moon had shown itself again from behind a billowing cloud dyed silver.

"Five-odd years ago, you would've been horrified to hear yourself say that," Daddy said, humming.

A very familiar notch between her brows cleaved for the first time. "How's that?"

Gesturing with his cup, Daddy pointed over his shoulder toward the kitchen—Annie glanced inside, where Mother was bent in concentration over the checkbook spread out across the table. "Need I remind you of the catastrophic terror of your multiplication tables?"

Annie rolled her eyes. "That was *once*."

A low, oaky laugh rumbled from Daddy, hugging around Annie's insides like a broad, encompassing embrace. "That was *foundational*."

"Fine. I'm done talking about numbers."

Daddy swirled the dash of amber left in his glass, watched it whorl around. Annie had the sense this was not his first pour. "Fine," he said simply. "What do you want to talk about?"

Annie thought about that for a moment. A rare bolt of honesty shot through her, a reckless urgency to peel up one of her edges. She would still have to be tactful. She bit her lip.

"When you were my age," Annie said, staring straight up through a perfectly dark space between the stars, "you liked girls, didn't you?"

Daddy chuckled. "I suppose I did."

Focusing on not swallowing her tongue, Annie kept staring at the sky. "How did you know?"

"How did I know I liked girls?"

Annie nodded. A thoughtful silence settled in between them. From the steady focus of Annie's stare, distant prickles of light faded gently into visibility through the infinite dark.

She risked a glance at Daddy. Swirling his glass and looking pensive, he peered quizzically at Annie. "I couldn't say. You just know."

Annie scowled. "I thought you were a scientist."

Daddy laughed. Annie settled in against his side and thought of how delicate Peggy Lipton's wrists were under Annie's roving, curious fingers whenever they held hands.

"How do you know," she said steadily, "when you *know*?"

"Patience, jellybean." Daddy smoothed his hand over the back of Annie's head. "You can't force the stuff time teaches you. Sometimes you just have to wait for the lessons."

Well, that sounded like a cop-out, but Annie didn't have any proof of her own to the contrary. The dark sang softly around them, side by side in the garden chairs, and it only broke when Daddy gave a long, quiet sigh.

Annie peered up at him. He was staring at the moon and looked terribly young for a fleeting moment—washed clean, his face an open book of some deep preoccupation. An old fear of her father's fallibility reached up through Annie and latched on. She glanced away again.

"The moon must pity us," Daddy said gently.

Annie stared at her thumbnail as she plucked at its cuticle, the way Mother hated to see her do. "Why d'you say that?"

Daddy took one more slow sip from his glass, draining it. "Everything we're worried about, every problem we cause down here with all our grappling and overreaching—money, land, power, oil—it must seem so goddamn futile from up there."

Annie ignored the curdled feeling. "Do you think we'll ever go there? To the moon?" she hazarded, steering away from gravid things.

Daddy looked down at her. Good humor shone from behind the shadow in his eyes.

"You're the one who said it's possible," Annie added around a nervous, angular chuckle, "and you never tell me about what you do at the lab, so as far as I know y—"

"I've never worked on things made for exploration, chickadee." The hitching behind Annie's breastbone must have shone through. His gaze eased, and he reached out to tap his thumb against her knee. "But *you* might someday," he amended, "if you work hard enough. Keep that Fisk curiosity primed. Sorry, you got it from me."

"Apology accepted," Annie sniped back fondly. She jogged her knee under his hand as though shaking it. Daddy smiled.

"You keep looking up, okay, Annie?" he murmured. "You gotta keep looking for the better option."

He was being serious. He only ever called her *Annie* and not *chickadee* or *jellybean* when he was trying to bring a point home. She nodded.

"Okay."

She nearly told Daddy right then about the strange spot in the rosebushes at the far end of the garden, to prove how deeply curious she found the world around her—but when she drew breath to say so, Daddy let out a subtle, weary sigh at the sky, as though begging it to drag him away. The impulse died.

Annie slid from the chair and squeezed into Daddy's seat alongside him, thigh to thigh, like she was still small and not the springlike gangle of joints she had grown into since last summer. Daddy let out a dramatic groan.

"Whoa there, cricket legs!" He laughed, but Annie leaned into his shoulder and tucked her knees up as she wrapped her arms around his neck.

"Don't go that far," she said into his collar. An inexplicable urge to cry rose up in her throat. "Don't go where I can't reach, too. Okay?"

Daddy seemed to hesitate for a moment before he let out a silent sigh and wrapped an arm around Annie, as tightly as she was holding him. He pressed a kiss to the top of her head and placed one broad hand over the back of her neck. "I promise."

They sat there in the garden chair for a long time in comfortable silence, the familiarity of Daddy's warmth and the smell of his cigar smoke and cologne. When Mother called them both back inside, Daddy helped Annie to her feet and put the chairs back in their places around the little porch table. Everything was where it belonged: Daddy home from work, the furniture re-set, and Annie's heart finally pulled back down from her throat to sit once more in her chest.

I promise, Daddy had told her, and so she trusted him.

✳

1949—THE APODACA HOUSE, THE KITCHEN TABLE
Santa Fe, New Mexico

There had to be something wrong with Annie's brain. What else could explain this agony?

The numbers on the page before her had been swimming in one great, swirling mass of pencil strokes, eraser shavings, more pencil strokes, more eraser shavings—every time Mother came in from the den to check her work and gently told Annie her answers were still incorrect, a piece of Annie broke off and slid to the floor.

She was never going to get the hang of her multiplication tables.

The door opened from the front of the house. Annie's instinct to vault from her seat was arrested by the sharp sense of obedience that struck her still to recall Mother's stern expression and expectant tone of voice: *You have to stay there until you're through, Annie. Use your head.*

Annie wanted to cry, *But how!* Mother always trusted that she would just . . . *know* things, and Annie had begun to highly doubt that Mother had ever been a child herself. It seemed like Mother and Daddy and their neighbors and the rest of Daddy's friends from the lab had simply burst into the world fully formed, and that Annie was the only human being who ever had to suffer the slings and arrows of childhood.

It was, she thought secretly to herself as she carefully picked up the word she'd heard Daddy groan to himself last Sunday while the ballgame piped out from the radio, *bullshit*.

The low murmur of Mother and Daddy having a quick exchange at the door floated down the hallway into the kitchen. Annie strained her ears with her cheek propped miserably on one hand, but she couldn't make out a single word. Mother would be taking Daddy's coat and briefcase just now, and then Daddy would come into the kitchen to fix himself a tall, cold drink that she knew tasted even worse than the orange rinds in it.

With steady, measured footsteps, Daddy rounded his way into the kitchen. He didn't seem to see Annie at first. He placed both his hands flat on the counter and slumped his shoulders as he leaned forward until his forehead rested against the cabinet door above him. He stayed there for a moment with his eyes shut and a pained shape to his features. He looked so *tired*.

Annie squirmed in her seat. "Daddy?" she hazarded, her voice small.

Daddy's eyes opened and he turned his head to face her, as though he was returning to his body from very far away. After a moment, his smile appeared—kind, calm, slightly conspiratorial.

"Hey there, jellybean. What's got you down?"

Annie crossed her arms and stuck out her lip just a little, only because Daddy's heart was a soft and yielding thing when she was upset. "Math," she grumbled.

"Well now." Daddy came over and folded his long limbs down into the chair across from Annie. "That's some serious stuff. What kind of math?" He fixed her with a serious look, his eyebrows up slightly over the top edge of his glasses. Annie had done her darnedest to match those frames with her own, as closely as possible without being allowed to buy a pair from the boys' side of the optometrist's.

Annie pushed the paper over to Daddy as though she was sick of looking at it anymore, the way Mother would sometimes scoff and push away the newspaper with her morning coffee. "Multiplication."

Daddy whistled low, frowning down at the page. "Serious stuff indeed. You need to finish all these problems tonight?"

Unable to hold it in, Annie's eyes welled up. "Yeah."

"Whoa there, hey." Daddy reached across the table and put a hand to her cheek. "Don't cry, it's just numbers."

"The numbers are the problem!" Annie wailed. "I'm no good at them!"

As she wiped her eyes with rough pushes of her little fists and forearms, Daddy looked down at Annie's sheet again. "Nobody is no good at numbers," he said steadily. "Numbers are meant for everybody to understand, no matter what language they speak. It's the way people *teach* numbers that makes math hard. Do you like your teacher?"

Annie sniffled. "Yes."

Daddy leveled his gaze at her. "Be honest."

Chewing on her lip, swiping at her lower lashes again, Annie shrugged. "She talks too fast. The numbers get all swimmy."

A slow, understanding breath came from Daddy's nose. "You should always raise your hand when you don't understand something."

Tears welled in Annie's eyes again, traitorous things. "I know," she said. Her voice cracked hard.

Daddy's thumb tapped twice on the round part of her cheek. "It's okay, Annie. It's okay. One thing at a time."

Spinning the paper back around to face her, Daddy took up the green crayon from Annie's pencil box and circled the number one in the first equation at the top of the paper. "What's this guy?" he asked. Annie wiped her nose with the heel of her hand.

"One."

"Good. Say it out loud with me."

She and Daddy said it three times together, his low and gravelly timbre beneath Annie's higher, tear-wobbled voice — *One, one, one.*

"Now," Daddy said, tapping the number twice with the crayon. Annie sniffled. "Doesn't it look like this guy is saying his own name when you look hard enough? *One.*"

One.

Onnne.

With his pronunciation slow and clear, Annie began to see it. The little hook at the top was like a top lip; the slim serif at its foot, the flat onto which an imaginary tongue would hum to make the long *n*.

One.

Annie looked at the number three just past the multiplication sign beside it and found, after a moment of concentration, that it also looked frozen in speech — *three*, its two lips and teeth opened flat and wide around its own name. *Three.*

"Yeah," Annie said softly. She looked up at Daddy. "Do all of them do that?"

Daddy grinned. The one tooth at the very back of his mouth with a silver filling winked into view. "All of them," he said. "See? You've got a pretty good head for this stuff. You're a Fisk, aren't you?"

The weight of the world on Annie's narrow shoulders lessened by a half ton.

With his green crayon and steady instruction while Mother's radio program muttered softly from the den, Daddy reframed Annie's entire perception of numbers in one short half hour. By the time she scrawled in the last answer on the worksheet, it felt as though she could solve any problem the world threw at her.

"Let me check," Daddy said, gesturing for the paper. Annie handed it over and nearly vibrated from her seat to know if she'd gotten them all correct. The sound of the numbers talking to one another rattled in her head, an exhilarating cacophony: *one times three, four times four, six times five, eight times nine.*

Daddy's smile gave it away before he could deliver the news. Annie beamed as he nodded. "*Very* good job. Initial there."

The green crayon was easy in Annie's hand, warm from Daddy's grip when he handed it over. She scrubbed bold, careful letters on the bottom corner of the worksheet: *A.F.*

Daddy kissed Annie on the forehead when she turned the paper to show him. "Atta girl," he said, and ruffled the back of her hair. "Now, would you be so kind as to get your old man a glass of ice?"

Happy to assist, Annie hopped down from her chair and hunted in the cupboard for the drinking glass Daddy liked best. She chipped several chunks of ice into it and delivered it to Daddy at the bar cart across from the kitchen table.

"I want to do what you do when I grow up," Annie announced.

The line of Daddy's back twitched into stillness. He glanced over his shoulder at Annie as he began to prepare the Old-Fashioned he could probably mix in his sleep.

"I want you to do *more* than what I do when you grow up," Daddy said, a little haltingly.

Annie cocked her head at him. "What do you mean?"

Daddy dropped a couple of the larger ice chunks into the shimmery sunset-colored mixture. He stirred it with his pointer finger for a moment before licking his knuckle and taking a sip, his brow creased in honest thought.

"Well," Daddy said, "they'll probably aim to get someone to the moon and back within your lifetime. Think you can help figure out how to get to the moon?"

"Why would someone go to the moon?" Annie asked. Daddy took a thoughtful sip on his drink and added another dash of bourbon.

"Same reason humans do anything impossible: just to see if we can." He kissed her on top of the head again. "Good job with your homework, kiddo."

He went to the den, where he settled down next to Mother on the couch across from the radio. The sound burring from the transmitter jumped, the familiar voice of the evening news anchor cutting directly into the sound of a serial as Mother flipped the channel.

Annie returned to the kitchen table and peered at her math worksheet like it was a rare bird she had somehow caught. The way the equations seemed to flow now, every number singing to the next like passing a melody along a chain, made her feel powerful. Even more powerful than when Mother allowed Annie to stay up late and listen to *Yours Truly, Johnny Dollar* when she got good grades back from school.

Now, math tests were going to be easy. She was going to be allowed to listen to *Johnny Dollar* almost every night.

Annie wondered if her friend Diana also knew her multiplication tables.

1967—THE MANNED SPACECRAFT CENTER, NORMAN HALE'S OFFICE

Houston, Texas

I was through covering up someone else's tracks.

It was the fourth time I had corrected one of Norm's Euler curves in a simulation memo, the hull pressure weakness issue apparently not yet grokked, and it was the first time I realized that if I didn't say something about it, nobody would.

I collected his latest file and yanked my transcription from the typewriter the moment I hit the last keystroke. It won me some eyes from the other secretaries, but I paid them no mind.

The walk to Norm's office was shorter than usual for how quickly frustration made my feet move—it was exactly forty-seven steps away from the secretarial pool, and I got there in thirty-three.

His door was shut. I didn't knock.

"Norman," I announced as I barged in, no introduction. Norm looked up from his desk, eyes wide and expression frozen—he had his pen held loosely between his teeth and, if its weak mid-swing slow-down was any tell, had been idly flicking it to and fro as he stared at the sheets spread out before him.

He snatched the pen from his mouth and cleared his throat, straightening immediately. "Afternoon, Miss Fisk." Norm eyed the file in my hand as he smoothed his hair with a hasty, half-attentive motion. "What do we have here?"

I flopped open the folder and slapped it onto his desk, sending the pages beneath it aflutter. *"We,"* I spat, "have the calculations you've bungled on every single report I've transcribed for you since February."

Norm squinted at the sheets and pushed his glasses up his nose as he flicked through the pages. "Which part?"

I could have throttled him. Instead, I drew up tall beside his desk and flipped immediately to the page with his boldest offender. "Your coordinate transforms in your memos. You keep trying to use Euler angles when you should be using rotation matrices, you'll be unstable at ninety-degree pitch angles. *That's* why hull pressure keeps failing."

I snatched up the pen from beside Norm's hand and scrawled the corrected matrix layout in the margin of the top sheet. I circled it for emphasis.

Norm stared at the page.

"Well," he said after a stretched-out silence, "indeed I think you're correct." He glanced up at me with a confused frown and shuffled around through several other pages at once. "How has this not gotten me my ass on a platter?"

I crossed my arms and leveled a look at him. "I've been fixing it for you."

The light in his eyes shifted ever so slightly, like the sun flashing against the siding of a test module.

"You've been *fixing it for me*," he scraped out, frowning, not a question. I mirrored his expression, a sour thing that pinched my mouth.

"You should be thanking me." I nodded once, tossing my head to indicate the whole of his office. "This little oasis could have been reassigned to someone else! Forget about launch. You'd be punted to number-crunching fuel loads."

Norm stared at me for a moment while my pulse pounded softly up and down my neck. He didn't seem angry at my presumption, but I didn't know him so well—all I knew was the universal tenderness of mission control's collective ego. He looked down at the papers again and brushed his fingers with a strange reverence across the tidy shapes of my numbers.

"I apologize for the inconvenience my lapse in attention has caused," Norm said steadily. The way his eyes hitched so easily to mine when he looked back up was like a puzzle piece slotting home—a faraway current meeting its match, eddying together in waves. I resisted the sensation even as it shuddered sideways through me.

"Don't apologize to me," I insisted, my arms still crossed. "Apologize to the men you might have gotten killed if I hadn't caught it."

Norm looked at me for several moments with intrigue stirring at the corners of his mouth.

"Will you come to dinner with me?"

The non sequitur sparked like a sharp shot of gin to my system. There was no way I had heard him correctly. My glasses slipped down my nose as my brows knit fiercely at their center. "I beg your pardon?"

"Come to dinner with me," Norm repeated. I stared at him.

"With all due respect," I sputtered once my mouth caught up to my brain, "I don't want *dinner*. I want the—the *frat house* responsible for getting our country to the moon to have their simulation protocols on a tighter leash!"

I had turned and wrenched the door back open before I paused, cringing at myself. When I slowly faced him again, Norm was giving me a beguiling little grin with the files held up jauntily in one hand. "Might need these back."

I marched over and snatched at them, intent on not giving him another breath of attention, but Norm's grip persisted. He raised an eyebrow over the frames of his glasses when I glared down at him. "Think on that dinner," he murmured. I ignored the way my belly warmed at that voice.

"Study up," I hissed. The file came free, and I tucked it back into the crook of my elbow.

I hurried back to my desk. The keyboard swam before me gently when I sat, my pulse still pounding. *Think on that dinner.*

I had done enough thinking. Norm had no idea how much goddamn *thinking* I'd done, and none of it to do with him.

Well. *Little* of it. Not much at all.

With a sniff and a slam of my drawer as I drew out my box of Pall Malls, I decided I didn't need him. I didn't need anyone but myself. I was perfectly fine on my own.

I didn't need him. Perhaps part of me *wanted* him, but there were plenty of things I wanted that I couldn't or simply shouldn't have for one reason or another. It wasn't my business to question it or rail against it too broadly, because that was just the way life worked: give and take—and take, and take, and take.

1955—THE APODACA HOUSE, A SUNDAY
Santa Fe, New Mexico

By the summer between Annie's first and second years of high school, Sunday's routine could only have been broken by an act of God. She would wake with her alarm clock at eight, help Mother prepare breakfast and have a pot of coffee ready for Daddy by nine, and by nine-thirty Daddy would be moseying into the kitchen in his flannel robe and Mother would be unrolling her hair. Daddy would either take a rare day of rest or sequester himself in his office to get ahead before Monday—*Idle hands*, his eternal refrain—while Annie and Mother went for their weekly afternoon walk around the plaza.

With her shoes already on, Annie sidled up to Daddy's office door. It was the only room in the central hallway beyond the open archway to the kitchen. She knocked twice. "Daddy?"

A vague hum came from inside. Annie twisted the knob and squeezed in between the door and the jamb to peek in.

Daddy looked up from a sheaf of papers on his desk, his glasses down at the tip of his nose as he bent over a slide rule. He pushed the lenses back up between his eyes and set his pen down. "Heading out with your mother?"

Annie nodded as she fiddled with the doorknob. Daddy noticed her looking at the papers on his desk and smiled as he held one up.

"They teach you this stuff in school yet?"

"I dunno. We got to quadratic functions and matrices," Annie said. Daddy and Mother had enrolled her in math classes a year ahead of her own grade, which certainly hadn't helped her socially but finally gave Annie enough abstract concepts to take up the space in her brain where friends might have fit otherwise.

"How long do you think you'll be," Daddy asked, eyes turning back to his papers, "lots of things to see today?"

Annie shrugged. She began to swing the door back and forth shallowly on its perfectly oiled hinges. "We're making a roast for dinner, so we'll be back by two o'clock. And Mother promised I could look for a new bracelet from the artists."

"Remind your mother that we're low on tonic water," Daddy said. "And could you bring me the paper before you go, too?"

"Roger," Annie announced, and spun on her heel to shut the door again behind her.

"Hey, jellybean?"

She stopped with one foot out the door and turned to find Daddy looking at her.

"I love you," Daddy said simply. He looked right at Annie and offered a flicker of a smile. Annie beamed and finished stepping out into the hall.

"I love you, too, Daddy."

The door sighed shut with a soft click, and Annie hurried down the hallway, out the front door to where Mother already had the car idling.

The radio news was cranked up high enough to hear through the windows.

Annie snatched up the paper by the front gate, ran back inside to shove it under Daddy's door, and smiled at the distracted *Thanks* from behind the heavy wood.

* * *

Once they got back from the plaza, the ritual of supper began.

Sunday dinner was as close to sacred as the family was wont to get. And church-minded or not, Mother might as well have been laying out an altar with the way she tended to her mouthwatering, perfectly prepared roasts.

Annie always helped in the kitchen on Sundays unless there was something important to study for school. Trusted with scalloping potatoes by seventh grade and wielding the Starmix by last summer, working in the kitchen in tandem was the only time Annie felt as close to her mother as she did to Daddy.

The kitchen was a holy sort of place in more than one way, but partly also because it was the only time Annie ever heard the comforting strains of Mother singing to herself.

Annie had a jukebox memory of Mother humming all sorts of tunes while she gardened when Annie was much younger, tending the budding flower beds that now swallowed the backyard in perfumed Technicolor. While Mother didn't garden as much anymore, Sundays brought old tunes to her throat—"Moonlight Serenade," "Begin the Beguine," "Heart and Soul." Annie knew the words to none of them, but the melody to each and every one.

"Beautiful," Mother said as she lifted the gratin dish filled with Annie's carefully laid potatoes to the stovetop. Pride tasted thick like mousse as Annie watched Mother whisk the cream mixture to pour over them, her wrist quick and graceful. On Annie's own wrist, she fiddled with the pretty silver cuff she had bought that afternoon from an old woman with a kind smile.

"Would you find your father and let him know we're about twenty minutes out?" Mother glanced over her shoulder as she poured the cream, not spilling a drop.

Annie undid her apron and folded it carefully on the countertop. "Sure."

Daddy had still been working when they got back, and neither had bothered him since returning—when he was head-down like that, it was best to let him decide if he would be able to join them. There was no extracting Daddy until he deemed the work complete and emerged on his own.

Annie estimated there was just a hair over a sixty-percent chance Daddy would take his dinner in his office tonight. She hoped he didn't, though; it had been a long time since Daddy joined them for a Sunday dinner.

She stopped outside the office door again and knocked twice. "Daddy?" she called at the jamb. "It's twenty minutes 'til dinner."

No answer, not his usual lost-in-thought *Thank you* or even a grunt. Annie knocked again. "Daddy?"

When she tried at the handle just to peek inside and pull his attention up, the knob resisted. Locked.

Annie frowned.

The sound of Mother cooking in the kitchen persisted, busy and cheerful. Annie heard a soft sound of her humming "Night and Day," so Annie figured she could handle the lock herself.

Up on her toes, Annie groped around for the prying key. She made easy work of the latch, looking over her shoulder to ensure Mother wouldn't round the corner of the hallway and scold her for meddling with the lock to bother Daddy. It clicked open. Annie replaced the key on the lintel with careful fingers.

The hinges were silent as she pushed in. "Daddy?"

She stepped in sideways through the small gap in the door. There—

No.

That wasn't right, no. Not at all.

No.

No?

Annie stared at Daddy's desk as her chest tightened, confusion clamped around her like a vise closing, closing, closing around her lungs. "Daddy?" she breathed. He was—asleep?

No.

He wasn't sleeping, but he was slumped, he was—

He was slumped and he was staring, his glasses skewed, eyes open, and—

And.

Red, there was *red*. There was red everywhere.

Annie's heart pounded so fiercely she was sure it would burst. She fought for breath, gasping in and out, *one, two three, four*—"Daddy?" she tried once more, pleading, her voice going watery and so very small, smaller than the pinhole at the far end of her tunneling vision.

Don't go that far, she heard herself tell him, but *everything* was growing far away, wasn't it? Everything was far away, everything was fracturing, everyone—Annie stumbled back against the wall, the door falling open as she slid to the ground. *Don't go where I can't reach, too.*

He had promised her. He had *promised*.

Somebody screamed. Perhaps it was Annie.

She heard Mother's feet coming quick down the hallway—

And then.

And *then*.

All she could remember was the snipped-wire sensation of everything from that moment falling black.

✦ ✦ ✦

Whenever I tried to remember, when I cradled myself close in the confines of nighttime in the aftermath and tried to recall the day that devoured my childhood, I found only a sealed box left behind—locked, as though I had left my own key behind in Daddy's office.

An arch cannot hold without the center piece. A dropped stitch on the loom of my life, a ragged hole left fluttering with untended threads.

A piece of me, many and various pieces of me, missing.

Even when I wanted to see it, wanted to recall the feeling, the fetid rush of loss in my mouth like bile rising, it was gone. Ruptured. Cracked in half. My mind would never cross that frayed synaptic gap, because to do so would be to disappear along with those lost years.

To look was to lose my way and never come back. The fear of it threatened when I was alone, and I was terrified of what lay beneath the veneer of contentment, of putting away, of turning away. I had looked upon its work, ye mighty, and I had despaired and despaired until my mind washed it clean.

Like the sands of Jornada del Muerto, of Trinity blown to glass, to terror, to ruin itself—become death, destroyer of worlds, my father had known sin and it never let him be. Dragged him down into its mouth, barrel-first, and ended him with a hammer stroke over a headline plainly declaring war again, war stirring in the Pacific, right alongside the latest from the stock exchange. Sticky. Clinging. Impossible to wash away.

My body would not allow me to remember. Out of sight, out of mind, out of memory and left alone.

I was so *alone*.

Everyone I loved would leave.

And the longer I let that box of forbidden recall sit inside me without reaching for it—without bearing to pry at the lid, the further I grew from the years that it held—the more infallible I believed that truth to be.

Someday, eventually, everyone I loved would leave me.

Everyone.

03:00

1967—THE MANNED SPACECRAFT CENTER, THE EAST BREAK ROOM
Houston, Texas

Norman Hale was a genius, a gentleman, and so unshakably patient he could make a boulder weep.

It was small things at first: asking after my day as he held the door for me, hand-delivering his notes to my desk, swinging by with a coffeepot from the kitchen to top up my cup without my asking. The other secretaries were having a gossip field day. My ears were constantly burning as whispers found me from the lumpy red sofa across from the microwave while I came and went for my breaks.

Norm proffered a fresh pack of my preferred cigarette brand to me one morning—I was still digging through my purse while the coffee machine burbled.

"Here."

I turned and narrowed my eyes at him before dropping them to his outstretched hand. "*You* smoke Pall Malls?"

Norman shrugged and tapped one out for me. "I keep them handy."

He smiled after lighting it for me. The coffee machine had dripped a full pot before I could collect myself enough to take a drag of smoke.

Norm escalated his efforts soon enough, the thrill of the chase evident in the bright flashes of mischief I so often caught from behind his glasses.

"And what do *you* need from the data stacks?" I asked two days later without looking up from the memo in my hand. Norm had dashed into the elevator behind me as the doors slid shut to take us to the basement. In my periphery, I saw a victorious smile at the edge of his mouth.

"You know," he said. When he didn't elaborate, I snorted.

"You're about as subtle as a gas giant."

"At least that'd make me noble."

I bit my lips to hold in an unexpected spasm of laughter and only looked over at Norm when the doors trundled open. "That wasn't funny."

He opened one arm with a flourish at the basement and grinned at me. "That was *very* funny. After you."

He stayed behind as I stepped out ahead of him. When the elevator rolled shut again to bring him back up to the ground floor, I lingered for a little while staring at the ugly mint-green paint that had begun flaking where the doors met in the middle.

He persisted. I softened. Norm started stopping by my desk to ask me about equations he was allegedly struggling with, leaning in to peer over my shoulder at my typewriter as I felt the eyes of every other secretary on me—the intrigue in the copier room and around the coffeepots had risen past whispers and graduated to a painfully obvious over-under on when I was finally going to acquiesce to his doting. I gave them as little fodder as I could and simply ignored it. I was good at ignoring what my heart wanted. I'd had practice.

But Norm was sweet, and I was weak to sweetness.

It was autumn when I buckled. Night fell on the first truly brisk day of the year, and Norm was waiting alone in the lobby. He jerked a thumb over his shoulder at the parking lot outside. "Did you drive?"

I held up my keys as Norm pushed open the door. I followed him. He walked me to my car and didn't even try to put a hand on my elbow.

Norm held open the driver's side door for me after I flipped open the lock and I looked him straight in the eye. Knocking the heel of my hand twice on the edge of the door, I chewed on my lip and sighed. "Damn it. Fine. Let's do dinner."

Norm *bloomed*.

Puffed up from the inside out, he visibly scrambled to rein in his excitement. "Brenner's Steakhouse," he blurted, smoothing his skinny tie with one fussy, compulsive hand, "tomorrow night?"

So I said yes, and I pretended not to notice the spring in his step as he crossed the parking lot to his own car in the dark. I hid a smile in my elbow as I turned over the engine.

Tomorrow night arrived more quickly than any passage of time had any right to. I forced myself to quit fussing in the mirror at the circles under my eyes and figured my glasses would help hide them anyway, moving and re-setting one errant curl of hair that wouldn't sit right across my brow until Norm rang the doorbell to my walk-up.

He drove a shiny black '65 Barracuda with a cherry-red interior. Our conversation was starched and fussy at first; I was using the flashy car as a shield.

"And it's real leather?" I ran my thumb along the seam of the seat. The space between Norm and me was about as wide as it could get with two in front. I had myself nearly plastered to the door like I might have to tuck and roll at any moment.

Norm looked terribly amused by that. "Real leather." He hummed and smiled to himself. "You didn't grow up here, did you?"

"No," I said tidily, and didn't try to bring anything else up for the rest of the drive.

Lucky me: Norm was perfectly happy to fill the air with a running list of every single thing offered on the menu at Brenner's. The variety boggled me. It had been a year since I'd had a proper sit-down dinner at a place with cloth napkins instead of a sandwich eaten standing up at my kitchen sink. Norm insisted the food was all good, and I only hoped he was right. If he was anything like his compatriots at the Center, I could at least keep my mouth full and smile and nod as he talked about himself.

Norm opened the car door for me and didn't seem offended when I didn't take his arm. The maître d' seated us in a chintz-filled dining room, where a band was playing smoothly on a shallow stage and conversation purred like the Barracuda's engine.

"Do you drink?" Norm asked, scanning the tall menu open before him. The musicians were all wearing suits. I fidgeted with the hem of my skirt, a plain linen trapeze dress, and wondered if I might be able to sink into the deep plush of the chair. I should have worn something nicer. I wasn't nearly fine enough for a place like this.

"An Old-Fashioned, occasionally," I said. The names of dishes swam before me, unintelligible through my nerves.

"They have *fantastic* Old-Fashioneds here." Norm shot me a quick smile, his voice sticking long on the *n* of *fantastic*. I nodded.

"Sure."

My mother would have throttled me for such shortness on top of the wardrobe gaffe, my manners becoming a shambles the more and more time I spent on my own. Luckily, Norm seemed unfazed. He either didn't care too much about etiquette or was willing to overlook it for a chance to make a pass at me.

"Old-Fashioned it is then." He folded the menu shut and gave me another smile. I wondered, searching his face subtly, if he even remembered the Christmas party; if the subconscious prickling of our kiss was what made him so dogged in his pursuit. "How are you liking Houston?"

"Well." I folded, splayed, and re-folded the napkin in my lap. "After about a year, it's finally started growing on me. I don't think I'll ever get used to the wet, though. I grew up in the desert."

Norm's grin widened, but whatever he was going to pick up and say was paused by the waiter stopping to take our order. "Two Old-Fashioneds," Norm said, checking his menu, "and do you know what you'd like to eat, Annie?"

A blush rose beneath my cheeks. My bluster roiled as it bent in half under the weight of my nerves. "You seem to have a handle on what's good here. Order for the both of us?"

Norm's posture straightened. He ordered a first course of soup, another course of gulf fish, and a steak each. I sat in a stiff, professional silence as I traced the edge of my salad fork and couldn't manage to unstick my tongue from the roof of my mouth.

When the waiter returned to deliver our drinks before bowing away again, Norm angled for my gaze and fixed his attention on me in full. "So, the desert. You're from further west, right?"

I couldn't remember when I had told him that, but then he had likely pulled my file for a peek at me. *Touche*, I thought. "New Mexico. Santa Fe. My father was a scientist."

Norm perked up, impossibly. "Aerospace?"

I rolled the corner of my napkin into a tight coil against the side of my knee. "Not really."

With his brows furrowed and his lips pursed slightly, the small dimple in Norm's chin became a touch more prominent. He scrutinized me. "Military? Did you move around a lot?"

"The bomb," I blurted. I squeezed my napkin in my lap. Norm's eyebrows went up. "Los Alamos," I said. "He . . . worked on the bomb."

I chased the truth with a wide sip of my cocktail, holding in a cough. Bourbon burned a little more brightly than I remembered.

Norman's gaze flicked across mine with tight and tidy elucidation.

He offered me a soft, earnest smile. "Well, Annie, I'm glad you're here at Control instead of out on base with the meatheads further south."

A smile skittered onto my mouth. "Yeah. Me too. How about you?"

My digging had been correct: Norman Hale, son of schoolteacher Addie-Mae and Master Sergeant Robert Hale, black sheep of his family, grew up right here in Houston. He began as a boy obsessed with comic books and found his way into physics through those far-flung fantasies of diving into the stars. His father and brothers were all pilots, and Norm had dreamed about following in their footsteps as the baby of the brood, but he told me over the soup course about a few faulty valves in his heart that kept him out of the cockpit—engineering and navigation were the next best thing, which had deposited him at MIT to seize a pair of master's degrees as quickly as he could earn them to balance out his envy for those who could get up into the clouds. He was just over thirty years old, only four or five years my senior if I was counting right.

I watched him talk and decided it was his boyish energy that made him so endearing. He didn't seem to care about the impossible, viewing it as ripe for solving instead of a flight of fancy. By the time Norm was telling me a story about a simulation last year in which Aldrin completely blanked on how to start the damn thing—he arranged his cutlery and several other elements of the table to mimic the flight control board, adopting a couple different voices for each of the operatives as he acted it out—I was laughing too hard to hide it. Looking at Norm was like looking at all my better parts held up in a mirror.

We were each on our second cocktail and tucking into the fish, flaky and white, when Norm wiped his mouth and leaned one jaunty elbow on the table. "So," he said, a preamble. I raised my eyebrows.

"So," I replied.

Norm smiled to himself. "Contrary to what you may think, I didn't just ask you out to boost my ego."

I snorted. "And here I thought it was because you figured me nothing but a pretty skirt to chase."

The drinks were loosening me up—I had meant it when I said *occasionally*. Norm didn't seem bothered as he shook his head with good humor.

"You *are* pretty, although I'd probably add a few more adjectives to do you justice. But I also think you're brighter than the folks at the Center know."

I raised my eyebrows. The pivot blindsided me. Heat spread from my neck down to the spaces between my fingers. "How do you mean?"

Norm laced his hands together and rested his chin on the lattice of them, a gesture that might have looked patronizing from anyone else but that felt full of tart expectance on him. "I mean, I think you're being wasted as a secretary."

Fondness and fury twisted together in my gut with a quick thrash, dashing the pleasant buzz behind my breastbone. I opened my mouth to say something sharp, but our waiter arrived to sweep away our fish and deliver a pair of succulent, perfectly seared steaks on two huge plates. Norm whistled low and sat back slightly in his chair. I wasn't hungry anymore.

I waited until the waiter finished explaining the cut of the beef and left with a flourish before I dug out my cigarette case from my purse. Norm fumbled at his breast pocket and leaned across the table to offer me a light. "How do you expect me to take that?" I finally said when I had drawn smoke and the lighter clicked shut again. "'Wasted'?"

Norm made a brief, pained face. "There's a reason I'm a flight controller instead of the poet laureate."

"Are you one of those guys who gets his kicks by cutting girls low?" I said as I exhaled, crossing my other arm over my chest. "I won't waste my time with you if you are."

Norm looked at me and gave a short, tight sigh. "No, Annie, I'm not. I'm just a guy who gets tongue-tied when he talks to a smart woman."

I didn't respond, just watched him. My pulse was still tingling, yearning, the larger half of me wanting to reach out and drag my fingertips along his face, trace the lines of his palms, feel at the hems of his sport coat sleeves. I tamped it down.

"What I was trying to say, and clearly failing at," Norm said, fussing with the stem of his glasses, "is that the sims quit failing on hull pressure warnings after your changes, and I think you'd be a better fit in programming instead of typing. I told Glynn as much, and he agrees."

I blinked. I was shocked the ascent lead even knew who I was, busied with Norm's launch team below him and the rest of the flight directors alongside. "Glynn Lunney?" I clarified, and Norm grinned, victorious.

"That's the one. Showed him my hand-notes against your corrections. He's sold. Wants you to take a test with the lead programmer, Ros, as soon as possible to see if you'd be a good fit. Only if you're interested."

The programmers. The cabal of women who worked the computer banks—whip-smart, no-nonsense, the subject of whispers and backhanded remarks from the secretaries—faced resentment for the fact they were the entire reason the Center could work in the first place, and they were one of the only integrated groups within Apollo.

They were geniuses, all of them. My mind went blank trying to imagine myself in their ranks.

"You're joking," I said, but my voice had no bite. Norm took up his fork and knife and sliced into his steak, looking quite pleased with himself.

"I only joke about things that bore me," he said. He gestured at me with his fork. "You, Fisk, are the furthest thing from a joke."

I watched him take the first few bites of steak before stubbing out my cigarette in the crystal ashtray to my left. "What did he say?"

Norm looked up at me as he chewed, his face inquisitive. I swallowed down the rest of my drink in one mouthful and cleared my throat before trying again. "Glynn. What did he say when you told him about me?"

Norm wiped his mouth tidily and squinted his eyes in thought. "If I can recall correctly, he said, 'If she's got enough moxie to tell you where and how you've fucked up, I want her on a computer.'"

I was halfway through a sip of water and almost choked to hear the fricative pleasure Norm took in the word *fuck* in his copycat of Glynn's Pennsylvania drawl. Norm laughed. The tight fist in my gut began to loosen. I didn't even care that the people sitting near us were staring.

My appetite came back. We left nothing but T-bones on our plates.

I insisted I was too full for dessert when the waiter asked, and Norm relented to closing the check without a slice of chocolate cake.

He gave me his jacket on our way to the car. This time, I sat much closer to the center of the seat. I stared straight ahead through the windshield and watched how deftly Norm steered the car through my periphery, his hands gentle and sure on the wheel.

The watchful moon hung over our drive. When we reached the quiet little sickle-curve of my street, the Barracuda slowed so gradually it was as if the entire night had gone liquid with Norm's reluctance to say good night. A soft protestation began panging in my chest, too.

"Well, Annie," Norm said with a sigh, sliding the car into an idle at the curb across from my door, "I've had a lovely time with you tonight."

I smiled, nervous but clear. "So have I. Thank you."

The up-lit glow of the headlights reaching out ahead of us caught Norm's glasses at an angle as he watched me across the real red leather seat. "I would offer to walk you to your door, if you didn't strike me as the type to find that patronizing instead of forward."

With a sniff of a chuckle, I reached out and patted him once on the cheek. "I appreciate the offer."

Norm nuzzled almost unconsciously into my palm. I left it there. His eyes bored into mine, searching. My heart leapt into my mouth.

"If I don't walk you to your door, how will I ask to kiss you good night?" he murmured. My breath caught high in my throat. He was so familiar, every bit of his warmth like coming home. How could I deny him? How could I deny myself?

"Well," I whispered, "as long as you're asking."

This time, I shut my eyes before his mouth found mine.

It was slower, a far more purposeful thing than it had been at Christmas—his hand came up to cradle the back of my head as he crowded softly into me. We didn't mash noses or glasses for the foresight of tilting our heads properly. His lips moved slowly, as patient against my own as his campaign to take me to dinner.

I thought of the last time I had kissed somebody. I thought of Evelyn but shook the memory away. I reached up to Norm's hair, short and fine, and found it softer than I had expected it would be.

He pulled back first. Half-breathless against my bottom lip, he gave a little huff. "*Really* been wanting to redo that properly."

I leaned down and tucked my forehead into his shoulder. We clung to each other. The car door was flush at my back and the warmth of his jacket still sat across my shoulders. "I wasn't sure you remembered," I admitted.

Norm sat back and leveled a look at me, his eyes impossibly bright. "You think I could forget kissing you, Annie Fisk?"

A tectonic shudder within me bid me to behold him in the tender night; remember him here, right now, licked by moonlight and a long shadow along his entire left side.

"Well," I said.

Norm leaned in and kissed me again. I forgot what I was going to say. It was probably a weak argument anyway, if it left me so easily.

He was the first to pull back again. I wanted to invite him upstairs.

I wanted to remember what it felt like to have someone else's hands on my skin.

"I gotta let you go," Norm rasped. He ran a hand over his hair with an abashed smile as he shifted in the driver's seat. "We stay here any longer and I think I'm gonna make an ass of myself."

I shrugged out of his jacket, handing it across the seat. "Rescue your dignity if you'd like," I said, "but I was going to invite you upstairs."

Norm let out a long and agonized sound as he hunched forward and pressed his forehead into the top of his steering wheel. "Don't say stuff like that to me, Fisk," he moaned, "I'm only a dog chasin' a fancy car. Wouldn't know what the hell to do if I caught it."

When I laughed, he turned his head sideways against the wheel and watched me with a dizzy grin on his face. "I think you'd figure it out okay," I said, but relented. I paused with my hand on the door. "Thank you," I said again. I ran the edge of my thumbnail over the edge of the latch handle. "Honestly. For . . . seeing me. Not just for dinner, or this do-over of Christmas."

I gestured between us with a flapping hand. Norm chuckled as he caught it softly by the wrist, and he held my gaze as he kissed me gently on the heel of my palm.

"It is and would always be my pleasure, Annie," he murmured.

Damn it. I surged forward and left him with one more kiss.

"Okay," I said against the corner of his mouth, and then with my head thrown back as Norm smacked lingering, piquant little kisses along the line of my neck, "*Okay!* Okay. I have to go. Really, I do."

From my doorstep, I waved goodbye to the rumbling Barracuda. I watched as Norm shifted into gear and disappeared down the dark ribbon of the street.

When I got upstairs, my vision felt endless in the dark. I didn't bother turning on any lights.

I hadn't let myself risk feeling this way since leaving St. Christopher.

I had assumed my heart began and ended with Evelyn, but now a drop cloth had been thrown off its surface to reveal potential still sparkling and fresh in my rib cage, as though it hadn't been collecting dust.

Maybe it was the bourbon. Maybe it was the promise of a change from the mundane, a thrown stitch in the orderly row of my routine that I was quietly afraid I would never break. Maybe it was just Norman.

Truth be told, I was surprised I could feel this for a man. My attraction to women was a comfort to me, a safety despite the taboo. Desiring a woman could not ever lead me to a husband, nor to a child, to the terrifying potential of a father who might disappear like mine had.

But Norm felt different. He felt familiar, obvious, like my favorite sweater I hadn't pulled from its storage box since leaving Santa Fe for lack of mountain cold here.

Perhaps this could be different. Perhaps I could keep someone close, just this once.

I toed off my shoes and unclipped my garter belt to roll down my stockings, used the toilet, brushed my teeth, and washed my face in the dark. I stripped off the rest of my clothes and wriggled into the warmth of my bedcovers in my underthings. When I tipped my face sideways into my pillow, I smelled the soft cling of Norm's cologne in my hair.

The moon was a thick white tooth in my window. I stared at the pearly shaft of light and, like counting sheep, compared the ways in which kissing Norman was both so very familiar and entirely new: his gentleness, the soft play of his fingertips along my face, the shape of his lips smiling ever so slightly under mine; the fine grit of clean-shaven skin, the baritone burr of his voice at my jaw, the way he said my name so delicately.

1959—ST. MARY'S STREET, HEADING SOUTH
San Antonio, Texas

I slapped a hand to my forehead. "Oh, goddamn it."

Evelyn glanced over at me from the driver's seat. "What, are you okay?"

We slowed to a stop in the yellow pour of a streetlight. Evelyn's station wagon idled with a low, boat-bellied grumble. I shut my eyes and sighed. "I'm fine. I forgot to call my mother."

A sound of commiseration came out from between Evelyn's gritted teeth. "Do you need to go back to campus?"

A note of regretful apprehension was heavy in her voice. I shook my head. "No, but there's a phone booth just back there." I jerked my thumb over my shoulder and winced. "Would you mind?"

Come on, Evelyn had harried me as I cast about my room for the necklace I wanted to wear to the gallery, *we're already late!*

She sighed lightly and glanced over her shoulder as she pulled the wheel around. "No, it's fine."

I leaned over the seat and kissed her shoulder. "Thank you."

Once we had U-turned and pulled up to idle beside the phone

booth standing opposite the empty sidewalk ahead of us, she fixed me
with a look. "You owe me."

I slipped out of the car and into the little box, nickels in hand. Evelyn was taking us to a gallery in King William, the cool district downtown full of interesting people and even more interesting art, and I
hated to make her wait on me—but my weekly call with Mother was
the least I could do.

The operator connected me, and I listened to the line trill as part of
me hoped Mother wasn't in. I checked my wristwatch—eight o'clock in
Santa Fe, what would she usually be doing at eight? I kept telling her
to pick up new hobbies, make friends with some of the other women on
the block, give herself something to do that wasn't just radio programs
and work and the daily march of the horse pills that kept her mood
managed.

"Hello?"

Regret clashed hard with relief as Mother's voice piped down the
line. I licked my lips and shrugged up against one interior corner of the
booth. "Hi, Mother, it's me."

"I wondered if you'd forgotten." There was a tired smile in her
voice. The idea of her waiting on me made the regret win out a little.
"What are you up to tonight?"

I caught Evelyn's eye from outside the booth as she lit a cigarette,
watching me evenly. The last time I spoke with Mother, she had asked
after the men on campus. I spun a white lie about a handsome adjunct
from the Midwest, and then spent the rest of the evening making up
the sordid story of his imaginary life while twisted up in hysterics on
Evelyn's floor.

Expected to inherit the family sausage business, Evelyn declared, her
voice very serious, as I laughed so hard I teared up, *but the poor guy has
no stomach for Chicago any longer!*

"A date," I said, not looking away from Evelyn. The risk of it made my tongue tingle as though I'd just sipped on something too hot too soon.

"Oh!" Mother sounded like she sat up a little on her end of the phone line. "That young man from Chicago?"

In the brief silence between us, I tried to focus on the crackling buzz of the phone line and see if I could hear the radio turned down a few clicks or the ice in her glass. I chewed on my lip.

"We're going to an art gallery."

"That sounds lovely. Remind me what he looks like, what's his name?"

I kept my stare on Evelyn, who was looking down the arterial bend of the road reaching through the dark toward downtown. "His name is Eddie. He's blond, tall. He's a humanities major."

"Is he a writer?"

"Oh, God no." A genuine smile flickered at my mouth.

"What's so bad about a writer? Your father had a beautiful way with words. I think I still have some of his letters somewhere from his Oxford days."

The mention of my father made the back of my neck burn as though under a titration of acid. I shifted on my feet and crossed my free arm tight around my middle, leaning into the handset. "How's the house?"

I deflected. I always deflected. Even *thinking about* thinking about Daddy made it feel like I was peeking over the ledge of a chasm. The back of my mind clammed up. Not a single lick of anything deeper than my surface-level goings-on made it down the phone line. I was an immovable boulder, and all my mother wanted to do was understand me.

It was terrible. I had no idea how to fix it. I told myself there would be time enough later to figure out how she fit into the rest of my life.

Mother told me about the house—nothing was new. I fed a few

nickels into the box to keep us connected when the line prompted me. I asked which serials she was listening to these days. She asked about my classes, and I told her that astronomy was particularly interesting She asked about Professor Laitz; she always liked what I had to say about Professor Laitz. I thumbed another couple of coins into the slot.

When we eventually said good night, I settled the handset chunkily back into its cradle. Beneath my glasses, I pinched at the inside corners of my eyes and counted to six before blowing out a heavy breath.

I blinked quickly and rolled my shoulders back. Rapping twice on the glass, I drew Evelyn's attention and nodded at the door of the phone booth as I shouldered it open.

Evelyn moseyed up and stood just outside the opening. "How is she?"

I scowled at nothing and kicked the toe of my shoe against the edge of the booth, running my thumb over one hinge of the folding door. "Oblivious."

Evelyn took a shallow breath, drawing air to say something, but stopped herself. I looked up as she jammed her cigarette back between her lips and drew deeply on it. I frowned at her. "What?"

"Nothing," she said. She pistoned an exhale out from the corner of her mouth.

"No, what?"

Evelyn let out the tightened sigh I hated to hear her make—her passions swung broadly. She was content or she was exasperated, with little in between. I was still learning how to skate around her spinier edges without being pricked by them, like skirting a flowering burst of cholla in the middle of a footpath.

"Don't get mad," she preempted, which made me roll my eyes.

"Hell of an opener," I groused. Evelyn gave me a flat look.

"I've overheard the stuff you talk about with her, Annie. I've never met your mother, but you can't get upset with her for not knowing you if she doesn't have anything to go on," she said. "What can you expect from conversations with a woman who doesn't know who you are, besides this . . . constant, low-grade misery?"

"My relationship with my mother is none of your business," I snapped. Evelyn raised her eyebrows, coolly impressed at me biting back.

"I'm not saying it is. I'm saying you clearly have a habit of trying to bury yourself in your own reservations, but your mother's got one hell of a shovel on you, doesn't she?"

My stomach made a tight knot. Over the past several months as the people we had become to each other—companions, girlfriends, whatever my undefined but boiling affection wanted to call it from day to day—Evelyn had never turned the barbs of my own shortcomings against me like this, held the mirror up to my face.

I clenched my teeth. "It's not that simple."

"I never suggested it was," Evelyn said. "Don't put words in my mouth."

"I'm not putting words in your mouth; I'm trying to stand up for myself!"

"And I'm trying to make you feel better, but clearly we both need a little more practice!" Evelyn threw up her hands and turned on her heel to stalk back to her station wagon, her embroidered boots clacking briskly over the concrete. She sat hard beside the hood ornament. I glared at nothing in the opposite distance as the crickets chorused around me, rising alongside the angry white noise between my ears. The soft flicking of Evelyn's lighter precluded its faint glow. She smoked another cigarette down to its filter in silence as we stewed separately.

Her passion awed me into a soft sort of fury. Evelyn could care so deeply about such specific things, but she never let her caring twist her up like it did me. I envied her detachment, the privilege to possess feelings rather than falling slave to them. I always wondered if I might be able to learn that skill. My problem was I cared too much, but I didn't have Evelyn's intuition for direction or action. She acted, and I just . . . drifted. Maybe *misery* was the right term after all.

"Evelyn," I finally called out, weak with surrender. "Please come here." I watched her kick off the hood of the car and flick the burnt-out butt between her fingers into the street before coming back over to me.

"I know I poked a tender spot," Evelyn said, "but it's the truth. I've told you I'm not in the business of lying to you, and I meant it."

My heart squeezed so tightly into the low space of my throat I thought I might choke on it. I prodded my tongue at my lips and stirred up the explanation she deserved. "I don't . . . go home anymore. I owe my mother time, at the very least, but I can't give her the truth," I finally spat into the night.

Evelyn said nothing and watched me. I made a blind gesture into the space between us. "It—there's a lot of . . . sad ground between me and her. No-man's-land. Neither of us is any good at walking on it. If I forget to reach out, she forgets that I need her to and we just . . . stay in our foxholes. I don't know. It's easier to ignore than to do the work. Does that make any sense?"

Evelyn's eyes softened slightly. "Sounds like one of you might end up with trench foot," she said. I snorted, a smile twitching onto my mouth.

"Gross."

With a small, quiet sigh, Evelyn stepped closer and smoothed her hands down my upper arms until I uncrossed them. She carded our fingers together where our palms met and angled for my gaze until I finally looked up at her. "Take it from me, Red. Don't let the fact she knows you love her stand for nothing."

"I know," I muttered.

We only spoke about her mother when Evelyn was loaded, taken by the occasional dust devil of self-pity. *She doesn't let me come home*, Evelyn told me once with her face buried in my waist. *Unless I show up with a guy on my arm, I'm as good as dead to her. Like I was never even born.*

When I tried to look away again, Evelyn ducked her face down slightly. Those soft brown eyes of hers were deep and earnest, through and through. "I just think, hell, you've still got something precious, so why don't you use it? Why not just talk to her?"

"Sometimes," I admitted, "I think it would be easier if there was just . . . some other reason we didn't talk. I don't know."

Evelyn shook her head and bundled me into her arms, holding me close enough that I could smell the leather of her jacket beneath the layer of fresh smoke around her. "Don't wish for that," she murmured into my hair.

"I'm not wishing," I insisted, where my face was bowed into her shoulder.

"She loves you." Evelyn stepped back to look at me hard through her curtain bangs and hold me steady by my shoulders. "Be patient with yourself, Annie."

I nodded. "You're right."

"Broken clock, twice a day." Evelyn reached up one hand to rest on my jaw, stroking her thumb softly along my cheek. I twisted my face to catch her palm with a kiss to its center, pulling her closer.

"I'm not telling you to drag me to Santa Fe and have me introduce myself to her while I'm fucking you on the doorstep," Evelyn clarified as she followed me back into the booth and jostled the door shut behind us. "I just don't think you deserve to hang up after every conversation with a frown on that gorgeous face." She ran her thumb over the seam of my lips, and I nipped the pad softly. "She wouldn't want that. Right?"

I looped my arms up around the back of Evelyn's neck and tugged her down into a kiss, melting into it as she relented in kind. "Right," I said against her mouth. "Now let's be done talking about my mother, please."

Kissing devolved into soft petting, the soft petting turned heavy, and after a handful of breathless minutes, I found myself pressed back against the cloudy glass of the booth with the edge of Evelyn's jacket lapel humid under my panting mouth. Her hand was between my legs over my skirt, her fingers nimble and skilled, and her mouth played a dangerous game along the cords of my neck.

"I'm sorry," I gasped when I knew I was toeing the line of my limit. Evelyn looked at me expectantly, her cheeks pink with her efforts. I swallowed and tried again as my brain continued to slide to pieces: "I don't—like arguing with you."

Evelyn sniffed a chuckle and nuzzled against my ear. "Consider us even, Red."

I leaned helplessly into the heel of her palm. She rounded me off with quick, absolving accuracy in the phone booth, and I trembled and gasped nonsense into the bend of Evelyn's collarbone as I broke.

She kissed me slowly while I returned to myself, lingering and sweet, and pushed my hair away from my flushed face, my skewed glasses.

"I thought we were late," I panted, hoarse and heady. I reached for Evelyn's chunky silver belt buckle, but she batted my hands away.

"We were already late when we left." She nodded her chin up over my shoulder. "That pearly eye's gonna watch us get there safe anyways."

I twisted to see the moon, replete in the dark sky through the scratched and clouded glass of the booth. Still held in place under Evelyn's protective lean, I twisted my arm up to give it a middle finger. "Voyeur," I quipped. Evelyn laughed.

"Didn't know you were into that scene, Fisk."

I straightened my glasses as I wriggled upright, combing my fingers through my hair. I shrugged. "Can't know anything until it's tested."

Evelyn rolled her eyes and pulled me to her for another kiss, where I felt the curve of her smile. She tasted like cloves. "*And* we're back. That head of yours." She tapped me twice on the temple with one knuckle. "Too full all the time."

1967–THE MANNED SPACECRAFT CENTER, THE OFFICES AND DATABASE WING

Houston, Texas

The Monday after my dinner with Norm, I pulled up to the Center far too early. I was trying to avoid tempting fate with a new and concerning fussiness in my car's starter. The hatchback had a unique tendency to give up when doing so would cause the most inconvenience, but not before lingering for about two or three years after starting to show symptoms. I would take care of it later.

I had a test that morning for the programming team, and not a bite of breakfast in my belly for the nerves. I had fixed the Project Y pin to my buttonhole before leaving the house in a bid for luck.

The sun was barely up. The parking lot was sparse and silent. As I crossed through the lobby, the morning janitor and I nodded hello at each other while he finished putting away his mop.

Through the beehive halls of the building, I passed the empty secretarial pool and kept going down the east corridor. Stopping at the junction, I hitched my purse high onto my shoulder. Shoulders straight; eyes on the door facing me less than twenty strides away.

The programming suite.

I could do this. I could *do this*. I had four years of experience and two bachelor's degrees. I knew computers. *Hello, world*. I could *d*—

As I passed Norm's office, his door swung open. *Shit*. I hadn't even noticed his light on.

I danced out of the way with a yelp and narrowly missed a slosh from the coffee cup in his hand as he stopped short.

"Jesus and Mary on a *fuckin'* rocket—*Oh*." Norm froze halfway through licking a splash of coffee from his wrist. He straightened and fussed at the cuff of his sleeve, flicking at the drop with his fingertips instead. "Morning, Annie."

I dug my fingers into my palms and managed not to crack too wide of a smile. "Morning, Norm. I thought we kept baby bottles in the break room for the navigators; you sure you can drink from that without using both hands?"

Norm rolled his tongue into the side of his cheek. He gestured at me with his mug, liquid dangerously close to the lip again. "Funny! You're a funny gal, Fisk."

"Why are you here so early?" I said, narrowing my eyes.

"I always get more done in the morning before the rest of the crew starts coming in." He nodded at the programming suite. "Ready to get obliterated?"

I snorted. *"Obliterated."*

"You haven't met Ros?" Norm's eyes widened gently as if in awe of the woman. "Imagine Marie Curie," Norm said as he began to count the fingers of one hand, his voice low, "Ada Lovelace, Amelia Earhart, and Dorothy Dandridge all combined into one person. That's Ros Washington."

My mouth went dry. "She's the one testing me?"

Norm clapped my shoulder. "She'll love you! You'll do great."

His hand lingered a little. I gave him a benign frown and ignored the fact I wanted him to leave it there. "It isn't a personality contest. Computers don't care if I have a nice smile."

Norm shrugged. "Don't need a computer to see that."

I kept frowning at him, even as I felt a treasonous blush give me away. "You're not helping."

"You'll do great," he said again, and sauntered past me. He paused after four more steps and turned to face me again, whirling easily on the freshly waxed morning floor. "And if you pass," he said, "I'd love to take you to dinner again sometime."

I raised my eyebrows. "Only if I pass? What if I fail?"

"If you fail, we split the bill."

I watched him for a moment, my heart twisting sweetly. I swallowed. "You'd better not have jinxed me."

Leaving Norm backlit by the pale sunrise, his silhouette sure and pleased as he disappeared down the hall toward mission control, I turned on my own heel and hurried to the programming suite.

The left-side double door sighed inward when I leaned on the latching bar. A low throb enveloped me at once: the planetary hum of processors at work.

The room was huge, broadly hexagonal, with a small company of desks and transports on one end before the rest of the space rose into ranks of power racks and transistor cabinets more numerous than I had ever seen. It smelled of thermal adhesive and heat sinks. The mild charge in the air made the small hairs on the back of my neck stand up.

Jesus and Mary *and* Joseph on a fucking rocket. This place was Eden.

"Good morning! Are you Anne?"

I turned to face the greeting and found a petite Black woman in a maroon A-line dress standing up from a large desk beside a monitor the size of a small television. She had a beauty queen smile and the most immaculately pressed hair I had ever seen. I stuck out my hand. "Yes, hi. Annie, Annie Fisk. You're Rosalie?"

"Rosalie Washington, Ros for short. We like brevity here. Nice to meet you." She shook my hand and gestured at the room, the strangely harmonic wheeze of processors at work making it feel as though we stood in a pair of iron lungs. "Let's show you around, shall we?"

Ros led me through the room and pointed out the parts worth knowing, as though I was surveying a place to live in—here were the memory banks; there were the power supply racks; those were the cords for the computer desks, careful not to trip on them.

"The code comes to us from the folks at MIT," Ros said when we were settled at an empty desk with a test booklet resting on the keyboard. Memories of midterms and finals swam at the back of my head. "Marge, Marge Hamilton, she's the one who runs it all over there—she was one of our first *human* computers."

Ros woke the sleeping transport with a hefty *chuk* from the switch on the back of it and rested her hand on top as though showing off a game show prize. The screen looked like infinity staring out at me, ocular and black. It flickered to life with convex text scrolling and blinking and skimming across the screen. I stared hard into its depths.

"And this," Ros finished with an amused smile, "is one of our own little spacecrafts."

She gestured at the chair, and I sat carefully. Ros loaded an answer slip into one end of the computer and smiled at me when she saw me watching. "Pretend it isn't here," she said. "It's only an hour-long test."

The screen awoke with a grainy spurt of noise and the scuttle of tubes waking up with current. "Is it terribly difficult?" I asked.

"Oh, I shouldn't think so. Just a little tedious. Here, let's get you set up."

Ros leaned over my shoulder and typed a cluster of three- and four-letter packets that made a grainy little *breet* sound when she executed the command line. The whirring of a fan kicked up. From inside the monitor, the faintest chirp of cathode collision scored the letters that furled across the screen.

"Press this key to begin," Ros said, pointing at a broad, flat button by my right hand, "and go until you're done. Let me know if you get stuck."

I managed a small smile. I was already focused on the instructions that now ran across the screen. "Thanks."

"Good luck!"

Ros returned to her desk. For a few seconds, before tapping the button to begin, I watched her, the stacks of notes and memos on her desk in tidy piles, the confident set of her shoulders as her fingers flew across her keys. Typing on the computer was a blockier sound than I was used to hearing in the secretarial pool, like plastic pebbles knocking together rather than the sharp razorbill pecking of metallic hammers.

It calmed me.

I took a deep breath, held it for a moment, and pressed the start button as I exhaled.

Question one: *What are the two parts of the computer processor's instruction set?* Opcode and operand.

And two: *If there is an instruction of 12 bits with 2 bits for the addressing mode and 4 bits for the operand, how many instructions can you have?* 64.

The test moved into syntax prompts after I got through the basics of the language, easy enough to pick up as I went. Assembly was mnemonic rather than binary, which meant I was able to make little mental pictures of the shorthand as I made my way through each code prompt—for instance: *msg* stood for message. I imagined the three letters pressed together until they could fit into a mailbox. It made *sense*.

I was rapt.

As my fear of this all being a fluke gave way to a reluctant ease, I melted into the familiar rote of test-taking. The chirp and whir and rhythm of the work captivated me entirely.

After long enough that the edges of my vision had blurred a bit with focus, the monitor gave one last clicky beep. I was done. I sat back in my chair and glanced at my watch: ten minutes to spare.

The slip spat itself out from the side of my transport. Ros came over to retrieve it, her shoes clacking smartly across the floor. "You made good time, huh? Come with me." She gestured over her shoulder at the door.

I took up my purse and bustled after Ros to get to the scanner room. Now that I knew what the programming suite felt like, how deeply and immediately it smacked of a home for the way I ticked, I was terrified I'd failed and would never get the chance to be in there again.

I must have been fussing with my pin. Ros glanced at my hand and gave me a warm grin as the scanner began to churn with an awful, nasal screech.

"Thank you for your time, Ros, I really appreciate it," I said over the noise.

"It's not a problem." Ros waved a flippant hand. "It's not much earlier than I'm usually in."

"Is it always so quiet in there?" I said.

"Pardon?"

The scanner was really chewing on my results. I raised my voice a little more; "Is it always so *quiet* in there?"

"Betty Eagan will talk your ears off about her cat if you let her, but otherwise we tend to keep it pretty library-like. Why, does it bother you?"

I shook my head with a hasty toss. Ros watched me for a moment. "How do you find the secretaries?" she asked. She was eyeing the pin on my lapel with an intrigued fondness.

I drew my brows together. "How do you mean?"

Ros considered this for a moment. "Are they particularly friendly with you?"

I peered at the machine for a moment. "I don't know," I admitted. "I never really gave it much thought."

She pulled a considering face. "Well, they don't tend to care for our little corner here. I'd hate to ruin any friendships of yours."

I turned that concern over for a moment. Recognition dawned as my chest tightened, a giddiness I didn't want to feel until I knew for certain. "And why is that?" I asked lightly.

Ros's smile tipped up at one edge. The machine quit growling. My test slip had floated down the floor—with every single question marked correct.

With her hands on her hips, Ros looked pleased with herself. "Well done, Ms. Fisk. Can you start Tuesday?"

That was tomorrow.

✦ ✦ ✦

God, I could hardly focus for the rest of the day.

I decided I would wait until everyone was gone before I packed up my desk and returned my drawer key to Fran Greene. I didn't want to cause any waves—not that anyone would miss me, but I would hate to be a distraction.

Now that I knew to watch for it, I could mark how none of the other girls came up to talk or gossip *with* me—it was at me, or about me. They had their little units and cliques, buzzing in their own combs in the hive, and I was a lone worker bee with a little too much pollen stuck to her elbows and knees. I had never belonged, not really. The notion didn't bother me. I had a new chapter to start tomorrow.

I stayed late, poring over more of Norm's notes, a particularly valid excuse given that new landing module tests were starting in a few months. When I was the only one left in the secretarial suite, save for Fran in her office probably wondering when the hell she'd be allowed to lock up after me, I covered my typewriter and made quick work of packing up my desk.

When I sidled into Fran's office with my box in my arms and my drawer key hooked on one finger, Fran looked up over the edge of a pulp novel. "Sad to see you go, Annie."

Are you really? I dangled the key between my thumb and forefinger. "Yes, well. Winds of change and all that."

Fran pulled a bit of a dramatic face. "We'll miss you. I hope you don't hate it there."

I shifted the weight of my box in my hands. It was filled with mostly paltry trinkets—a plastic puzzle cube, a framed photo of my father and two of his friends when they were still bright-eyed, some file folders of calculation carbons I still needed to keep on hand. I frowned. "Why would I hate it?"

Fran peeked over my shoulder out her office door, in the direction of the computer bank. "It's . . . different," she whispered with a saccharine brittleness.

I followed her sight line to see Ros at the double doors locking up behind herself. The fluorescent lights bounced off the berry color of her dress, a jewel-toned complement to her deep brown skin. She noticed me with my box in my arms and waved. "See you tomorrow, Annie."

"See you, Ros," I called back. Fran's lips had soured more tightly together when I turned back around.

I narrowed my eyes and stayed quiet until Ros's footsteps retreated. "If all you see are assholes, Fran, perhaps give some thought to the common denominator."

I put the key down beside her typewriter and marched out.

1967—THE MANNED SPACECRAFT CENTER, THE PARKING LOT
Houston, Texas

The night was on its way to a deep, brisk navy-dark as I crossed into the parking lot. Someone was standing next to my car—I hissed a low oath when I realized what time it was and hurried over at a shallow jog.

"Sorry," I huffed as Norm turned to face me with the last of a cigarette at the edge of his mouth. He smiled. I forgot how to talk for a moment. "Have you been waiting for me since six?"

Norm made a flippant sound as I yanked open the back-seat door on my side of the car. "McCabe has us all at full-steam these days, I finished pretty late. Haven't been out here long, just one smoke."

I shoved my desk box in the back seat and shut the door again. A yawn took me by surprise, and I leaned against the edge of the roof to keep it as demure as possible. Norm chuckled.

"Hey, so congratulations," he said, reaching over to chuck me gently on the shoulder. "Passed with flying colors. How about that dinner?"

I gave him a tired grin. The parking lot was nearly empty. I hitched my purse carefully up my shoulder and waited an extra second before

I nodded. "We could pick up something on the way if you'd like. Want to come over for a drink?"

Norm's cheeks blushed a bold red even in the half-dark, his eyes widening for the briefest second before he caught himself. "Of course," he managed, "absolutely."

We took my car—the Barracuda was less noticeable staying late in the lot than my snub-nosed Nash. I promised to drive him back later and wondered if I wanted *later* to mean *tomorrow morning*.

After swinging by the liquor store for a bottle of red and then taking a swing through the Whataburger window down the road, we arrived at my building with a pair of bright-orange paper bags in either of my hands and the wine tucked in Norm's elbow. In the little nook of my kitchen, I fetched a pair of plates to arrange our food while Norm perused my eclectic collection of records.

He made a bright, intrigued sound from in front of the right-side shelf. I looked up at him. "What?"

Norm glanced at me. "Just browsing, you got a bundle of letters here beside your Baez. Don't want to stick my nose in your business."

Alertness shot through me. I blinked. My letters from Evelyn.

"You could look at them if you want," I said, not really meaning it. Norm barked a laugh.

I looked at him through the slot of the galley kitchen. "What? That's not weird?"

Norm looked a little beguiled from his crouch near the *N*-thru-*P* section of my records. "Annie, you had an entire *life* before you even knew I existed. Of course it isn't weird."

"I don't do this very often," I blurted, and busied myself plating our food. A few seconds later "Tombstone Blues" was spinning.

I brought two plates to the coffee table, piled with burgers and fries and onion rings. "I didn't read you for a folkie," I said.

Norm lowered himself to sit on the floor beside me. He unbuttoned and rolled up his sleeves tidily. "What can I say," he said with a sigh, taking up the wine bottle and the opener I'd laid beside it, "I love a good story."

I turned around in place, thought for a moment, and bustled back into the kitchen. I hunted through the cabinets and only found one wineglass. "Damn it."

"All good in there?" Norm called over.

"I forgot to do my dishes," I admitted. "I only have one wineglass clean."

The bottle popped as Norm twisted out the cork. He cast a look to where I stood with the single glass in my hand at the edge of the kitchen.

"We could share, if you aren't bothered." Norm gestured with the bottle, shaking it jauntily. "Already kissed, didn't we?"

I blushed and returned to the table. He poured a single glass for us, clinked the edge of the bottle against it with a mocking toast, and let me take the first sip. We tucked into our food as Bob Dylan warbled from the record player.

Under the even tread of conversation, our dinner went to nothing but greasy paper and used napkins. The wine was almost empty by the time I got up to put the plates in the sink and exhume a half-eaten pint of ice cream from my freezer and, thankfully, two spoons.

Norm and I ended up flopped on opposite sides of my sofa opining about air resistance. The ice cream was gone—I'd let Norm go for most of it. The record player had long gone to fuzz in the background of our conversation. Neither of us cared to switch the album over.

When Norm glanced at his watch for the first time all night and made a regretful sound, my heart ached.

"I should go," he said, levering himself up to sit. He wrangled a few scraps of wrappers and napkins onto his empty plate, tidying a little aimlessly.

I chewed softly on my lip. "You don't have to if you don't want to," I said. Sweet apprehension rattled the spaces between my tendons. "I'm not kicking you out. *Yet.*"

Norm smirked, carefully setting the empty wine bottle back on the coffee table from its place on the floor at our feet. "You're a nice girl, Annie. I don't want to impose."

I sat up a little and fixed Norm with a look. "I want you to stay," I said clearly.

Norm watched me for a moment. His gaze was noisy with too many possibilities to pin down from where I sat. I scooted closer. He swallowed.

"You have chatty neighbors?"

"Yeah, tons of eyes out here in nowheresville. Worried for your reputation, or mine?" I laid a gentle hand on his bare forearm, warm and still. "I don't care what some old uptight someone thinks about the company I choose to keep," I said.

What I didn't tell him was the whole truth of it, the piece that dug its fingers into me whenever I looked at him: he felt familiar in such a sharp way, carved in relief against the back of my mind. I couldn't tell him the whole of it. I just couldn't.

So I touched lightly at the fine fabric of his shirt, pulled him down to me, and kissed him the way I'd wanted to the other night.

He responded like I was water in the desert. He tasted of wine and the tart tang of mustard. The hair along the back of his head was still soft as down when I reached up to cradle him there. Norm hazarded at the seam of my lips with a careful press of his tongue, gently beckoning me, and I opened to him with a sigh.

We shuffled together on the couch, crowding each other with slow shifting and gentle touches, until I muttered, "The bed," against Norm's mouth. My heartbeat was pounding under my skin. I was leaning up between the arm of the sofa and Norm's body, clinging to him as he held me close and kissed me to a dizzied flush. "Come to bed."

Norm nodded and slid back. His hand still lingered on my flank, playing at the edge of one garter strap beneath my skirt. Very few decisions before had ever felt so firm and perfect to me.

I took him by the hand and kept the lights off. Norm's silhouette stood out in the bedroom doorway as he came through it, backed by the hall light. The moment struck me like a leap into the deep end of the swimming pool. He was so *right*.

Norm moved to stand between my knees. He slid my glasses off as I looked up at him, and he eased me back onto my covers. I leaned into the thumb he swept over my cheek, chasing friction.

"Can I touch you?" he murmured.

I nodded. "Please."

His hand slid up from my knee to my thigh to the gap in my skirt, and I gasped silently when his fingertips tested softly between my legs — it had been years since I'd had the privilege of someone else's body warm and present above, or beside, or below me. I melted into Norm's hand and spurred him forward with my knees gripping his hips as his fingers set to work.

Norm unclipped my stockings with his free hand. He slipped the soft nylon down to my ankles, leaning down to kiss me as he kept his hand slow and steady between us. I helped him unzip my skirt and he pulled it away along with my girdle and my shorts as I maneuvered in quick, wriggling bursts, desperate not to be parted from him for too many heartbeats at a time.

"Have you done this before?" Norm asked, his breath ghosting along my neck. He was peppering a string of kisses there. I was putty in his grip and had to try twice before I found my voice.

"Yes," I gasped, so much crammed into one syllable — *Yes, with a woman; yes, with hands and mouths and some lovely sleepless nights; no, not with a man, but you're so sweet and terribly handsome, and I think all you really need to know is that I've had an orgasm before, and you seem to want to give me one.*

He kissed me and dipped one fingertip into me, shallow and gentle. I tightened my legs around him, digging my heels into the backs of his thighs, and Norm breathed approval into my mouth.

My legs began to tremble after several minutes that felt like years. Norm had two fingers and an expeditious thumb at work with devious accuracy. "Norman," I panted, clinging to him. He kissed my neck again where my collar curved, leaning into me as he angled the shape of his touch to pull me even closer.

"Come on," he whispered, more encouragement than demand. I had but two, three more desperate gasps—and then before I could even realize it was fraying, my thread snapped and sent me reeling.

I dug my fingers into Norm's shoulders and cried out softly, the first swell crashing like sparks through my limbs. I rode the second wave with a roll of my shaking hips, pressing against Norm's hand. The third, fourth, fifth pulse of ruby-red contentment tightened my arms around his torso, lifting myself to him.

When I settled, I released the vise of my arms to lay back and stared up at Norm. His expression was bright with pleasure, alert, and he was loosening his tie with one finger hooked at his collar. The half-moon carved a sharp stripe of light across his body. He still had his hand braced gently against me, cradling me through the aftershocks.

"God," I panted.

Norm paused. "Do you want to . . . ?" His hand stilled on his belt buckle.

"Absolutely," I insisted, wrestling my blouse off my arms and shuffling out of the rest of my underclothes. Norm set to the buttons of his shirt as I rooted my way out of my brassiere.

I shuffled back against the bed and welcomed the soft nudge of his fingers again. Apprehension gnawed on me shallowly, enough to sting but not hurt, and I tightened my grip on Norm's shoulders beneath his open shirt. "Go slow," I whispered.

"That's the plan, darlin'."

He kissed me as he began to ease himself inside, breathing a low oath at the back of his mouth. I hissed gently at the breach—he stilled and soothed me with a nuzzle of his nose.

"Been a while?" he hummed. There was a smile in his voice against my ear. I swallowed down my nerves, focusing on the way my ache for him had become a sharp burn.

"Something like that."

"It's okay. We're going slow. I've been—*ah*—out of the game for a bit, we could say, so apologies if I get too excited."

A giggle burbled to my surface, and I buried my face in Norm's neck as he huffed his own laugh. His hips shifted, sliding in by each aching second. I bit my lip and finally relaxed into it when the warmth of him shifted just so, sliding home with a ripple that shuddered up my spine.

The bedframe creaked slightly. Norm's buttons hung open, and I watched the moonlight peer through the crisp cotton and paint my skin silver beneath him.

"Christ, Annie," Norm gasped, his hair falling in pieces across his forehead. His left hand gripped the skewed pillow by my head and his right was flat against my lower back to angle my hips up into him. "There you are."

His voice was shorn hoarse. I was dazzled. The only response I could muster was to reach up with my mouth and kiss him in messy desperation. Norm made a beautifully shattered sound, and tipped over his edge.

I shut my eyes as well, like I could feel it, too. Maybe I could. Drunk on my own satisfaction, I wondered how close two people could get before they became the same body.

In the bathroom, while Norm caught his breath in a sprawl on his back after we carefully slid apart, I peered at my reflection in the mirror as I rinsed my hands. I had tidied myself up and had come away mottled, blushed, smeared like the edges of my lipstick and ruddy with bliss. I scrubbed off my makeup and spent an extra moment with the drying cloth over my eyes trying not to come apart with the hum of newness still making my pulse pound.

When I returned to the bedroom, Norm was stretched out in the long lance of moonlight.

"You know," he said, his voice heavy, "this may just be the sex talking, but I'm gonna say it anyways: I've felt drawn to you ever since the night we met."

My heart fluttered. I folded my legs up under myself on the foot of the bed and stared at the long, pale lines of Norm's body in repose. "Did you know that planets sing to each other?"

He lifted his head to peer at me from across his torso. "Space is a vacuum, ain't it?"

"Not singing in a way we would understand, but each one emits its own . . . ultra-low frequency as it turns. The music of the spheres." I reached out to trace the fair hair lining Norm's stomach with light fingers. He shivered, curling closer to me. He was beautiful like this, prone and marmoreal. "Sometimes when their orbits intersect, they resonate with each other."

Norm was giving me a smile that all but melted my heart when I glanced back up at his face from the ridge of his ribs above his navel. "Can I be Neptune?" he asked. He yawned. "Neptune's my favorite."

He fixed me with that tender look, his face pressed sideways in the sheets. I wanted to hold him until the world ended.

I gave him a smile, my whole body alive. "Of course you can." I leaned down to kiss him.

Perhaps I wasn't the only one who looked for invisible lines that connected people. Maybe Norm wanted to know if connection could be quantified, too. Maybe he was Neptune, singing low and long from the endless blue of its surface, and I could fix myself to his orbit and never tire of his song.

✦

1957—THE APODACA HOUSE, NEAR MIDNIGHT
Santa Fe, New Mexico

The engine cut its grumbling as I twisted the key. From outside, the muffled sounds of crickets and other night things scuttling through the low scrub brushes bled through the skeleton of the Cadillac. I stared at the yellow wash of the headlights dying out against the gravel path as enchantment still thrummed through the high points of my body, mixing with a sour sort of regret.

It wasn't that Peggy Lipton and I were doing anything groundbreaking. Twice a week we would listen to reruns of *X Minus One* sprawled out on her bedroom floor after school, share the gossip from the opposite ends of our social strata—she was a cheerleader, and I was studying for the Putnam Competition in a few weeks—and eventually end up with our limbs all tangled as we kissed each other silly on her bright pink throw rug.

It's just fun, Peggy had said earlier that evening when I finally drummed up the courage to ask her why, especially now that she was going steady with Michael Young?

"I don't want to be fun," I said out loud in the private clutch of the car. I chewed on the inside of my cheek and killed the headlights with a *clik*, listening to the engine cooling down and the pebbles loosening themselves from its mechanism with soft little *tnk-tnk-tnk*s. I heaved a sigh and knocked my head back against the headrest.

Honestly, I couldn't blame Peggy for keeping it to strictly kissing-only and never letting the truth of what we were doing upstairs pass across the threshold of her bedroom. We were just girls being girls, as far as she was concerned.

It was useless to bellyache over it. What we were doing could never be anything more than idle fun, and that was simply the reality of it. You kissed girls, and it was fun, and then you got engaged to a man. Life went on.

I swallowed my frustration and gathered my bookbag. Creeping quietly through the front gate into the house, I was sure to open and shut the door as softly as possible to keep from waking Mother. All the lights were off, and I was about to make for my bedroom when I paused at the soft glow of the reading lamp in the den.

Damnit. I sighed to myself and steeled my guts to face my mother head-on.

"You're a little late, Annie," Mother announced when I stopped in the doorway of the den. She had her hair in rollers and a cigarette burning down in the ashtray beside her. A glass was sweating softly in her hand, ice clinking in a low amber pour. I hadn't seen her drink in weeks.

"We were studying," I said, gesturing back over my shoulder. "Got tied up in differentials. Peggy's not so quick with them."

Mother hummed and took a sip. It didn't matter whether she believed me, only that I gave her something worth mulling over. *I* was afraid of the truth, so I couldn't imagine what it felt like from the outside. A swaying stack of white lies was better than baring the whole of me at once.

Mother regarded me steadily across the carpet between us. She let the silence hang for a moment, still as glass. "You'll have to be sensible about setting your own rules on things like curfew when you're away."

I bit down on the flutter of surprise that lit up through me to hear her inviting a conversation about me leaving. She didn't like to talk about it, not since my acceptance letter to St. Christopher had made her cry in the kitchen. She insisted it was because she was proud of me, but I knew the difference between her joy and her mourning.

Clearing my throat shallowly, I nodded. "Sure. That's—we've had assemblies at school to talk about preparing for it. Time management, scheduling, things like that."

Mother nodded. She picked up her cigarette and tapped off its long stem of ash, took one drag on it, and stubbed it out. "Humor an old lady," she said. "What are your plans?"

I resisted the urge to pluck at the skin around my thumbnail. "Well, my degree. And then from there, I . . . well, maybe my master's, or—a job, out East?"

Mother raised an eyebrow at me. "Are you asking me, or telling me?"

"Telling you." I drew my shoulders back ever so slightly.

She watched me intently as I avoided looking her directly in the eye. I wondered if her rare indulgence in a drink that night meant she had forgone her mood pills. That would explain the lucidity, the third degree.

"I thought your father was going to save the world someday," Mother said plainly. The ease in her voice hit me like a slap, cold and prickling across my skin. Mother *never* talked about Daddy.

I lowered myself down to sit on the bottom of the shallow, carpeted steps that led into the den from the hall. "How's that?"

Mother sighed to herself. "He *cared*. It wasn't just numbers to him. He really believed in what he was doing—before, well. When there was something worth caring about. Before they really knew what they could do."

I stayed judiciously silent and stared at Mother's composure. I would have never believed she could trust me with something like this.

"The reason we fought," she said, not meeting my eyes as the years showed in the lines of her face, darkened by the long shadows of a lone lamp to her side, "was because I never let him quit being that . . . paragon, in my mind. I demanded he present a side of himself that didn't exist anymore, or maybe never existed at all."

A beat of silence sat heavily in the den before Mother looked at me, singular and exacting. A shiver rushed down my spine with the acuity of it. Her gaze pared me open—had my mother demanded the truth of me in that moment, I would have spilled it at her feet.

"At the end of the day, he was just human," Mother said, her voice low and fierce. "But you, Annie—there's something about you that I can't shake."

My breath stuttered in my throat. "What, something not *human*?"

Mother sniffed and smiled. "Don't be silly. We're all human; we all make mistakes. You're bound to make a mess of them yourself, Lord knows I have. But there's . . ." She paused, staring at me; through me, as though she was reaching ahead to pick apart some piece of me yet unseen. Mother shook her head, once. "You're unbound by the things that held your father back," she finally said.

"Unbound," I repeated, my pulse hammering.

"You know how ugly it can get, chasing down answers to the things that don't make sense to the rest of us. I don't think he ever let himself admit that it got to him," Mother said.

Did I know anything of that ugliness? I could hardly remember the sound of my father's voice, the shape of his mouth when he smiled. Thinking of him made the roots of my teeth itch, so I didn't.

A fusty stillness nestled between me and Mother. I could hardly find my words, bowled over by the weight of being seen. It was alarming, to discover that the one person from whom I had hidden myself most carefully had been able to see me the entire time.

"I don't think I . . . know," I stammered, my face hot, "not really. I can't even remember him, Mother."

Mother's expression softened with regret. "I know."

"Do you?" I looked right at her. She looked right back.

"I'm used to being on the outside," Mother said carefully. "You and your father . . . you're smarter than me. The both of you. There's so much of him in you." Her eyes welled. I looked down at my shoes.

"You always say that."

"I always mean it. It scares me that I can't reach you properly."

"What does that have to do with my plans?" I asked carefully.

Mother took a shallow sip of her drink and set it on a coaster beside the ashtray. She ran an idle thumb over the back of her other hand, subtle and bird-boned. When did my mother become so small? "Just don't forget I'm here."

I felt terribly young again. I wanted to curl up and let my mother cradle me in her arms like she had when I was little.

"School won't be easy," Mother said. "It's not like what you're used to, you won't be able to pass without effort. But promise me you'll be careful with how closely you sew yourself to the work you do, Annie, because work like that—digging so deeply, playing God—it can swallow you whole before you even notice it happening."

I stared at her in muted bewilderment. "Where is this coming from?"

Mother watched me for a long moment. "You've become someone I recognize from a long time ago," she finally said, "and I wanted to say my piece to her."

A traitorous film of tears sprang up across the bends of my eyes. I blinked in a flurry before turning away to swipe a finger along my lashes. Giving a sharp sniffle, dispelling the tightness in my throat, I looked back at her and did not flinch. "What happened to Daddy? Be honest."

Mother stood and idly fluffed the couch cushions. I noticed the shape of her posture beginning to stoop somewhat, a brassiness drawing into her hair, vitality sapping from her edges ever so gently. "We have to let the past lie, baby. It doesn't matter. All you have to do is keep those Fisk genes in check. Alright?"

We shared a long look. A low rumble roared between my ears. *It matters,* I wanted to cry, *everything matters so much all the time!*

Mother started forward to brush past me up the low steps to retire into her room, but I stopped her with a hand around her wrist. "I don't want to leave you alone," I said.

Her soft skin was warm in my palm, the hairs on her arm fine, and I leaned in to press my forehead to her knuckles from my huddle on the step.

"I can't ask you to stay," Mother murmured. Her hand was very still in mine. "Don't worry about me."

She seemed to hesitate for a moment, and I felt her palm tighten in a hesitant squeeze around my thumb. "Remember, Annie," she whispered, "none of this was your fault."

And then she slipped from my grip, sliding away like silk on the wind, and disappeared into her bedroom.

I sat there alone and stared at nothing for a long time. The grandfather clock across the room chucked its low-bellied way through the minutes, steady and constant and blind to anything but the passage of its hands.

1960—ST. CHRISTOPHER, A LECTURE HALL
San Antonio, Texas

"Fisk?"

I froze as my pencil scratched sideways across the calculation I was noting down. A work-study runner stood at the rear of the low-lit lecture hall, two rows back from where I was sitting. The professor paused. Nobody said a word.

"Ah. *Miss* Fisk?"

My face burned several degrees hotter. I gave an abortive little wave over my shoulder and swept my notes and my purse into one arm. The runner smiled at me as I slunk into the aisle and up the stairs, straightening my skirt. I wasn't smiling back.

"Call for you," she stage-whispered, as though my mortification at being pulled from the middle of a particularly dense lecture on molecular bonds wasn't already rolling from my shoulders like a stench. She held out a note for me and pushed open the lecture hall doors.

"From whom?" I winced against the daylight streaming in through the hallway windows. The young woman was still holding the note out to me. I took it as the lecture hall door fell shut beside us with a dull, heavy sound.

"Not sure. Operator said it was from New Mexico."

My stomach lurched. "Did they leave a name?"

"No, no name."

I clenched my teeth and looked down at the page: four numbers, and a title: St. Vincent's. The lurching in my stomach heaved into a churn.

"This is a hospital," I said. The runner cocked her head at me. She would be prettier, a thought far in the back of my mind said, if she didn't fasten her collar right up to the top button.

"Is it?" As though I had told her there might be rain later this afternoon. My fingers clenched, crimping the corner of the note.

"What else did they say?"

"To call back."

"Yes, but what *else* did— Never mind." I crammed the note into my purse and hitched the strap on my shoulder, pushing my glasses up as I started down the hallway at a clip. "Thank you."

"Have a good day!"

I made a beeline for the ground floor, streaking down the wide bend of the steps. At least the stairs were empty. At least the pursuit of knowledge left the rest of the building mute to the noisy panic that was beginning to rise through me like a tide.

A fucking *hospital*. I hoped it was a minor mishap, involving someone connected to me only by the most tenuous thread. By the time I crammed myself into an empty phone booth on the far side of the lobby, I had gone through the very short list of family left and only one of them still lived in New Mexico. The privacy screen clattered as I bullied it shut behind me.

I dialed the exchange with a shaking hand. Statistically speaking, the person in the hospital was my mother.

We hadn't spoken in two weeks. The last time I called, it had gotten tense—I had clammed up and been ornery because Mother wouldn't quit asking about men.

I tried redirecting her, talking instead about classes and work, but she was always so quick to remind me there was life beyond work.

Remember, she had chided me, *be careful about being too involved. There are other things worth pursuing besides your labs.*

Like what? Marriage? I sneered so violently I could almost hear Mother flinch on the other end of the line. *Marriage won't get me to NASA.*

Mother was very still for long enough that I thought the connection had dropped. When her voice finally came back, it was thick; *Well, Annie, you hold yourself so far away from everyone you might as well leave the planet.*

It was me who killed the call then, a furious slam of the receiver back onto its cradle. I sat and stewed in my own rage for a long time until one of my hallmates tapped on the screen to ask if I was finished.

Each day Mother didn't call back, I figured it was just another one of our stalemates—boil low in our separate pots of salt water until one of us reached out to switch off the burner on the other's range. And repeat, ad nauseum.

Now I wasn't so sure.

Worry gripped me hard as the call connected. My body scrunched in a rigid fold on the little bench. I roved my thumb over and over the curled edge of the runner's note. "This is Anne Fisk," I said when the receiver came to life, "calling from St. Christopher in San Antonio. I received a call from St. Vincent's with an extension . . ."

"Connecting you now." The operator's voice crackled after I gave her the numbers.

Distantly, I thought of how we were hearing each other on a delay, how there were dead handfuls of moments stacking up between the two of us with each relay. How many lifetimes must have grown to exist in the spaces hidden inside every phone call mankind had ever made, the sum of every millisecond stacked into something like a body? How many chunks of sixty, seventy years at once were walking around in the unseen places between matter, colliding with those unaware and alive?

The line clicked and buzzed for a moment before fuzzy ambience found my ear. "Hello?" someone answered, a gruff voice. I set my thumbnail against my teeth.

"This is Anne Fisk at College and Academy of St. Christopher," I said, gnawing sideways so I could be understood. "I was told there's an urgent message for me from this extension?"

"Ah."

I should have tasted the reservation there, one syllable to wedge itself sharp and immediate between my teeth like a popcorn kernel, *Ah*. A hissing sound on the line told of a shallow drag on a cigarette, a shuffle of papers.

"This is Dr. Jack Doore at St. Vincent's. You're the contact for Mrs . . . Helen Fisk, her daughter, correct?"

"Correct," I parroted. My pulse began clouding in my ears. "Has she been hurt?"

Another short pause, another inhale. I could imagine him, white-coated and half-bald, perched at a desk and leaning into the handset with a frown on his face. This was not the first such phone call he'd had to make.

"I'm sorry, Miss Fisk. Your mother was found deceased on a wellness check."

The back half of me knew it before *sorry* finished coming through the line. My stomach wrenched itself into a sharp knot and some place behind my eyes and my nose prickled sharply, but tears didn't form along my lashes like they had when Mother told me that Daddy was dead.

I took a breath to speak, faltered, and paused before I swallowed and took another. "Oh," I managed. I put my free hand in my lap and adjusted my seat. My ears began to ring. "I— What happened?"

"Heart failure. It's very hard to catch in women, even if she hadn't been alone."

Alone.

I don't want to leave you alone, I had told her, and yet what had I done? I had left her.

I wanted to peel my skin away from my ribs and dig my fingers in between each bone. The air felt as though it were compressing around me, vacuum sealing me in my own body.

"Sure," I said. None of this could be real, this was all just a bad dream. It had to be. If this was real, it was too cruel. I stared at the creased slats of the privacy cover in front of me. My last conversation with my mother had been an argument. I had hung up on her, and now she was dead. My mother was dead. She was—

"Miss Fisk?"

I blinked back into presence as the doctor cleared his throat. "Do I need to come home?" I blurted.

"Oh. Ah. Probably, yes, if you want to organize a ceremony. Take care of assets, all that. We can hold the body for up to four weeks."

I was still staring at the cover slats. I might as well have been watching this happen on a television screen. My body was not my own. My mother was dead. "I can be there next week. We have Easter off. It's a Catholic school."

"That—well, that'd work just fine."

"Did she say anything?"

"Beg pardon?"

My fingers were aching, gripping the handset so tightly that my knuckles had squeezed to ghostly pale. My mother was *dead.* "Did my mother say anything, or—I suppose she was gone. When they found her, I mean."

I couldn't help but imagine Apodaca Street spangled with a flurry of ambulance lights, drawing the neighbors awake in morbid curiosity at something the matter with Mrs. Fisk. It was the second time that front yard would have been a mess of solemnity and chaos. How many of them would have remembered the first time? I still couldn't.

"I'm sorry, miss, she was gone when we found her. A neighbor called in the check."

I nodded. *My mother is dead.* "Alright. Well, thank you for letting me know. I'll—I guess I'll be there soon. Have a good afternoon, Doctor."

"Good afternoon, Miss Fisk. Again, my condolences."

I hung up, the handset chiming with stark finality to leave me in the quiet of the empty lobby.

My mother was dead. I supposed I was an orphan then, which was ridiculous because orphans were children. I was in college. I was, ostensibly, an adult.

I couldn't find it in me to cry. I was hollow, a step past devastation. The cleansing freedom of tears was very far away.

After a long silence spent counting my pulse in the dark, I threw back the privacy screen and stood from the seat.

"Is everything alright?"

The receptionist by the front doors was looking at me with temperate concern. I stared at her for a moment, my mind blank.

"No," I said simply, and exited into the obstinate sunshine of a perfect spring day.

My feet moved on autopilot. I careened like dust through atmosphere across the quad and did not cry. The dormitory building opened before me, smacking me full in the face with a wall of canned coolness from the air-conditioning hard at work in the window units. I still did not cry.

My fist was shaking when I brought my hand up and knocked briskly on Evelyn's door. The music humming through the walls dipped a few clicks lower and her latch opened.

"Annie! What happened to molecul— *Oh.*"

Evelyn was wearing nothing but her fluffy blue robe and had been painting her toenails. She was smiling. How could she be smiling? My mother was dead. I stumbled over the threshold of the door and pulled Evelyn hard into a clinging hug.

I dug my chin into the collar of her robe. It fluffed against my cheek. I could smell the traces of her cypressy Halo shampoo, but no other sensation punched past the shock that coated me. Not the softness of the cloth, not the warmth of her skin, nothing.

"Annie," she said again, one hand flying up to smooth my hair and the other out to shut the door behind me. "Hey. What happened, Red?"

I burrowed my face deeper in the side of Evelyn's neck and breathed hard through my mouth. The terry cloth caught on my teeth, and I couldn't even bring myself to bite down. Around what was there to close my teeth anyway? The anger with which I met grief when I was younger was nowhere close to tenable. All I could feel was nothing.

I stared through the window over Evelyn's shoulder and saw the daytime moon hanging alone in the blue sky. The thought struck me: how utterly alone must my mother have felt lately, with me as distant from her as every planet and star wheeling out beyond our reach? It was my fault. I had pushed her far, far away.

And now she was gone.

I crumpled as I clung to Evelyn and finally began to weep.

1968—THE MANNED SPACECRAFT CENTER, THE PROGRAMMING SUITE
Houston, Texas

The programming suite had its own sort of witching hour. The hum of the computer bank was so low and large, like the massive throb of a bedtime story, and it was easy to drift into the lull of it when I stayed late.

Ros would shut the lights as she left, leaving me in the glow of my screen. I would either work until Norm came around to pry me away from the lines of Assembly or I would drive myself home if I was still awake enough. If I missed my own boat and found myself too drowsy, I would slip into Norm's office—he'd given me a copy of his key when he'd found me conked out at my desk the month prior—and sleep on the sofa across from his bookshelf. The spines on his shelves would sing me to sleep as I read them over and over again like turning over pebbles in my palm: Resnick & Halliday, Sears & Zemansky, *Rocket Manual for Amateurs*.

Another Christmas party at the Center had come and gone. This time around, Norm and I snuck off to the copy room rather than Gibbs's office to neck and trip all over each other in giddy mischief.

Here, he'd teased me, with that perennial scent of cherries on his breath that came from an almost criminal amount of grenadine in his drinks, *let's see what happens if we take some leisure on the machine while it's running.*

I promise you we'd be far from the first to try it, I'd said, pulling a face at the sleeping copier as I reached down to undo Norm's belt and he locked the door behind us, *how about we settle for the counter?*

Despite my best efforts, amid all the dinners we shared and the hours at night we stole beside each other after long days spent with the mission, I was falling in love with him.

There wasn't a single part of me I could turn over to find the crawling creatures of regret at how quickly and willingly I had opened myself to him. All I found was belonging, whole and encompassing.

Just as with Evelyn, I was terrified to open my mouth and say as much. All I had to do was tell him how he made me feel — but each time I thought I might try it, fear won out. My lips stayed sealed.

I shook the errant thoughts out of my head and scowled at myself as I went through my desk again. I had somehow misplaced a sheet of matrices I knew I'd referenced earlier, and I was methodically scraping every drawer and cranny in the suite for it.

"Goddamn it, Annie." I pressed a hand to my forehead and cast another look around the computer bank. Misplacing things always made me feel like I was losing my mind. "Think."

I had: written a few particularly long strings to chew through the pertinent report; taken a sip of coffee; checked my code from top to bottom; taken another sip of coffee, now going cold; dug through my desk for a fresh notepad, not found one, borrowed one from Betty's desk; taken another sip of coffee, all dregs; and then stood up to stretch my legs and take a lap over to the power banks to keep my knees from protesting.

I bunted the heel of my hand twice against my forehead before dropping my arm with a sigh. I needed to quit pulling such ridiculous hours. I needed to start sleeping more consistently in my own home.

Damn it. I shook my head and started on another lap of the bank, hawk-eyed and squinting—perhaps I'd had it in hand when I cycled the racks, put it down somewhere while my brain churned? I had a knack for forgetting what my own limbs were doing when I got absorbed in the work. Particularly in the flow of programming, my thoughts took on a rhythm that worked together with the computer's hypnotism— *global, start, selection, .text, mov, mov, mov*—

There!

At the far end of an alley between two of the larger power units, a sheet of paper sat alone on the floor. I hadn't squeezed back there to check on the cabling at all, but our notes sometimes got kicked around by the cooling fans, swept into all sorts of strange places throughout the suite.

The page sat, edges fluttering gently, in the center of a single linoleum tile at the end of the narrow aisle. I slid into the walkway with the metallic tang of transistors hard at work sharp in my nose. It wasn't dangerous to be back here, Ros had assured me the first time she coached me through the power cycling pattern the last of us still working in the suite executed once a week—it was almost always me.

The clicking and whirring of the brain center of our space race made me feel very, very small when pressed so close to it. My pulse seemed to meld with the computers from so close, as though I might have grafted myself to the machines I was spending so much time wrangling.

I knelt down and gingerly plucked up the paper by one curled-up corner. Before I stood up again, I paused. Waxy pathways of green crayon rambled across one side. I turned the paper over.

Multiplication Tables—Unit 2
A.F.

I dropped the sheet like I'd been burned. The back of my mind quivered, as though a fuse plugged into my memory outlet began to flow with energy.

The page twisted in the air and landed back on the tile. The wiggly march of numbers from a child's hand and another set of tidier, more elegant arithmetic danced together to peel back the wonder of mathematics at work.

A memory I had never once recalled before bloomed through me like a needle-drop as I stared: I had left this worksheet in the rosebushes after my teacher graded and returned it, my proud *A* in red pen tucked like a message in a bottle for my friend Diana to find.

This had no business being here.

One, I heard in the rare gut-punch of my father's voice, *one, onnn-e.*

"What in the hell?" I breathed. A cooling fan beside my left ear kicked up to a faster whine, as though replying in kind.

This was ridiculous. I needed to get some sleep.

A tickle at my periphery pulled my attention, perhaps the amber warble of an LED status light or one of the monitors kicking up to life. I glanced away, and the sharp smell of the computers grew more intense for the briefest moment.

When I looked back to the paper on the floor, it was gone. The tile was empty, mocking, pristine. Not even a jot of dust seemed to gather on the square.

A chill took me, sudden and cold on the backs of my arms despite the warmth of the hardware hemmed around me. I hurried back out to my desk and leaned on it with both palms flat.

One times three, four times four, six times five, eight times nine.

"Fuck!" I whispered, squeezing my eyes shut and tossing my head so sharply I almost sent my glasses flying. I leaned back and peered into the power units again, but saw only empty space.

The roots of my eyelashes prickled as tears sprang up alongside a fogginess in my nose. I bit down hard on my lip. My father's handwriting burned my mind, the quick shapes of his numbers some sort of sick joke. It was bad enough I could hardly remember what he looked like—his face stood blank in my memory as though something had scraped away his features in every snapshot with the edge of a coin, a cruel tease, and now—

Why now?

Don't go where I can't reach, too. Okay?

"Enough," I snapped out loud. I shoved the heel of my hand up under my glasses and pressed it to my eyes in turn until spots burst pink and red behind my squeezed-shut lids. *Enough.*

It was time to get some sleep.

I stalked into Norm's office and kicked the door shut behind me with a touch more force than might have been necessary. My head was reeling. A numb, cottony sensation plugged my skull, stuffed and empty at once. I settled roughly on the sofa and threw my jacket over my legs as a makeshift blanket. There was no way, not on this earth.

Resnick & Halliday, Sears & Zemansky, Norm's bookshelves mocked me as I stared at them, my jaw tight. *Mov. Mov. Mov.*

If there was something at work in the computer bank, it was not any of my business. I was a programmer. A translator. I simply told the machines what to do.

There was no such thing as fate. The cosmic joke of predestination held no water here.

And yet.

Sleep evaded me, fixation snared about my ankles, and I could do nothing but recite multiplication tables to myself in an endless loop, over and over again, as I stared at the ceiling and tried to recall the color of my father's eyes.

04:00

※

Discovery had hooked me through the cheek. I couldn't ignore it. If only I could call up my father and ask if this was how it had felt for him—half-manic, lit from within, desperate for answers.

I was lucky Norm didn't take it personally that I kept kicking our next dinner date down the line with the excuse of more work, always more work. At least he had his own endless march of problems to solve with the navigation team—the optical subsystem still had a few ghosts in its machine that needed working out.

For four straight workdays after finding the multiplication sheet, I stayed late enough to find myself alone in the power supply racks. That single floor tile confounded me. I placed all sorts of objects throughout the rest of the aisles as my control variables: pens, binder clips, balled-up memos and notes from wastebaskets scrawled with things like *THIS IS A TEST* and *HELLO, WORLD* in my messy scrawl. The first night proved my initial thought: Only the single tile by the UPSes made things disappear.

But they didn't just disappear. Some of them came back.

Once I focused on the tile, I took to timing the strange hiccups in slapdash experiments. From the first attempt to the last, every single disappearance lasted exactly six minutes. Down to the frantic second hand on my watch, six minutes. Three hundred and sixty seconds, every time. I hadn't managed to net results this exact even when I'd massaged my numbers for an agonizing organic chemistry lab in school.

I filled two legal pads with observation notes, and then two more. By day, I stowed them underneath the Assembly handbook in my desk drawer. I was on my fifth pad of notes by the second week, scrawling differentials and cross-referencing Einstein texts about wormholes.

Wormholes.

It was equal parts exhilarating and embarrassing to let myself even think the word. It felt impossible.

My palms itched incessantly. I was a distracted mess when the sun was up.

"Annie."

I blinked, back to myself in an instant. Betty Eagan, the programmer with her desk nearest mine, had stopped in the middle of talking her way through a thorny bit of syntax. It was always easier to pick apart the vagaries of Assembly packets when there was someone looking back at you—or some*thing*; Darla across the aisle tended to talk through her code at a little porcelain sculpture of the Virgin Mary she kept beside her transport.

"Sorry," I muttered. I mashed my fingers up under my glasses and pinched at the bridge of my nose. "I've been . . . tired. Lately."

"Yeah," Betty hummed, "no kidding. You sure you're getting enough sleep?"

I gave her a wry smile. "Does *anyone* in this place get enough sleep?"

She commiserated with me, but still drafted Ros later that afternoon to check if anything was the matter with me.

Ros took one look at me and said I looked like a walking head cold. When I tried to insist I was fine, she proceeded to soft-lock me out of my transport.

"Go home, Annie," she said, scooting my empty chair in and leaning against it. "That's a directive."

She was right. I wasn't fine. My eyes would cross if I didn't quit staring at the racks, and I wouldn't be any use to anyone if I couldn't look at a screen properly. I took Wednesday off.

By lunchtime at home, I was about ready to climb my own walls.

I had brought my notes with me to pore and pore and pore over them again. The knowledge that something wasn't quite right spilled between my ears. It threatened to tip out and drown me. But who could I tell? Norman? My pride held me back. If there was even the slightest chance I was wrong, that this was a glitch with *me* instead of a glitch in reality, I wasn't going to risk our relationship by talking about it. Besides, I hadn't been to dinner with Norm in almost two weeks.

Maybe it wasn't even a relationship.

A relationship. I paused in the middle of picking up the handset of my phone.

The dial tone rang twice, three times; *a relationship.*

Imagine that.

The operator picked up. I cleared my throat. "Hello, College and Academy of St. Christopher, San Antonio. Please."

I waited for the line to latch, *chk-chk-hmmmm,* and gnawed shallowly at the edge of my thumb. My coffee table was a mess. I caught my reflection in the mirror above my sofa as I paced with the phone carriage hooked over two fingers and almost let out a laugh. Ros had been right. I looked like hell.

I asked for Dr. Laitz at the university exchange and waited again. A low buzz, the line clattered softly, and then: "This is Ed?"

"Hi, Dr. Laitz!" I blurted. I slammed my eyes shut and tossed my head. "Hello. Sorry. Good—afternoon, Dr. Laitz, this is Annie Fisk from the class of '62. Do you remember me?"

"Annie Fisk!" There was a smile in his voice. My chest tugged hard. "Of course I remember you. How is life treating you?"

I drew my shoulders back and shut my eyes as I remembered how it had felt to sit across from him in that perfect pocket of space in which everything felt possible. I tried to put myself back in that sensation, that boundlessness. I cleared my throat and opened my eyes again. In the mirror, I looked determined. "Pretty—quite well, actually. I made it to NASA. I'm a programmer."

A little chuckle crackled the phone line. Dr. Laitz was silent for a moment. "I'll be," he murmured. "I knew you could do it. For how long?"

"I started as a secretary two years ago, and just a few weeks back I got moved to the programming team."

"Foot in the door, alright. Are you allowed to tell me what sort of things you're working on?"

My mouth wobbled into a smile, and I gave my own little huff of a chuckle. "No. Well—okay. If I were to throw some hypotheticals at you, would you be able to hypothetically lend some perspective?"

A steady sigh fluttered across the receiver, as though Dr. Laitz was leaning back in his chair. "Hypothetically, yes. Theoretically, even. I'd be honored."

I settled myself on the sofa with my knees drawn up tight, my grip a vise around the phone. My notes sprawled out before me like shed feathers of some massive bird roosting in the rafters. "Suspend disbelief for a second and tell me the basic properties of a wormhole."

"A *wormhole*."

"Suspend disbelief. Just for a second."

Dr. Laitz made a thinking sound, the way the computers whirred and clicked when they got to chewing a particularly large hunk of data.

"Two mouths," Dr. Laitz said, "connected by a single throat. The throat provides a topologically distinct pathway that can't be moved. It's a fixed point, a rigid body in space-time. Enter one side and exit on the other, and vice versa—traverse the fourth dimension. Time travel. Hypothetically."

I grunted, shuffling through some of my notes. "So it always connects the same places in space-time? The mouths never move?"

"Correct. At least, that's what the most common theory says."

I stared through the couch cushions for a moment. "What if this . . . hypothetical wormhole wasn't playing by the rules?"

"Playing, how?"

"What if—alright." I paged feverishly through the latest sheaf of notes: last Monday's and Tuesday's tests. Monday night, a woven bracelet I made for my friend Diana for Christmas when I was eleven years old had appeared, and Tuesday's results were a folded paper frog Mother taught me how to make when I was nine. My own past, the intangible line of it, stretched like a drumhead. "What if the mouth was fixed in space on either side, but moving freely through time?"

Dr. Laitz was quiet for a moment. "Space and time, uncoupled?"

"Well, not entirely uncoupled." I pawed fiercely through my notes, timings riffling past like a skipping record: *6:00, 6:00, 6:00, 6:00.* "Just. I don't know, *slipping.* Like they're hitched to parallel rails but moving back and forth at different speeds. I don't know what's driving it."

"An anomaly."

"Exactly."

A long silence fell.

"Annie, what have you found?"

My skin prickled all over. "I don't know yet," I stammered. "It feels—so much bigger than me, but it also might have everything to do with me." I sniffled and wiped a hasty wrist across my nose. "Hypothetically."

Dr. Laitz went quiet again for a moment, the line hissing softly with its own signal transduction. I rested the mouthpiece of the handset against my shoulder so I could sniffle sharply without making it too obvious. Why the hell was this making me emotional? When I put it back to my ear, Dr. Laitz was saying, "—continually impressed by you. Always have been."

I bit my tongue briefly. "Thank you, sir."

"Oh, call me Ed, Annie. We're colleagues."

A jittery burble of laughter leapt from my lungs. "God. Imagine that. It's weird, Ed. It's all so—fucking *weird*."

"Of course it's fucking weird! The greatest stunt reality ever pulled was convincing us there was any such thing as normal." I could picture him leaning back in his chair, one hand tucked into his elbow, smiling out his window at the open stretch of the quad. "People have been hypothesizing over wormholes for ages. There were a few of them I caught wind of, the possibility of them, cropping up over the last, oh, fifteen, twenty years. Nothing concrete, though. That's the big secret, Annie: Time goes on, agnostic of all our own mess, and it just keeps getting weirder."

"You're telling me," I said as I lay long across the couch, propping my head back against the arm.

We talked for nearly an hour then—about wormholes, about rockets, about the college, about life. It quit being hypothetical. My face hurt from smiling so much. My sense of curiosity began singing at a frequency it hadn't since the day I sat down to my interview at the Center.

"Well, I hate to cut this short," Dr. Laitz said finally, "but I've got a class soon."

"Please, you've given me more than enough of your time." I sat up and combed through my tangled hair with my fingers. "Don't let me keep you."

"Call any time you'd like, Annie, I'm always happy to talk shop with you."

I bit my lip and nodded. "Yeah. This was helpful, I really—thank you. Truly."

"My pleasure. You stay safe now, okay?"

"Okay. Bye, Ed."

"Bye-bye, Annie."

The line clicked to quiet. I held the handset in my lap and stared at it humming softly with dial tone. It seemed like just yesterday I was in one of his lectures, listening to his calming and present lilt narrating planetary orbit all the way to my seat in the back row.

✦ ✦ ✦

I stopped in Norm's office first thing the next morning back at the Center. He opened the door at my knock and beamed at me.

"You're feeling better!"

"Can you stay late tonight?"

Norm toasted me wryly with his coffee cup. "And good morning to you, too. What is it, more navigation updates?"

I tossed my head a little and shrugged. "Something like that."

With a touch of sneaking suspicion in the angle of it, Norm leaned against the doorjamb. He crossed one toe over his other ankle. "What do you mean?"

Glancing briefly around the hallway, ensuring it was all clear, I leaned in to murmur at his chin. "There's an anomaly in the power racks."

Norm's mouth tipped up gently at one side. "What," he whispered back, "like one of 'em's broken?"

"There's a wormhole."

Norm leaned back to level a look at me. *"What?"*

"There's a wormhole," I said tightly, "in the last aisle of the programming suite."

I watched Norm's expression go through several angles of amusement and disbelief until it settled into a stunned sort of intrigue. "You're serious," he said, and didn't take his eyes off me through a slow sip of coffee.

"Stay late and I'll show you," I said. I took a step back and fussed at my collar.

Norm furrowed his brow. "This isn't you hallucinating from a staggering lack of sleep?"

"This is the entire reason I haven't been getting any sleep."

Gnawing on his lip, Norm's gaze narrowed. I knew that expression. I had given it to every physics exam I had ever taken: a heady mixture of awe and horror.

Or maybe it was adoration.

"Fine," he said. "I'll meet you back there at eight."

I nodded. "Good. Great . . . thank you."

"Have a good day, Annie," Norm murmured, leaning in close in a fond mimicry of my own low tone. His door shut with a soft click. I realized belatedly that I was blushing.

The programming suite felt overfull during the workday now, as though we were going to spook some delicate, unseen creature hiding in the power racks with our work on the launch. My awareness that something else outside of time might pop into existence and blip right back away again before I had a chance to notice still weighed heavily on my attention span.

"Back to rights then?" Ros asked as I came in.

"Caught up on sleep, yeah. Thanks again."

Ros made a passing joke that I didn't quite catch as I managed to avoid looking in the direction of the blank tile.

Two mouths. One throat. A rigid body. I thought of trees falling in the forest with nobody around to hear them. Whenever I wasn't looking at it, what was it doing? Why trinkets from my mother's rose garden?

By eight o'clock the Center had slowly, slowly emptied of its swarm. Norm took his sweet time coming down—I was starting to think he had just left me to my harebrained bullshit, and I was almost ready to just get to testing on my own before I heard the distant creak of his office door. I tracked the leisurely approach of his footsteps ambling down the hall from the engineering offices.

Norm stopped in the doorway of the programming suite. He had his hands in his pockets and looked at me from there. "You look like one of us," he said.

I held in a yawn. "How's that?"

"I can read your screen backward through your glasses, and you could use a solid year of time off."

Norm came over and softened the ribbing with a kiss to my forehead. I leaned into him briefly.

"Ready?" I asked without ceremony, leaning down to slide out two sheets of letterhead from the bottom drawer of my desk. I was up from my chair and two steps away before Norm caught my wrist.

"Whoa there. I need you to walk me through it, slowly. Like I'm an idiot."

With just the safety lights on, half of him illuminated by the tepid glow from my transport screen, I could tell he was simply humoring me. He didn't believe me.

I would make him believe.

"Like you're Gibbs?" I sniffed. Norm chuckled.

"Sure. Like I'm Gibbs."

I held up the papers. "I place something on a particular part of the floor in there"—I pointed to the west side of the room—"and every time, without fail, that thing disappears. Exactly six minutes later, no more, no less, every single time, that thing comes back."

A notch formed between Norm's eyebrows. "'Disappears' how, exactly?" he asked. I ground my back teeth together.

"I'm ninety percent sure it's a wormhole."

Norm's eyebrows went up. "That's a lot of sure. And you discovered this possible wormhole how . . . ?"

I set my jaw.

"Because a sheet of paper I *know* I left in my backyard for my imaginary friend when I was eight years old turned up before disappearing as well," I said through my teeth.

Norm laughed. Steamed, I shouldered past him.

"Annie!" He got me gently around the waist and stopped me. "Annie. Hey. I'm sorry. I didn't mean to laugh. I didn't mean that."

He took up my left hand and kissed the backs of my fingers. I was still holding the letterhead page.

"Do you want to test it with me, or not?" I demanded.

Norm released my hand gently. He gave me a shallow, dramatic bow. "Lead on, maestro."

My irritation ebbed into a low rumble of excitement as I led Norm to the end of the power banks. I could fit through easily but he, all broad shoulders and lanky limbs, had to wedge his way through. I held out an arm to stop him when we reached the four-by-four opening of the floor—empty. Nothing else had come through.

"Ready?" I asked gently. The power units clicked and whirred at our ears as Norm drew up close beside me.

"Whenever you are," he said, amusement light in his tone as he glanced around the cramped racks. I was looking very forward to watching him eat his heart out.

If it still worked.

I knelt down carefully, balanced on the balls of my feet as the heels of my shoes slid off, and prodded the first sheet of paper out onto the floor. It rustled as it stuttered and came to a tenuous rest just left of the blank tile.

With my hands braced on the racks on either side of me, I inched forward and barely, gradually, nudged it forward bit by bit with the edge of my foot.

"Do we need to say a magic word?" Norm teased. I turned to hush him sharply with one last push. He glanced down at me, his eyes dancing, but his gaze stopped short—his pupils flashed. My heart leapt, and I turned back to the tile.

The sheet was gone.

"Start counting!" I hissed, immediately looking to the watch face on the inside of my wrist.

"Annie." Norm's voice was pale.

"It should be six minutes exactly."

"Annie."

"Six minutes, and then it comes back."

"*Annie!* What the hell kind of trick are you pulling?"

I faced Norm, my cheeks hot. He looked stunned, like I'd peeled back a curtain and shown him the real Big Rock Candy Mountain. "I know the navigators have the collective sensibility of a fifth grader, with all those goddamn pranks you get over on each other, but I'm not *pulling* anything, Norman, I'm showing you something amazing! Shut up and watch!"

I wouldn't be able to count it exactly with Norm distracting me, but I could get it damn close. To Norm's credit, he was silent as a monk as we waited three minutes . . . four minutes . . . five . . .

We glanced at each other, Norm's stare sharp and flicking nervously across my face—my eyes, my nose, my lips, back to my eyes—and then *there*.

The paper appeared right where we'd left it, a bit wrinkled around its edges but fully intact. It alighted on the edge of the tile, wafting as though whatever pushed it into reality had just sighed.

"Jesus Christ," Norm whispered, awestruck.

My heart raced with success as I waved the other sheet of paper. "Want to see it again?"

Norm stopped my hand as I moved to slide the second page out on the floor. "We have to write a message," he insisted. He was all but vibrating in place. "Do you have a pen?"

Norm patted his pockets awkwardly before he stopped and reached into the front of my blazer. I squawked when he drew out the copper bullet tube of my lipstick. He raised an eyebrow. "This will work, right?"

I wanted to protest that I was terribly fond of Coty's Cardinal Red—as was he, given the randy suggestions he had made last time I wore it when he took me dinner—but the rush of discovery overtook my vanity. I nodded. Norm uncapped it carefully.

"What should we write?" I asked, and Norm took the paper from me with a triumphant smile and my lipstick tube brandished like a fountain pen. He flattened it against the power bank beside him and wrote a simple greeting in a smear of bright red:

HELLO, WORLD!

"Have to stick to the basics," he explained, "something everyone knows, even the computers." Norm winked. "Trust me, I read the comics."

I snatched the paper back from him and plucked the lipstick to sign the bottom with a flourish—*Annie H. Fisk.* "Lest we forget," I said briskly, leaning forward to smudge a dash of the color across Norm's lower lip like the tail of a signature, "whose discovery this was."

Norm surged forward and kissed me, knocking the breath from my lungs and making me drop the bullet tube. We both pulled back and turned our heads to watch as it rolled into the center of the floor—the feeling of a sneeze built somewhere at the back of my skull, and when I blinked to chase away the itch the lipstick had disappeared.

"You bastard, I liked that color," I groused, but I was smiling.

"Send the note through, too," Norm bid me, a murmur at my temple.

I crumpled the paper quickly in one fist and tossed it down onto the floor. Again the itch, again the unshakable instinct to shut my eyes . . . and again it was gone.

I held up my wrist, wagging my watch. "Six minutes."

"Six minutes," Norm hummed, and kissed me soundly.

We necked against the power rack for one . . . two . . . five minutes.

As the sixth rounded the 12 on my watch, I pulled back to peer at the anomaly space again. Norm cleared his throat and straightened his tie.

Five minutes and fifty-one, fifty-two, fifty-three seconds . . .

. . . Nothing.

"It's still gone," I said, staring at the empty tiles.

"This is incredible," Norm breathed. I shook my head and frowned.

"This hasn't happened before. They always come back."

Norm took me by both sides of the face and turned me to look at him. His expression was giddy. His mouth was red. "You found a rift in space-time hiding right under our noses, you beautiful genius," he said with forced evenness, "and you're concerned with being unable to replicate an *experiment*?"

I looked from the empty floor back to Norm's face. "It's always six minutes," I said, at a loss.

"I love you," Norm blurted. I gaped at him.

"What?"

He searched my face and shook his head before planting another kiss on me, as though he could hardly believe it. "You," he said against my mouth, "I love all of you."

Confusion, conquest, delight, and ardor clashed in my gut all at once. When he pulled back again, I floundered for words. *Love.* I had never made a habit of saying it. My parents were so particular and specific in how they harbored their affection, and gone now.

I thought fleetingly of Evelyn. I had known how to love her. Hadn't I?

Was this the same? Could I know how to love Norm the way he needed me to?

Hell. If I could find evidence that space and time were more malleable than we thought, I could learn how to love one man.

I wrapped a hand around his tie. "You have the strangest sense of timing."

Dragging Norm close as though pulling him across all of reality itself, we shared another haphazard kiss. Our teeth knocked together. We were both smiling too hard to care.

The paper never returned, nor did the lipstick.

We slept at his place that night.

1960—THE APODACA HOUSE, EMPTY

Santa Fe, New Mexico

I stopped with my hand on the front door. A tanager trilled from somewhere in the skinny ponderosa by the gate behind me, its song like a nudge to the backs of my knees; *go on, go on, go on.*

The house loomed, the husk of a life that felt very, very far away. I hadn't returned since I had pulled away with my father's pin in my pocket and my heart in my mouth. I couldn't bring myself to.

And now the house was mine.

I wasn't going to keep it; I knew that much. Every moment I spent back in Santa Fe wore on me deeply. The quiet streets weighed me down, as though something loomed just over my shoulder and grew closer the longer I was here; the flat-roofed houses that used to look so cheery to me now only looked empty, dead-eyed with their square windows, doorways like slack-jawed, narrow mouths. Loss had sapped away the beauty of this place for me.

But I wasn't going to linger for longer than this week, and after I washed my hands of the Apodaca house I would never have to come back. I could finally move on.

It was what I had always wanted, wasn't it?

I pushed open the door. A cool silence greeted me, welcoming as a brittle handshake.

Wasn't it?

The hallways waiting open before me felt like three dead ends. To the left, I felt my empty bedroom echoing with the angst and confusion of adolescence. Ahead of me, Daddy's office waited past the kitchen like a black cloud, the quiet terror of unfound memories threatening over the threshold. And to the right sat Mother's room, layer upon invisible layer of regret rolling out from it like the tide on an empty beach.

This was a sad house. I was eager to be rid of it.

I floated through a cursory pass, cataloging in my head the immediate yes or no of what I would keep. After the first half hour of drifting through the silent innards of the place I used to call home, I brought the empty boxes in from the car.

The side door into the kitchen creaked when I came back in. I was determined to comb through every little cranny of the house and find the pieces that I knew had been hidden from me—the small and soft-bellied things we had never talked about before Mother died. I told myself the sooner I got this done the sooner I could get back to Texas. Back to a life worth living.

I started in my old room. It was empty save for the bedframe, but I could still imagine the places on the walls where photos and the few posters from girls' magazines Mother allowed me to put up had hung for so many years. Nothing to do there except to say goodbye—I left it with a press of my fingers to the doorjamb.

The den held a pair of vases I wanted to keep, and the record cabinet I would cart out with me when I left again.

Mother's room next.

It felt strange to know she wasn't going to just get back from her shift at the dry goods store, put her purse on top of her dresser as she unclipped her earrings and toed off her shoes, and tell me about her day while I lingered in the doorway to watch her.

As I marveled carefully through her drawers, I came away with small prizes of tangible proof my mother had lived as full a life as she was able: a bundle of letters she and Daddy had exchanged during his graduate studies in Britain, a fresh pack of her cigarettes, a short pile of her favorite noir novels—*Thieves Like Us. The Big Clock. I Married a Dead Man.*

At the back of the empty nightstand, I found a small wooden frame with a photograph inside it. Three men slung their arms around one another's shoulders, their legs put up in a campy imitation of a chorus line. I slid it up through the slot in the glass so I could see the back of the photo itself and found a caption penciled there: *With A. Brooks & W. Harris. July 16, 1945. Before Trinity.*

I turned it back over and looked at Daddy in the middle, searching for the man I couldn't quite remember.

I felt strangely closer to Mother than I had in a long time as I stared at the photo. Cruelly, the clearest solution to ugly feelings came well after the statute of limitations on acting on them had expired. The agonizing march of closing out a life—collecting linens and clothes for donation, storing the flatware, organizing the furniture I had no reason to keep—she had done this same slow deconstruction for Daddy.

I had Mother cremated and scattered in the wind, per her wishes. She had told me once as a kid she didn't like the idea of being worm food, and did we even have worms here in the desert? She had learned to love dearly the sunset-red of the dirt.

The frame and the photo went into the *Keep* box.

I skipped Daddy's office. I had told the estate agent to save anything that looked official or worth keeping, but Mother had done the real legwork of that room after he died. I couldn't bring myself to enter it even after so much time had passed. The thought of accidentally filling in my memory's blank spot scared me bloodless. I refused to risk it.

When the *Keep* box had barely been touched and the *Donate* box had already spilled over into a third, I sat back on my heels in the den and wiped sweat from my temples. I sighed and rolled my eyes up to the ceiling, where the exposed eaves looked back down at me impassively.

"Couldn't have gone during a more temperate season instead," I called out to nothing, "huh?"

My throat went thick and lumpy enough to choke me briefly on my own sorrow. I sniffled it away and swiped at my eyes as I stood and made for the kitchen, where I poured a glass of water from the tap. I took it into the backyard for a break.

The sliding door out from the den stuck a little, like it hadn't been opened in years. A layer of dust coated the patio furniture in one thick, uninterrupted coat. Daddy's chair sat at the same jaunty angle as ever, like it was simply waiting for him to top off his glass in the kitchen and come take a seat in the purple dusk again.

The garden clearly hadn't been tended in any meaningful way since I left. Plants and petals were perhaps too wild, too hard to predict for Mother. She had let everything go.

The roses had gotten wilder, ebullient with bursting freedom. I peered at the ground beneath them, where their leaves and roots and thorns ran thick, and found traces of the clutter that had enchanted me as a child: a paper clip here, a pen there — and, trapped by untrimmed tangle, a few snared pages fluttering in the breeze.

I moved to them slowly, as though approaching one of those cats that showed up the winter of my junior year and would spook whenever I tried to coax them closer. Wary of the pricking thorns, I plucked the pages out from the leaves and smoothed them flat against my knee where I knelt on the gravel.

The first sheet was a legal pad scrap that made me squint: a mess of calculations and nonsense, scrawled in a tight hand that made my brain turn over on itself even after years of sitting through Professor Laitz's classes. I could understand the thrust curves, but otherwise it was Greek to me. Was this old homework of mine? But it wasn't my handwriting.

Perhaps one of Daddy's notepads had found its way through the window—the paper looked weathered; it might have been here even before Mother passed. I turned it over, but nothing on the back clarified anything. A glance at the far end of the house confirmed that neither Mother's bedroom window nor Daddy's office window—if it had even been unsealed since he died—would have led out this way. Anything dragged by the breeze would have ended up in the front yard.

I looked down at the second, more tattered page and fully intended to see another wash of unintelligible scribbles—but I frowned at its simplicity.

HELLO, WORLD!

The words were written in a strange red script. I scratched at it with my thumbnail and it came away, waxy and yielding—crayon?

There at the bottom in the same bold red:

Annie H. Fisk.

I cast my memory wide, scraping for when exactly I had written this—and how recently, to still be in one piece in the bushes? I stared at it, a mounting sense of premonition at the back of my head like the buzz of static on a television screen in the moments after switching it off: *HELLO, WORLD! HELLO, WORLD!*

I tossed my head and clamored to the third page. My pulse rang heavy and loud in my ears. At the top, the salutation proclaimed itself below a lofty address:

The Manned Space Center
Houston, Texas
July 16, 1969

Whenever you are, this is for you.

Apprehension touched where my head met my neck. The message was typed in slim lettering from a dot matrix, not unlike the printouts from the teletypewriters in the mathematics basement on campus. I flattened a hand behind me without looking away from the page so I could balance myself down to my backside, the gravel scratching at my overalls as I crossed my legs and hunched over the pages, and read on.

Being alone is different from being lonely. You are so much more than the sum of your parts.

You will stumble and wander, but I promise you will find your way. It will be everything you had ever hoped for. You will read Einstein, Dirac, Sherman Morgan, Booth, and countless others, arming yourself for the life that awaits you.

Your world has been very small for a very long time. You should never fear it getting bigger just as you should never fear the endless expansion of the universe.

You have to love, jellybean.

You must. And how can you not? It will scare the hell out of you, but it's the only way. Even in the end. I promise. Every fiber of you will resist it—you still haven't cracked that fucking box open, but using it as an excuse to deprive yourself of what you deserve is a mistake.

You've always believed in something greater than yourself, a cosmic bargain. Everything may as well be sand in the desert without it.

Loneliness is a dangerous business, Annie. The only certain thing is uncertainty. Your ante against it must be love.

I stared at the page with tears in my eyes until my sight burned from not blinking. This had to be a sick joke.

So why did it make my core sing as though some great string in me had been touched, setting me a-song with the wheeling spin of the universe?

I thumbed back to the message in wax and stared at the shape of my name in red on the page—*Annie H. Fisk*. I traced it, feeling the shallow ridges of each letter.

Something shivered in my chest, toothy and rapt.

This was not meant for anyone else. This was no mistake. This was mine.

Perhaps Professor Laitz was right—maybe physics didn't exist for us to understand the universe as a whole. Maybe the deeply rooted parts of it remained so unbelievable in order to help the simpler topsoil of nature being nature make a little more sense.

I read the letter again and again and again. I read it until I memorized the shape of every word.

The only certain thing is uncertainty, I read, staring at the words until the delicate chains of their syntax dug so deep in my mind they would never let go.

Loneliness is a dangerous business, Annie.

I couldn't keep any of this. These pages were volatile. The longer I held them, the more they made my fingers tingle. I shut my eyes and recited the names back to myself—*Einstein, Dirac, Sherman Morgan, Booth.* And then I scrambled to my feet, forgetting my empty glass of water, and hurried into the kitchen.

My purse was on the counter where I'd left it, my lighter inside. I hesitated for but a single moment when I laid the pages in the sink. Then I flicked the flame to light in my hand. *HELLO, WORLD!*

A sense of calm inevitability filled me as I touched the dancing tongue to the edge of the shallow stack.

I glanced over my shoulder as the pages burned. Pinned to the refrigerator was a kitschy magnet from a café in Albuquerque—doubtless a place we'd loved as a family, but I could barely recall—and a crayon drawing from ages ago. The rosebushes burst up from a wobbly rendition of the garden wall in a blob of green and pink. In front of it stood the spindly stick figures labeled *Daddy, Mother, Annie,* and *Diana* in the corner with a rose in her hair.

You've always believed in something greater than yourself. I watched as the words burned away, curling to ash against the drain. *A cosmic bargain.*

I ran the sink when it was done and washed the evidence away.

I stalked back out to the car several minutes later with the drawing and the magnet in hand. I stowed the careful fold of it in the glove box and paused when my knuckles bumped against my father's pin. I let out a slow breath and counted to six. The pin was warm when I kissed it before fastening it to one strap of my overalls.

I grabbed another box from the back seat. Before going inside again, I tapped out one of the Encores from the unopened package I'd taken from Mother's room and smoked it down in silence.

The gravel whispered under my toe when I scrubbed out the used-up filter. I went back into the house to finish my delicate extraction, sawing carefully through the bone and sinew of it to free myself into whatever awaited.

1968—THE MANNED SPACECRAFT CENTER, ART McCABE'S OFFICE

Houston, Texas

So Norm believed me.

Now we only had to convince a man whose entire job consisted of making sure we got an American on the moon as quickly as possible to divert some very precious resources into studying a mystery in the back end of our own facilities that might very well lead to a great big goose egg.

If we wanted to make a proper case for ourselves, the directors would want more tangible evidence. Norm got himself an instant Minolta and got pretty handy with a shutter. Whenever we sat our nightly vigil in the racks waiting for something to come through, Norm would have the camera at the ready in his hands—I always told him not to waste film, but it was difficult not to be charmed by his snapping photos of the two of us while we waited.

One time, a paper star came through. I squeezed my eyes shut at the same time I started the counter on the stopwatch Norm had filched from mission control. Reaching back into the strange soup of my disparate childhood memories, the fractal mess of them unfurled like a patchy carpet.

"Nineteen . . . fifty-one?" I said, tilting my head slightly as though I could dislodge the truth of the memory by helping it wriggle free. "I was eleven, maybe ten, my friend Laura taught me how to fold these during recess. I brought one out to show to Diana and left it under the rosebush so she could have it next time she came back."

"Do you still remember how to make them?" Norm asked from behind the viewfinder, taking a picture of it. I smiled at him.

"Probably not. Had to carve out space for trig."

"Ah," Norm teased me, nudging my hip with his toe. Our legs were stretched out between the two of us as we sat back against opposite sides of the rack aisle. "That's first-grade stuff."

We drafted a proposal report of the anomaly findings over a few days of in-betweening, pulling late nights on the floor of Norm's office after wedging ourselves deep in the computer bank with our testing materials once everyone else was gone. We had pages and pages of readings from the strange tile square, which we measured any way we could without touching it directly: temperature, altitude, scrapings from its perimeter to send to the chemical lab under implied confidentiality, the whole nine.

We were armed with a folder nearly as thick as the sandwich Art McCabe paused on the way to his mouth as Norm swung the door open. "Art?"

McCabe frowned. "I'm a little busy, can it wait?"

"No." Norm held out an arm for me to enter first, and then followed behind as he pulled the door shut. He brandished the folder. "We've got a proposal."

"A *proposal*." McCabe set the sandwich aside and gestured at it. "Hale, I've got about twenty free minutes a day, and if you think I have the room to spend it approving any other projects instead of eating my fucking lunch, I—"

"Five minutes." Norm's stare was firm. He raised his brows at Art. "You owe me for the save with the CSM test on 9, remember?"

McCabe worked his jaw. He sat back in his chair. "Fine. Five minutes. How'd he drag you into this, Fisk?"

I flinched when Art addressed me directly, his steady blade of a stare cutting straight into me. He was a man made of squares: square jaw, square haircut, square carriage. I cleared my throat. "I dragged him into it, sir. I'm the one who found the anomaly."

Art's forehead creased like the belly of an accordion as his own brows went up and he swung his attention back to Norm. "The *anomaly*."

My gut prickled at the assumption Norm was the one he should be addressing. I took the folder from Norm's hand and a step toward McCabe's desk.

"We've got readings. Compiled and tested, repeated results, method-driven, all of it. Here."

McCabe looked between me and the folder I held out to him. "We gave you a promotion to the programming team, Fisk, not permission to go digging around."

"With all due respect, sir," I said, willing my hand not to shake, "those are the same thing."

I gestured with the folder. From over my shoulder, I could feel Norm buzzing with anticipation. McCabe hesitated for a moment before he stood up, muttered something low to himself, and took it from me with one square hand.

It was strange to see our notes cracked open in front of someone else. Across the front of the folder in heavy stamped typeface, Norm and I had dubbed the project *Aion*: unbounded time, the mystery of eternity, cyclical and confounding.

The office was dead quiet for a long time, broken only by the sound of pages turning.

"How the hell did you find this?" McCabe finally asked. Norm and I shared a look.

"Pure chance," I admitted.

McCabe squinted at me. "Is this another prank?"

"No, sir," Norm said with a nervous chuckle. "Trust me, the navigation team still bears the collective scar of thinking you have a sense of humor regarding anything in a sixty-mile radius of your office."

McCabe grunted. "I'll say." He turned back to me. "And how did you think to follow up on it? Prepare all of this?"

I held in a shrug, my back ramrod straight. I set my mouth in a firm line. "We used the scientific method."

McCabe narrowed his eyes. "Obviously. Why even test it in the first place?"

"Innate curiosity, sir," Norm said emphatically.

"Sure, fine, but *how*, Hale. Do they teach basic language comprehension at MIT anymore, or is it just numbers these days?"

Damn it.

I swallowed my pride and took the folder back from McCabe. I flipped to a photograph of a crayon drawing of Diana and me. "Santa Fe, New Mexico, 1948, I drew this picture and left it outside in my mother's garden. It appeared beside the uninterruptible power supplies at the back of the programming suite and remained for exactly six minutes before disappearing."

I flipped to another photograph, this one of a single celluloid doll shoe I had lost when I was nine. "Santa Fe, New Mexico, 1949, I lost one of my doll's shoes in the garden. It appeared beside the uninterruptible power supplies at the back of the programming suite and remained for exactly six minutes before disappearing."

I flipped to a third photograph: a red bauble earring. "Santa Fe,

New Mexico, 1956, I borrowed a pair of my mother's earrings to sneak out to a party with Peggy Lipton and got home late. I climbed over the garden wall because I knew the patio door would be unlocked, but one earring fell off and Mother found out about it the next morning anyways when I only returned one of them. It appeared beside the uninterruptible power supplies at the ba—"

"*Alright,* Fisk."

McCabe ran the tip of his tongue along the seam of his lips before pursing them tightly. He stared hard at me for a long moment, puzzling me out.

"You expect me," he finally said, "to divert resources from the most sensitive work this country has done since the bomb based on a—a what, a memory scrapbook?"

A dark place in me I dared not touch trembled at the mention of the bomb. I cleared my throat gently and took a breath. "Sir, it—"

Norm put a hand on the small of my back. "Art. This is serious stuff." A rankled shiver rushed up my spine and I stepped away from him by the barest inch.

"Not only serious, sir," I said, shooting Norm an adamant look from the corner of my eye, "this could change the way we approach future launches. Look at the summary, it's all there. The potential for travel across space *and* time. And let's say we ignore it; who's to say Russia doesn't stumble across their own anomaly and start digging into it first?"

McCabe's jaw twitched with tension. "How do you know there could be another in Russia?"

"How do we know anything about it besides the fact it's worth the research? That's why we need the resources." I set my jaw and rolled my shoulders back a little, forbidding myself from fidgeting. "Sir."

I held McCabe's stare.

Another silence fell. The slow march of his wall clock stole away the present, second by precious second. He didn't blink. Neither did I.

"Let me see that again," he muttered and held out a hand for the folder.

McCabe sat back down and read. I forced myself not to chew on my cuticle as we waited. Norm's thumb made steady, meditative circles on my wrist, which at least kept my nerves tuned to a manageable frequency.

"Say I decide to approve this," McCabe finally said, leaning back in his chair and lacing his fingers together across his broad chest. He regarded me coolly, a measuring look. "What do I tell my supervisors? How do I court *them* to give us what we need, convince them this isn't some crock of shit pseudoscience?"

I began pacing before McCabe's desk. "What did the supervisors say about the moon landing? About Apollo? Wasn't that complete pie in the sky at first?"

"The moon is real," McCabe deadpanned. "You don't need to run tests to look up and see it."

Norm cleared his throat. "If I recall correctly, sir," he said, "you had some doubts about Apollo."

"Can your proposal do what Apollo has already proved it's on its way to doing?"

"That depends on what you believe Apollo is doing, sir."

"Telling the rest of the world not to fuck with us."

Norm cleared his throat shallowly and, in my periphery, I saw him run a hand over his hair. I bit the tip of my tongue lightly between my teeth for a moment, still pacing.

"That can come next," I said. "First, we would need to run for the fences of this thing. Find the limits. Know where to press on it and how." I paused in front of McCabe's desk and looked him square in the eye. "And wouldn't you want to know? Aren't you curious? We're holding the door open, sir. All you have to do is walk through."

McCabe rolled his tongue over his teeth and riffled back through the report. He shut the folder gingerly. "Holding the door open, huh?"

A little breathless, adrenaline pulsing through me like shimmering oil, I managed a sideways smile. "What's your why?"

"What's my *why*?"

"The reason we do all this. Your engine." I turned to Norm and saw him looking at me with a tinge of panic coloring his awe. "Norm, what's yours?"

He gaped for a moment before visibly drawing himself up from the inside out. "Uh. Exploration. See all the—everything from the ground that I can't see from the sky. Giving myself wings."

I opened a hand at him and mugged an exaggerated impressed expression. "Giving himself wings."

McCabe regarded me from an inscrutable angle. He nodded his chin at me. "What's yours, Fisk?"

I thought of Evelyn, of the Mercury 7, of a broadcast we watched on the floor of an art studio nearly a decade ago. "A bargain," I said, my voice stark. "There's a power greater than I am that will see that I'm taken care of if I do my part of the bargain, and my part is to shove my weight at everything that tells me it's impossible."

I hadn't the faintest idea if McCabe was a spiritual man in any capacity, but his eyes flashed with recognition. I watched him soften by the most subtle amount—but that let me know I had done it. My heart surged.

McCabe stood back up and held the file in one hand to wag it for emphasis. "If this curiosity of yours kills the fucking cat," he warned, "if this is some sort of phony hoax, this will cost NASA a *lot* of money and a *lot* of time. Are you prepared for that sort of investment on an independent project?"

Both Norm and I blurted our own *Yes* at the exact same time.

McCabe looked as though he was holding in a withering roll of his eyes.

"And you understand that your work on Apollo will not stop for this? If we let every yahoo scientist in this building run off sideways with their what-ifs, we'd still be scrounging around in the dirt wondering how to get a thruster off the ground."

"Of course," Norm blurted, mostly breathless. I nodded wildly.

McCabe looked between us with reluctant approval. "Fine. I'll take this up the ladder. You're lucky I want to get back to my sandwich. Dismissed."

We slipped from McCabe's office with the wind of progress under our heels. Norm and I took but ten strides down the hall before Norm yanked me sideways into a supply closet and planted a fevered kiss on my mouth.

"Genius," he gasped, clinging to me in the half-dark, "you're a fucking genius. I love you. I love you, I love you, I love you."

I gasped halfway into a chuckle against Norm's chin. "Don't do that again."

He pulled back to look at me. Norm's gaze flicked quickly over my face, eyes-nose-lips-eyes, and he tipped his head as his chest heaved shallowly with excitement. "Do what?"

"Don't take the wheel while I'm still driving. In there, I—I had it under control. Don't try to hold me back."

He nodded and pulled me into another kiss. His fingertips pressed softly, sweetly into the ridge of my jaw. When we pulled back again, he swept his thumbs over my cheeks and nodded again. "Of course. You can drive forever, Annie."

Norm watched me for a long moment. From outside the door, a pair of engineers passed at a quick clip with their voices pattering.

"Marry me," Norm breathed.

My heart leapt so quickly into the back of my throat I could almost taste it. "Are you kidding?"

Maneuvering carefully, Norm shimmied down to one knee with his left shoulder crammed against a ream of paper and took my left hand in his. "Annie Fisk," he whispered, "will you marry me?"

I hadn't even told him I loved him yet.

But "Yes," I breathed, automatic and impassioned, because sometimes when the universe throws you a bone you take it in both hands and bury your teeth in it before wondering to ask which part of your own skeleton it came from.

I loved him.

I wondered if I would ever muster the courage to tell him so. Last time I told a man I loved him, I walked into his study and found him dead.

Norman gave me every opportunity to say it back: *I love you*, from across his desk when I had my brow pinched in concentration as I scrawled through an equation on my notepad; *I love you*, into the curve of my neck from the growing familiarity of Norm's bed; *I love you*, from behind the viewfinder of his camera while we waited for the impossible to happen two feet away from us, and I looked right up into the *click-chk* of the shutter catching me fully enamored.

I dragged Norm up by the collar and kissed him again. A bin of staplers dug into my shoulder and a stack of paper-clip boxes threatened to topple if I jostled it wrong.

It was perfect.

Everything was random, nothing could be known entirely for certain, but for one moment in a supply closet in Houston, everything was exactly as I ever could have dreamed.

1959—KELLER'S STUDIO IN TOBIN HILL
San Antonio, Texas

Come April, I needed a television. The only one in the women's dormitory was older than sin itself and predisposed to fuzzing with cotton-white static, and I wasn't about to miss even a moment of the Mercury 7 press conference.

It was bound to be dry. I could handle dry. I was rounding the home stretch of a calculus course that put western New Mexico to shame with its lack of moisture. A half hour of broadcast news would hardly be painful.

Evelyn's artist friend Keller had a television set at his studio. He was a bandy-legged, sightly loony guy I knew from forays into the Irish Flats accompanying Evelyn to all the homegrown artist gatherings in town. I saw his work at independent galleries and occasionally displayed with other contemporaries at McNay up the road from campus—he twisted wire into all sorts of shapes and scenes, some of them whimsical and others brow-raisingly graphic. Keller told me once that he studied in Greece to get the technique right, and then learned how to make it all a little more phallic on his own.

Two of the three times he and I had met had been in the back seat of Evelyn's wheezy Pontiac after she bailed him of jail. He had a penchant for punching cops during queer bar raids. Keller loved a spectacle.

He agreed to have me over to use the television when Evelyn asked—so long as we brought a six-pack and some of the weed Evelyn was still fleecing from poor Andy the hopeless lit major. Had I not already met Federico, the stunningly beautiful man Keller had wooed somehow with all his coyote-style mischief, I would have suspected he had more than a bit of a thing for Evelyn, the way he doted on her.

I made it down to the long stretch of road near San Antonio College with a quarter of an hour until one o'clock, but still I bounded off the bus and down the sidewalk. The address to Keller's warehouse was scrawled on the scrap of paper in my hand, and I hurried due south as though I was all but down to the wire. The door was unlocked when I tried the handle.

"Hey," I called out into the ceiling raking high, high up. The sound of a signal skipping arrhythmically between stations pulled me to the far end of the space, away from the windows, past a wall filled with Keller's latest dioramas, either half-done or waiting to be shipped out for showing. The huge yawn of the interior was probably once some sort of assembly space before Keller snapped it up, but I was too excited to marvel.

I found the three of them, Keller and Federico and Evelyn, around the corner of an exposed-brick wall, piled on an overstuffed red sofa on top of a heap of mismatched rugs. Evelyn was crouched in front of the set, flicking the channels, and Keller had his arm stretched lazily over Federico's broad shoulders. Keller was in an open chambray button-down and an undershirt, and the pink lines on his face told of his welding mask only just recently laid aside.

"Right on time," he crooned. A tightly rolled joint sat between his lips. Federico struck a match to light it, leaning close to him to let the flame catch.

Evelyn looked up at me briefly, a shallow frown creasing her concentration. "Hey," she hummed. "Which channel again?"

"Channel five, I think," I said, catching my breath. I shrugged off my purse and bent down to kiss Evelyn on the temple before holding out a hand to Federico. "Hi, I'm Annie. I think we've only met once or twice, at one of those house shows."

Federico gave me a sunny smile and took my hand to press a kiss to my knuckles rather than shake it. He had a broad, tan face with a heroic-looking brow and a pair of stunning dark eyes rimmed by thick, black lashes. His hair was coiffed in a glossy black slick-back and he sported a flawless mustache accenting the tart pout of his mouth. I looked between him and Keller, an odd couple, artist and muse, and tucked away a thought for later on what Evelyn and I might look like from the outside.

"I remember you, little scientist," Federico said, still smiling. "You're the one who makes Evie sigh about the stars, no?"

Evelyn made a suffering sound from her place on the ground. "Stop," she groaned. I bit back a grin and blushed.

"That may very well be my fault." I turned to Keller, who was exhaling a languorous set of smoke rings over his shoulder as he melted into the couch. He had the beginnings of a straw-colored goatee at work on his face and, as ever, an impish set to his sharp hazel stare. I leaned in and kissed him on one stubbly cheek. "Thank you again for letting us come over, I know it isn't really your thing."

"Can't say no to a lady in need," Keller drawled. He winked at me. "Call it a weakness."

Evelyn made a sound of victory as she found the channel, with a pair of news anchors giving a preamble to the broadcast with an intrepid-looking emblem at the bottom of the screen. "Channel *six*," she said pointedly. Rising to her feet, she brushed off the seat of her slacks. She had on a men's T-shirt with a faded logo she'd picked up at a consignment shop, and I noticed with a pleasant swoop in my belly that she wasn't wearing a bra.

She smiled and tucked an errant piece of hair behind my ear. "Glad you made it," she said, and kissed me hello again now that the television was tuned. I smiled against her mouth.

We settled in a line on the couch and I took the cigarette Evelyn offered me in lieu of sharing the joint—"She wants to stay *sharp* for her space-things," Federico said in a friendly mock whisper.

The press conference began with formalities and brief explanations of Project Mercury's mission: with Sputnik lighting a fire under the pertinent seats, the Air Force handed space flight off to the shiny new National Aeronautics and Space Administration and sought to put a man in orbit around the earth before getting him back safely, *before* the Soviets.

I was rapt.

They reached the question-and-answer section, reporters crammed into the back of a stuffy-looking room. Keller, Federico, and Evelyn chatted softly among themselves about art and upcoming shows when the questions got too technical, but I didn't mind. Evelyn was holding my hand, running a thumb across my knuckles like she wouldn't want to be anywhere but next to me.

Someone asked about the families of the men on the panel. One by one, down the line, I watched them talk about their wives. Their children. The people they were leaving on the ground.

"*I have no problems at home, my family's in complete agreement,*" said one of them. Laughter rang through the press room.

"That one sounds like a riot at parties," Federico snorted.

In my periphery, Evelyn patted his knee. "I don't think these guys go to the same tea dances you do."

The joint crackled. I kept my gaze fixed on the television, picking out the clean-cut all-American ease to each of their looks. The questions continued as I waited for one of them to talk about something a step past the mundane, to give a glimpse into what he felt about the stars and the long stretch of space. I craved evidence that I wasn't the only one with a strange pull toward the impossible driving my decisions. I couldn't be only one.

"It is noticed that three of our seven young men are smoking," the mediator said. *"What will they be doing when they get up in the capsule? Perhaps, Randy, you might tackle that one?"*

Keller barked a laugh. "Now here's the *real* meat of it! How do you reckon they do that, Annie?"

"They'll have to quit," I said with a shrug, not looking away from the screen. "You can't smoke in a vacuum."

Federico made a tetchy sound and exhaled as he declared, "I am never going into space."

". . . they are mature men," said an official in gray at the podium on the opposite end of the press table, *"and we will leave it up to them in large part. Of course we have a few months for an indoctrination program."* More knowing laughter threaded through the room, foggy through the backs of the microphones in front of the panel.

Federico got up and stretched with a yawn, his bare arms and shoulders bunching and reaching with almost feline grace, before heading to the bathroom closet across the studio.

"The question is: What is the motivation of these men?"

I leaned a touch closer to the screen, my heart twisting.

"Careful, Red," Keller teased me, tender and low, "you'll fall in."

Evelyn hushed him. He chuckled.

"I'm getting another beer," Keller mock-whispered as he slid up from the couch as well.

Here it was. One by one down the line, the men gave their names, ages, hometowns, and the peek into their motivations I was so desperate to hear—that perhaps I was not alone in my affinity for the unseen, my grasping for answers to which I didn't even have the questions in the first place.

Their reasons washed over me as my cigarette burned to a long tail of ash between my fingers, forgotten: *It is an extension of flight and we have to go somewhere, and that is all that's left; I feel it is an expansion in another dimension, much as aviation was an expansion on the surface of the earth; I am just grateful for an opportunity to serve; It certainly is a chance to pioneer on a grand scale.*

I tried not to feel too disappointed that their devotion was mostly drawn from service rather than curiosity.

A soft nudge to my shoulder knocked me out of my reverie and the ash from my cigarette to the floor. I swept it off the carpet as Evelyn's hand slid up the back of my neck. She kneaded me there softly until I looked away from the television to meet her gaze. "Yeah?"

She smiled at me, amused. "You look like you're about to try and crawl in to ask a few questions yourself."

I leaned back and sat up a little straighter to tug at the hem of my skirt. It slid with a soundless hasp against my nylons. "They all— I dunno. They're all military; it's duty to them. It's . . . different than what I expected. I thought they'd be more . . . curious."

Evelyn's fingers began a light, unconscious circling against my nape. She considered the conference on air. Federico returned and reached across the couch to pass Evelyn the joint waiting on the ashtray. She took a shallow draw of it.

"Is the military the only way to get into this stuff?" Evelyn shot me a grin. "You gonna enlist?"

Keller made a disgusted sound as he vaulted over the back of the couch to nestle back down against Federico's shoulder, beer in hand. "Annie, my dear, there's probably a smorgasbord of lesbians in the armed forces, but I'd be honor bound to never speak to you again if you enlisted. Nothing personal."

I snorted. "None taken."

"If you don't mind me asking," Federico said. "Why . . . space, why all these men who worship the Wright brothers as though they are gods?" He winnowed a graceful hand in the air, drawing a tiny pattern of smoke from the end of the punk between his fingers.

"I mean—" I stopped myself. I'd spent the past several years simply accepting that space was my own intangible North Star. But I didn't know how any of them would feel about me going off the deep end of destiny. I bit my lips together for a moment. "I don't know. It just feels right."

"Don't twist yourself up too bad," Keller offered as he took a swing from his bottle. He nudged Federico's knee with one foot. "Fede likes to think everything needs a 'why.'"

Federico shrugged. "It makes things easier to have one. You can plan accordingly."

"We all of us hang on to something as we go through life and feel that if we are risking our lives, it is worth it."

My insides lurched with sudden affinity. I extracted myself gently from Evelyn's arm and drew my knees up, peering even more closely at the television set.

"I would like to know if any of you have a religious, a strong religious feeling."

Down the long table they went again in order, expounding on the churches they went to and their reiterated faith in the program, until the camera wobbled gently as it stopped on the man I now recognized as Colonel Glenn.

He paused for a moment, thinking, and something in me hitched like an anchor catching on a rock deep below the surface.

"I was brought up believing that you are placed on earth here more or less

with sort of a fifty-fifty proposition, and this is what I still believe: We are placed here with certain talents and capabilities." Glenn leaned forward, one elbow propped beside a water jug, the explanation flowing easily. *"It is up to each of us to use those talents and capabilities as best you can. If you do that, I think there is a power greater than any of us that will place the opportunities in our way, and if we use our talents properly, we will be living the kind of life we should live."*

I swiped at my eyes under my glasses when my cheeks tickled—I had started crying.

"I look at it," Glenn continued, *"if I use the talents and capabilities I happen to have been given to the best of my ability, I think there is a power greater than I am that will certainly see that I am taken care of, if I do my part of the bargain."*

A bargain.

I had never before heard it spoken so clearly, so perfectly. When I looked up at the sky and felt my mind reaching toward something I could not see despite feeling my way toward it, a bargain was a good word for it.

Think you can help figure out how to get to the moon?

The warmth of Evelyn leaning up against me pulled me back down to the present. She rested her chin on my shoulder and said nothing, but her hands smoothed down my arms and the kiss she pressed to my shoulder was light.

"That," I whispered to her, "that's my why."

1968—THE MANNED SPACECRAFT CENTER, THE PROGRAMMING SUITE

Houston, Texas

I twisted my engagement ring around and around my finger as I checked over our table of testing materials for the fourth time—it had taken me and Norm about a month to realize I should have been wearing one.

It was my father's old wedding band, saved at the bottom of my paltry little jewelry box. It was a little loose, but the weight of it felt right. I watched the simple sterling silver winking in the fluorescent light of the programming suite.

Norm had suggested we go out and pick something pretty, but I didn't need pretty. If all we needed was a symbol, this was the only one I wanted.

Anyway, there was too much at stake lately to think about pretty. It was Monday, and there was reality to defy.

McCabe had gotten his approval from up top.

While we waited on the go-ahead to expand the Aion project, I had taken it upon myself to carefully tape out the tile in the power bank to keep other programmers from disturbing the anomaly or stepping on it during the day. The tests were now Tests, capital *T.* A strange feeling of ownership lived in me to see our work expanding, drilling down into the crux of whatever connected the anomaly to me, my childhood, the Apodaca garden.

We had officially labeled folders now, a film camera to log each test instead of Norm's photographs, and there was an actual Aion database instead of the slapdash repository I had thrown together on my computer terminal. We had a *team.* I never could have predicted this for myself from the stacks of the library or the back of a lecture hall at St. Christopher. This was more than simple Fisk curiosity. This was me doing something about it.

I was happier than I had been in a long time.

One of our teammates, Gene, was at work preparing the camera as I looked over the table of props for our tests. The spread was a mix of organic and synthetic material, dense and light, large and small. I was turning over a tiny plastic desk plant in my hand simply for something to occupy my nerves.

"Excited?" Gene asked. He was an infinitely levelheaded guy from the mechanical engineering team, a no-nonsense quick thinker. He was Louisiana Creole and hailed from Loyola with a comfortable croon like syrup. As another devotee of the dual degree, he and I got along like a house on fire.

I gave him a smile made wooden with the butterflies in my belly. "That's one word for it."

Today's test was for a new control group: objects sent through Aion at the same time. The potential for measured chaos was high.

We had exhausted our parameters for single-object trials and had progressed to multi-object tests earlier this month. The upper and lower limits of what counted as *the same time* had made themselves clear: If object A went through the anomaly within six seconds of object B, then A acted as an anchor and neither would return. If more than six seconds passed between placements, each object would return after its own respective six minutes had gone by.

No one had any working theories yet on the objects that appeared on their own.

Norm had devised a mechanism that would drop more than one object onto the anomaly tile at exactly the same time. It was made of slide rules, twine, and audacity: Test objects could balance on the "loading bay" of a wide base that straddled the anomaly tile. Moving quickly, one could then yank away the base with a string to let the objects fall at once to the floor.

Norm nicknamed it Bessie.

I looked up from the little plant in my hand to find Norm striding into our side of the programming suite as though he had caught the sun between his teeth like a Frisbee—there was nothing anyone could do to ding his happiness these days.

I shrugged away a tiny scratching of premonition and accepted the exuberant kiss he pressed to my cheek. Proximity to the anomaly always made me feel as though my own outline was blurred, like a thumb smearing a smudge of lipstick. I wondered if it was an energy field that raised the hair on my arms whenever I got close, or whether it was a call to the void sewn into me by the fact that my own past waited on the other end. I never quit wondering if Norm felt it, too. I always forgot to ask.

"Ready?" Norm reached down as he spoke and turned the plant over in the palm of my hand, drawing a thumb down one rigid little leaf.

"I think it's going to get really weird," I said, nodding at Aion's blue-taped edges.

Norm's eyebrows went up. "You mean it hasn't been weird up 'til now?"

I rolled my eyes and shoved him gently with my shoulder, which turned into a companionable lean when he reached up to wrap an arm around me. "Weird*er*," I said. "More funk. Twistier."

"Want to place some bets? What do you think will happen? Gene?" Norm looked sideways at Gene over my head and sallied a competitive grin at him. "You a betting man?"

At the mention of a bet, I thought of Evelyn. The shape of her smile was brief and vibrant in my mind. I wondered what she'd think of Norm, or of Aion.

"Only when I know I'll win," Gene said as he raised a deferential hand. "Rockets, I can parse. I'll leave this *weirder* shit to you, Hale."

Weirder shit was right. After the first official test, McCabe had hustled Gene down to the projector room to play back exactly what he had just recorded as though he didn't trust his own eyes.

I was just glad we hadn't been laughed out of McCabe's office from the first. But then I suppose when one was in the business of carving into space, the impossible was enticing. Addicting. Better than any vice around.

As I got my stopwatch in order, Norm set to preparing Bessie. Our first pair of objects were both small and synthetic with relatively low density: the plastic plant, and a compact mirror Norm had charmed from one of the secretaries — *We'll give it right back, Scout's honor.*

McCabe stepped through the plastic sheeting the Center had set up to section off this side of the suite, so the programmers could continue to work without us derailing them entirely. "Ready?" he barked.

"Just about," Gene said, threading the last of the film.

After several minutes of fiddling and checking and fiddling again, Norm nodded at me; I nodded at Gene, who nodded at McCabe, who nodded at me again. We were rolling. I cleared my throat.

"Aion Test B-31," I announced. "Timing trial three, synthetics in paired entry. Norman Hale on push mechanics, Gene Sutton on camera, Annie Fisk on timer." I adjusted the watch in my hand, readying my thumb on the start. "T-minus ten, nine . . ."

As we counted down, Norm looked up and caught my eye through the power banks. He grinned at me on *seven* and winked on *six*.

". . . two, one."

A yank on the slide rule, two quick clatters of landing; a soft itching behind my eyes made me blink. And then: the objects gone in the silent slippage that took them every time.

Clik. The seconds began to spool out from my watch.

Norm gave a victorious laugh from his crouch beside Bessie. "She works!"

Gene snorted behind the camera. "The intrepid spirit of discovery," he said flatly, "dreamed up on a lunch break and filched from the module engineers."

"Horse, cart," I called out, waving my watch as it ran. "We still need to see what comes back."

A particular idle chatter had come to take up the usual six minutes of these tests. Gene told us about the house he just bought in Clear Lake. McCabe waxed poetic about some trades the Astros were making this season. Ros passed close to our little cabal and warned McCabe we'd better not be messing with her transistor loads.

"One minute," I announced when the second hand sped past its last apex, and we all fixed our attention back to the anomaly spot.

Sixty seconds of silence persisted—I had never noticed how slowly a minute could pass before these damn tests.

"Ten," I counted back along with the clock as we approached the final stretch, "nine, eight, seven, six, five, four, three, two, o—"

Norm let out a whoop.

I stopped the watch.

6:00 on the dot.

"Look at this!"

Norm dragged both the plant and the mirror off the tile with the careful scrape of a straightedge. He picked up the plant and held it to the light in his long, careful fingers. Without looking away from it, Norm levered into a stand and hurried over to Gene's camera. He displayed it flat on his palm to the lens.

"*Look* at this," he repeated, enchanted. Gene focused the aperture, and I crossed over to see it for myself.

The plant had been bisected clear along its center stalk with a burst of impossible geometry. Like a glittering butterfly half-emerged from an odd chrysalis, a tesseract shape had burst from the plastic and split it like a fruit peel, as though whatever waited in the passage between here and Apodaca had squeezed the soul out of its center.

"That," Gene marveled, coming around the camera to peer closely at it, "is definitely weirder."

"It—how does it feel, is it hot to the touch? Cold? Did it melt?" I asked. Norm glanced up at me with his gaze bright.

"Feels all normal, except for the obvious. Come see."

He turned it over in his palm. The glimmering edge of the aberration caught the light and threw it in sharp angles that paid no heed at all to the way light usually bent. It was blue one instant, yellow the next, shivering like oil-shine as though my eyes couldn't pin its color down.

"What about the other one?" McCabe said, peering over Gene's shoulder. He tended to keep his distance from our tests with his jaw set and his hands in his pockets, holding the line of common sanity.

We all glanced over at the compact still waiting on the floor, and I couldn't help the giddy laughter that split from me. A spear of the same impossibility stabbed out through the mirror's center like a dagger, about three inches long and sharp as glass.

"Fran is gonna fucking kill me," Norm said, beaming.

The afternoon wore on through more tests, proving the strange phenomenon over and over again with each repeated trial—when two objects went through at once, the residue of passage hitched a ride back and stuck to itself like bladed jewels. No matter the material, synthetic or organic, high or low density.

I was elated. We forgot to take lunch.

Norm and I threw rock-paper-scissors to decide who got to keep the plant on their desk, despite McCabe muttering *unnatural* under his breath as we packed out the testing area. Norm won it.

"Don't worry," he teased as we wrapped up, wagging the anomalous plastic at me while I wound the cord of the stopwatch with careful precision, "half of it will be yours when we get hitched."

On our way back to his office to compile and store today's notes, Norm and I fell in step. "Thank you," I said. Norm grinned.

"Whatever for, darlin'?"

"For being here. For not . . . thinking I was crazy."

"'Course you aren't crazy." Outside his office, Norm leaned over easily and kissed me on the temple before he kept walking. "It's one hell of a privilege to watch you work, Fisk. Now wish me luck, gotta tell Fran I ruined her mirror."

The afternoon ripened while I was at Norm's desk typing up today's report. Gene knocked and stuck his head through the door. "We're going for drinks; Norm wants to celebrate."

"Celebrate what?"

Gene shrugged. "Fran didn't kill him; he gets to keep the mirror. You coming?"

I spread one hand out at my notes and combed the other back into my hair. "I'm not quite done here. I could meet you there?"

Norm's head popped in alongside Gene's, and he scowled at me. "Don't lose track of time. A guy deserves to buy his fiancée a drink with an umbrella in it after a day like today, don't you think?"

I couldn't help but smile at him. "You just want the umbrella."

"And what if I do?" Norm sidled in through the door to bend low and plant a kiss on my forehead. "Seriously," he said against my hair, "don't stay too late. I want my genius on my arm."

I twisted to peck him on the lips and pat his cheek. "Promise."

"We'll be at Sal's," Gene said.

"Don't get the table with the shitty legs," I warned them as I turned back to my notes. Gene made a noncommittal sound—apparently the rickety table had brought good luck to the team throughout Gemini, and he was hard-pressed to give it up. He shut the door to leave me in silence again.

I tapped my pen on my knee and stared at the keyboard for a moment. I glanced at the plant I'd propped up beside a frame that held one of the first photos Norm had taken of me in the power racks. There, the two things Norm Hale loved more than he really ought to: impossibility itself, and me.

Don't lose track of time. I stared at the plant until my eyes burned for not blinking.

The test notes crunched as I shuffled them together and crammed them into the open space on Norm's bookshelf. I snatched up my purse, straightened my skirt, and hurried into the hall to catch up to the boys.

1968–JOSKE'S DEPARTMENT STORE
Houston, Texas

My every waking moment became Aion. I learned to function on obscenely little sleep. My bloodstream was probably more coffee than plasma.

I was so happy I could hardly stomach it.

As summer turned its sweating heft into the slim margin of autumn, it felt as though there were two Annie Fisks born from a tearing down my midline: one half for the work, and the other half for living. One could easily guess which half I preferred, which half was more vital and ready to function.

But there were still checkpoints along the ribbon of the week at which I had to immerse myself in the mundane instead of the extraordinary. For those, I used the less-developed half of me that was body instead of mind.

I stood in the hosiery section at Joske's surrounded by mannequins and far too many options. When had nylons become more than just . . . *nylon*? The plastic limbs unnerved me, as though they were going to come to life and start walking at any moment.

Advertisements splashed with the pouty doe faces of Twiggy and Jean Shrimpton looked down from the walls. Disembodied display legs stood like radio towers on the shelves as the aisles ran on in several rows, encased in colorful options and layered weaves.

While my eyes weathered the assault, my mind chewed on Aion. Why did it defy the rules? It was a question that hadn't retracted its claws from the back of my mind since my initial conversation with Dr. Laitz.

I reached up and ran an idle thumb across the display hose, dragging the two layers of fabric over the stiff arch of the fake foot.

According to our testing, the anomaly behaved as he had said: two mouths, one throat. But it remained uncoupled, and there didn't seem to be any rhyme or reason as to the spread of *when* exactly the other mouth opened in Santa Fe.

The things that came through were from different times, but always from the exact same place.

Why one axis moving, but not the other?

Length, width, height, time.

Four axes. Four dimensions.

Then how could it . . .

How could it . . .

I froze with my thumb on the third display, a fishnet stocking layered over a pair of solid fuchsia. The edge of my thumb skimmed over the stretch and give of the fabric.

Stretch and give.

From across the aisle, a sale on miniskirts and wrap dresses announced itself with a bold photograph of a trio of laughing women mid-stride down a sidewalk. I took a step closer and peered at the display stockings.

Stretch. And give.

At the edge of one of the fishnet holes, I caught the fabric with my chewed-down thumbnail and dragged it gently into an oblong shape. The small diamond eyelet of it yawned to one side . . . pulling the others around it in shifting response.

Where there was stretch, there must be give. Relativity. Innate equivalence.

Something clicked.

I snatched up a bundle of fishnets in one arm and shoved them into my basket. As I hurried to the register, I could hardly hear the piped-in music or any of the pleasantries the salesgirl was saying with a smile. I nodded, volleyed just enough monosyllables in response to be polite, and almost left the counter without paying. I probably told her to keep the change that doubled the total; dinner on me this weekend, kid.

The swingback strap of my left shoe came unhitched, and I staggered into a limp ten paces from my car. I'd have to come back for the replacement hose I actually needed later. Or maybe just check the drugstore on the corner. Would there always be so many *options*? Would the world always be expanding like this? I unlocked my car and wrenched open the door, the paper sack of fishnets clung to my chest. The heat swallowed me greenhouse-hot in the driver's seat.

The earth was round. Reality, matter itself exerted constant pressure to keep it that way. So why shouldn't I have assumed that time would respond accordingly to that pressure?

A rigid body would not remain rigid on launch. All things must flex to keep from breaking. The atmosphere is a fickle thing, ready to swallow even the slightest mistakes in heat-warp and hull-melt and—

I tore open one of the double-packs of hose and shoved my hand into the leg opening. As I twisted my fingers, balled and un-balled my fist, pulled and shifted the fabric to and fro over my knuckles, the openings of the fishnet like hundreds of mouths connected by hundreds of throats stretched and gave, stretched and gave.

The world turned. The tides tugged at it, and the oceans bending to that grip made our planet ever so slightly oblong, an ellipsoid. Under the loving drag of the moon always hitched to the orbital thread that kept her close, the gaps between matter would widen or shrink accordingly.

How strange, to be so orbited, loved by something so far away that pulled so dearly at the very fabric of being?

My eyes welled inexplicably. I sat back in my seat. The driver's-side door was still hanging open and I had one foot propped out on the asphalt. I squeezed my fist tight from inside the stocking and bit down on my lip as emotion rushed hot and spiny up under my face.

I caught my reflection in the mirror. There was wonder there, and no small measure of fear—with existence showing itself, its *true* self, the lofty and half-terrifying pitch of infinity and all its twisting wiles, who among us wouldn't have cowered to behold it?

It seemed discovery was less a product of joy and far more often a cousin of fear.

I swiped my fingertips under my eyes and looked away from the mirror, sniffling hard. Staring at my hand, twisting and pinching and flexing, I spent one more moment hanging in the strange awe of it all.

I dug my keys out from my purse once I had mostly returned to myself. I spared a glance up at the rearview mirror as the engine woke with a grumble and found a familiar gaze looking right back: determined and fierce, eyes so sharp and beryl-blue I could swear they were my mother's own watching me carefully through the backward trickling of time.

You've become someone I recognize from a long time ago.

✦　✦　✦

In the next three months of our Aion tests, we followed the tidal idea like hounds to point. The evidence of it led me to believe that the anomaly had something to do with quasars, more specifically the exact distances between them at coordinates draped over the earth like a flexible lattice as the planet turned and the moon with it.

If the ratio between the gaps in matter at an atomic level was just barely wide enough, objects could slip through. Those gaps stretched and gave with the turning of the moon, the pull of its orbit. Like the vibration of a speaker head turned up a little too loud, rattling a wineglass steadily across the top of the record cabinet with each thump of bass, the resonance of those gaps could be just right in some places to push matter back and forth through the fourth dimension: time.

Norm and I were poring over sheets of calculations spread across his office floor as the afternoon seeped steadily into evening. "We need a chalkboard in here," I muttered, piecing together a mess of coordinates and distance calculations in a long shaft of lowering sunlight arcing across the carpet.

"I put in the requisition form last week," Norm said over his shoulder as he paged through a reference text on mass and time. He furrowed his eyebrows. "Your father was a physicist, wasn't he?"

My gut flipped, pitching like the fishtail swing of a car taking a turn a bit too sharply. "Yeah. Why?"

Norm shrugged. He was still intent on the book. "I dunno. You never mention him."

I swallowed carefully. I would have mentioned him more if I could remember anything about him. "He . . . died. When I was fifteen."

Norm fixed me with a tender look. "Sorry."

"It's okay."

In my periphery, he chewed his lip for a moment. He was staring past the edge of the book still open in his hands. "My mother is the brains of the operation," Norm said fondly, with a distant smile. "She doesn't remember too much besides her own name and some of her earlier debutante days, but she's still sharp as anything. Can finish a crossword in record time and clean out a whole bridge table without blinking."

I was quietly, briefly, incandescently jealous of him; to have a vivid enough image in his mind of someone he loved enough to have it show in his eyes like that.

"My mother always told me I got my curiosity from him," I said carefully.

Norm gave me a tender smile. "Good. It suits you."

We kept after it for another hour. Norm finally got what he needed out of the book and paused as he replaced it on his shelf. He turned, drumming his fingertips against his cheek with one hand while he propped the other on his hip, his jacket rucked aside. I looked up at him from my place on the floor.

Norm frowned at nothing for several seconds, and then peered down at me with conviction in his eyes. "What if—"

THOOM.

The low sound of impact, unmistakable, fired off from somewhere just outside the Center. Norm sharpened and immediately looked to the doorway. I scrambled to my feet as the ruckus of curious anxiety began to pour through the hallways, colleagues bursting from their offices.

"Missile?" I gasped. Norm shook his head and took me by the elbow, hurrying from the office and out toward the front door.

"LLTV crash. They're running patterns today."

Analysts and typists and commanders alike were already jostling one another toward the doors. The late-autumn sun blazed down onto the flat basin of empty land around us, and a dark column of smoke had begun to rise from the landing test vehicle wreckage, which smelled of fuel even from here.

"God almighty," one of the secretaries breathed from behind me. Two medics tore at a dead sprint toward the pyre, stretcher in hand.

"Is he alright?" I hazarded as I tightened my grip on Norm's arm. He was staring hard at the fire, something like fury in his sharp green gaze.

"I don't know, Annie."

The medics finally hurried back. When the pilot lain between them gave us a weak thumbs-up as they jogged past, banged up but alive, the tension trickled out from us all in one great sigh. Chatter and mutters and even nervous laughter filtered up into the stiff silence of miles and miles of nothing around us.

Norm couldn't look away from the wrecked landing test vehicle. A gaggle of engineers had run out with fire extinguishers to kill the smoke as it billowed angrily up into the sky, their ties flapping and their hair tossed by the wind that had knocked the lander off course. The crowd began trickling back into the Center.

"What were you about to say?" I tried to capture Norm's attention. My grip was sure on his arm. "Back there in the office, before the alarm started up?"

Norm didn't respond and just kept staring. After a moment, he blinked and rubbed at his eyes beneath his glasses. His shoulders sagged. "What if we could avoid this?" he said softly. I frowned.

"Avoid what?"

He gestured a wide, flat hand at the wrecked module. "This. The— risk, the angst, the crashing, all of this."

Norm turned and took me by both shoulders. His stare was ferocious, a brightness I hadn't seen so intense since the night I showed him what Aion could do — *HELLO, WORLD.*

Something in me buckled, a fuse overburdened with current finally shorting.

"How?" I asked. My voice was weak.

Norm's expression didn't falter. "People. What if people could traverse via Aion?"

My stomach dropped. I thought of my father's belief in the invisible lines that drew people together. Not fate, but a more organic devotion. Mountains yearning for the sky they would never touch but for the brief kiss of low clouds making mist along their peaks.

I couldn't stop this. All I could do was observe; a dutiful scientist watching my discovery grow legs and walk away from me.

I slid Norm's hand into mine and squeezed, wishing that the lines of our palms might speak that ancient language to each other and guide us unscathed through the throes of the universe's heaving.

"It's worth trying," I said. A bitter taste had filled me even as I resisted it, the tang of insatiable curiosity. The worst part was that despite the fear, the instinct to shy away, I wanted to know, too.

Norm pressed a kiss to my forehead. Another breeze raked past and made his tie flutter in the air between us.

I wondered briefly if the hunger to know, to hold proof in my mouth like a marble on my tongue, might kill me with the same hereditary cruelty.

But I shut my eyes and decided to hope instead.

If nothing else, I still had hope—a beacon in the dark, a vessel on which to weather the uncaring current of the universe, that I wished dearly my father might have also found before it was too late.

05:00

1968—THE GULF FREEWAY, HEADING NORTHWEST
Houston, Texas

I flicked at the radio from the passenger's seat of the Barracuda, scoring three stations in a row all playing Christmas carols. I groaned. Norm raised an eyebrow at me through his periphery. "It's not Christmas yet," he teased. "You can't complain about Christmas music unless it's playing *after* Christmas."

"We've hardly put Thanksgiving in the ground."

"It'd be weirder to sit in silence."

I grunted around a cigarette and blew a piston of smoke out through the slipstream of the open window, which was tossing my hair in a mad riot.

The freeway streamed past, bearing us into the city proper. I looked sideways at Norm again. "You triple-checked?"

Norm's mouth held in an amused little smile. "Quadruple-checked. They're open 'til four o'clock, hand to God."

I glanced at my wristwatch and chewed my lip. "It's three-thirty."

"And we're about fifteen minutes away, plenty of time." If Norm showed up anywhere even five minutes early, he would crow about how silly it was to arrive so far ahead of schedule.

Today, Norm had blurted that morning as I was tucking my blouse into my skirt. I gave him a look from across the bedroom, where he was already dressed.

What's today?

I don't have any sims running today, and our next Aion test isn't 'til tomorrow. We should play hooky and go to the courthouse.

I'd finished straightening my buttons and fussed with the fall of my hair for a moment, not looking at him even through the mirror. I glanced at the nightstand instead, where our marriage license had been waiting in a file folder for us to drum up the gumption to do something about it. *Today?*

It was his simple shrug, the why-not of it all, that really hooked me in—why not? How much stranger could everything get from here, and what did I have left to fear?

I glanced at my watch again: 3:32. I hunkered into the seat and watched Norm's profile. The smile on his face couldn't have wiped itself away even if the car suddenly exploded and took us both with it.

I extinguished my cigarette tidily in the door tray. The city proper rose like teeth against the horizon.

3:46. Norm parked in the empty stretch of spots outside the front of the courthouse. I fussed my skirt smooth and tidied the cuffs of my sleeves while Norm stood by with hot-footed eagerness before leading the way up the steps. He went at a quick, sketching gait, the license tucked under one arm. He held the door for me, where the interior echoed hollowly with the faint slap-back of marble tiling.

We scurried up to the receptionist, who gave us a sidelong look as she directed us down the corridor—whether for our pulling-in-by-a-nose timing or for the odd couple we made as a pair of squares with varying degrees of anxiety visible at their edges, I couldn't decipher.

We cooled our heels in a row of plastic chairs outside the judge of the county courts' office. Antsy, one knee bouncing, I checked my watch again. 3:52.

The edge of my thumb not laced into Norm's hand was at my front teeth, absently chewing. I jumped a little in my seat when the judge's office door swung open.

He was a sallow, slight man with an anemic comb-over and a deep stoop to his shoulders. One corner of his mouth drooped a little, as though he was made of wax put to heat. "Alright," he said, gesturing inside. "Cutting it close, aren't we?"

Norm grinned. "We work on rockets. Everything we do is a close shave."

I wished that I could have bottled the sensation of the moment: the split of it brisk and bracing, like peeling open an orange and finding an extra segment tucked between its pieces—but instead of a single segment it was a profusion of them, spilling out from my own center.

The officiant rattled off a litany of legalities and formalities in his dishwater voice. Norm said his vows first. I was so nervous I could hardly process the words.

"And, Anne, do you take Norman to be your lawful wedded husband?"

Norm clung to my hand, our shared grip bone-white. Despite the dry rote of the courtroom, the heavy tick of the clock on the judge's wall—3:58—tears glistened on Norm's eyelashes. I held his gaze unflinchingly. I wasn't crying.

"Do you promise to love and cherish him," the judge droned, "in sickness and in health, for richer or for poorer, for better or for worse, and forsaking all others, keep yourself only unto him, for so long as you both shall live?"

I nodded, willing myself to shed even the smallest tear. Nothing came. "I do."

"By the power vested in me by the state of Texas, I now pronounce you husband and wife."

The judge was looking at the certificate, signing his name even as he bid us married. He flipped the paper around to face us with a firm line pressed into his mouth, a smile if I squinted. "Congratulations."

I signed first, and then Norm. The judge ushered us right back out with the certificate in hand, shut the door firmly behind us, and that was it. We were married.

I was a wife. I had a husband.

I looked at Norm, his profile touched by the warm fingers of the lowering late-afternoon sun. The fine hairs on his face caught the light and burst into illumination, and the sides of his spectacles flashed as he turned to me.

I remembered him at the window that first Christmas, soused with Manhattans and too many maraschinos and a head full of ideas about the moon. I remembered the way he looked at me when I said I wanted to keep it safe.

I looked at him, my *husband*, and felt sharply as though I had reared back and bitten my own tail; something cyclical, once hanging open and fluttering in the breeze, now sealed.

Now came the tears.

"Hey, hey," Norm lulled me, coming forward in the empty hallway to tender a thumb up under my glasses and swipe away the rush of them. "None of that now, darlin'."

"Sorry," I hiccuped, "I'm sorry, I just—I'm *happy*, Norm, I'm so happy, we—"

Norm took me by both sides of my face and kissed me, a hard and silent plea. I shut my eyes and met him halfway, kissed him right back, and I clung to his lapel when we pulled apart. He roved his fingers softly over the back of my neck and kept his chin from wobbling too badly.

"I love you," he breathed. I sniffled sharply.

"It's going to be okay," I whispered. I ran my thumb over his top buttonhole and the weave of his jacket, staring at the thread pattern. "It's going to be great."

Norm's breath was soft and even through his nose. Unconsciously I matched the steady in-out, returning from the stratosphere.

"If my mother were still around," I said, hysteria half-held at bay, "she would kill me for not making a bigger deal of this."

Norm gave a damp chuckle. "Mine would say it's foolish for such a smart, pretty thing to hitch herself to her space-addled son. She'd say it with me in the room, too, and I think I'd agree with her."

I clasped my hand over my mouth, shrinking in on myself, and shrugged with a humored sort of disbelief as I sobbed through a smile, my shoulders jumping shallowly. *Look at what we've done*, I wanted to shout into the empty courthouse corridor, blame him for making me feel so much love it made me want to curl up and disappear.

The obvious clatter of a janitor's cart rang from the other end of the hallway.

"Congratulations," an old, rasping voice called, "now get yourselves home. We're closed."

Norm swiped at my cheeks again, thumbing away my tears. "Here," he said briskly, "let's go get Gene and grab a drink at Sal's."

I lifted off my glasses and dabbed carefully at my eyes with the corner of my sleeve. I nodded and forced a steady swallow. "Okay. Yeah."

"Yeah?" Norm squeezed my hand. He smiled, the certificate envelope secure under his left elbow against his side. I settled my glasses back onto my nose and ran a hand through my hair as I sniffed.

"Yeah. Let's go."

We had time. I told myself we had all the time we could ever need, and I held in the bitter taste of doubt in the desperate hope it might melt.

ALMOST 1961—BRADLEY'S PUB, OFF-CAMPUS
San Antonio, Texas

Of the many things I loved about Texas, one of the top was that I could celebrate New Year's Eve without a coat.

We were packed into Bradley's Pub like sardines, twelve minutes to 1961. I was pleasantly drunk. My vision was swimming, haloing everything in a warm, golden glow. Evelyn's arm was linked in mine. I couldn't recall ever being so happy in my entire life.

"This is nuts!" Evelyn said in my ear for the third time, indicating the bar at large. "I didn't think anyone else knew about this place!"

"You have good taste," I said with a stupid grin. Someone had cued up Del Shannon on the jukebox, and a few other students whooped as "Runaway" began. The crowd was a messy combination of students from St. Christopher, San Antonio College, and Trinity—the boys from SAC were tripping over themselves to find so many girls in one place.

I pulled out a cigarette. Three of those boys automatically stuck out their lighters, and as I shot a laughing look at Evelyn, I didn't see which of them managed to light it first. When my drink was almost upended by a wide-swinging elbow not two minutes later, I craned my neck for the nearest door outside.

"Come on," I said over the noise, pulling Evelyn gently after me, "fresh air."

The night was a godsend when we finally stumbled outdoors. The crickets were chirring and a few other folks had found their way outside as well. The shallow but limpid pool of downtown glittered faintly from farther south.

Evelyn had her own cigarette in her fingers, and I offered her my light as nobody else invaded our bubble this time. We smoked in silence, catching our breath—she watched me with those big brown eyes, her hair in a short shag cut she had snipped herself last month, and I stared right back, head-over-heels.

With the angle of Evelyn's smirk, I could tell I was making a moony face at her. "What," she hummed sweetly.

"Nothing," I snickered. "Nothing. You're just pretty."

Evelyn's grin split into a reluctant chuckle. She looped an arm around my waist—genial to an outsider, warm as wool to us both. "Talk about pretty, take a look at the moon tonight."

She nodded her chin up and I followed it, straight up into the near-midnight sky to find our pearly eye staring down huge and round. Only a slim edge remained in shadow. I smiled to myself.

"Feels lucky for New Year's to have it waxing," I hummed. Evelyn made a small sound of assent.

"How do you mean?"

I shrugged, our sweaters whispering together at the shoulder. "I don't know, it just feels nice. Something on its way, something we can't quite see in full yet, but we know will be pretty. It's nice."

Evelyn bunted my hip softly with hers. "Prettier than me?"

With a snort, I exhaled a cloudy drag of smoke and looked at her sideways. "No comment."

She wanted to kiss me, I could tell. "They're gonna get people up there someday," she hummed instead. "How soon do you think? In your *expert opinion.*"

I raised my eyebrows. "So I'm an expert now?"

Evelyn tapped our knees together. "My money's on sometime before 1970," she said.

"Only a decade to figure it all out?" I countered. Evelyn leveled a look at me.

"Correction, Ms. Mathematics, that's nine years."

"Nine years," I said. "You think it would only take *nine years* to — No. I'm gonna stop there. It's a holiday, I'll give you a break from me."

Evelyn looked like the cat that got the cream. "No, keep going. It's sexy when you talk numbers."

I flushed pink but did as she said.

Partway through explaining the detailed specifics of thrust patterns and timing the moon's orbit, Evelyn put her hand over my mouth in gentle jest. I licked her palm and laughed as she pulled it away again to wipe off on the leg of her jeans. "Make a bet with me," she said.

"A bet on what?"

"If we get someone on the moon before 1970, you, Annie Fisk, are hereby obligated to let me whisk you away somewhere to empty the overfilled file cabinet that is your brilliant mind," Evelyn murmured, reaching up to tap me twice on the forehead.

"And what does 'emptying' entail?"

"Judicious application of my mouth," she said, proud of herself as she sucked on her clove again, "on judicious parts of you."

I wanted to tell her I was in love with her; that I liked her judicious mouth on me, sure, but I also wanted to see what might happen if we tried sewing our lives together like other people did. I turned to her and took a long moment staring at her profile.

"What do you like about me?" I asked. Evelyn snorted.

"What do I *like* about you?"

"Yeah."

"Where do I start?"

I scoffed. "Be serious."

"I am."

Evelyn looked down at her boots for a moment and rolled the last sip of her cigarette over her tongue. She tipped her head and peered at the moon again. "You spend so much time," she said gently, "floating up in the sky with your numbers and your . . . plans, it reminds me there's more to it all than just the ordinary."

I stared at the shiny black snip-toes on her feet as well. "How do you mean?"

"I mean, there's more than just the next day coming around the bend when I'm with you. There's shit like planets and stars and moons up there, which is a hell of a lot better of a reason to stick around than just another fucking Sunday."

The undercurrent of that idea met me like cold water shivering backward. "Evelyn," I murmured.

She shrugged. "You make it easy to find things worth painting out there. It's the truth. I just like you, Fisk."

I just like you. Everything with us seemed to be *just*, plain and stark and perfectly understandable. Brass tacks. Nothing but the facts. It should have been easy.

I love you, I thought, a test run, and felt the phrase burn up in its own atmosphere at the back of my mind.

Evelyn extinguished her cigarette in the overfull tray in the middle of the table we were sitting on. She smiled at me, tipping her head as she swung her feet. "Did I tell you I started a new series of canvases? It's about lunar phases."

I loved her more than anything. I loved her so much it made my chest hurt. I just couldn't tell her. I darted my tongue quickly over my lips instead. "What's it called?"

"Working title so far is *Artemis by Night*."

The crowd inside began shouting down from ten along with the clock—*Ten! Nine! Eight! Seven!*

We both jumped. Before Evelyn could turn to me first, I took her by the collar and pulled her into the crush of our lipstick and the clash of disparate smoke still sticking in our mouths, heedless of anyone else. The countdown rounded off: *Six! Five! Four! Three! Two! One!*

We didn't pull apart until they'd already begun singing "Auld Lang Syne," and I was too far gone in my swirling head—overfilled, Evelyn had called it—to care about anything in that moment besides knowing that I was in love.

I was invigorated. I was terrified.

"I'll take your bet," I gulped when Evelyn finally pulled back, her face flushed and a pretty grin shining in the dark. "What do I get if I win?"

"You won't. I'm an optimist." Evelyn flicked me softly on the nose. She kissed me again, painting those first moments of 1961 with such perfection that my heart could hardly bear it.

For just a moment I imagined myself as one of her canvases, full of blues and golds and shimmering midnight-black in complex patterns rambling across my skin.

1968—ANNIE FISK'S APARTMENT
Houston, Texas

I shut the door after Norm as he came in behind me. Rather than take his coat, I simply slid my hands underneath it along his sides and pulled him down to me with a kiss. His heels knocked against the closed door and he made a pleased sound of surprise against my mouth.

It had been nearly a month since we had enough time and were awake enough. McCabe had finally started taking Norm's talk of human trials seriously, and every day it seemed there was some new hurdle to clear between the straits of the Center's red tape. But tonight, finally, we were home at a reasonable hour.

Tonight, I just wanted to take my husband to bed.

"*Whoa* there," Norm said, batting at my hands as I went for his belt buckle, both of us all but panting. He stilled me with a touch.

"What?" I sniffed, reaching up instead to steadily loosen his tie as he finished hanging his jacket all haphazard on the hook beside him. "It's been a while. My head's all full of work and holiday plans. Come to bed, help me empty it."

I kissed him again, and Norm indulged me for a moment before pulling back again. He knocked his head back against the door as I fixed my mouth to the column of his throat—but I paused when he set his hands to my upper arms with a gentle, steady weight.

I pulled back to rest my lips barely against his clean-shaven jaw. "Are you okay?"

"I'm—" Norm sighed. "Here, come sit down, Annie."

I took a step back but stood my ground. Norm lowered himself onto the sofa. I stared at him from above, breathing through my nose and fixing a curl on my forehead with flick of my fingertips. "What?"

"Come sit," Norm repeated. He had his elbows propped on his knees, the liquidy length of him folded up with tension. The soft smudge of my lipstick clung to his neck. I crossed my arms.

"I really don't want to have an argument tonight."

Removing his glasses and rubbing his hands across his face, Norm let out a soft groan. "It doesn't have to be an argument."

The silence clotted like bad cream. The clock ticking from the kitchen wall to my right wore against my pulse, which had started beating double time beneath it.

Norm flailed his hands in frustration and gathered one of my throw pillows into his lap, a corduroy that had long sat on the sofa in the den at Apodaca. "I want to talk about the Aion voyage."

My worry cooled, and on its heels came a super-heating of anger.

We had been over this before. Neither of us would be the human trial. I had *explicitly* forbidden him from volunteering for the human trial. "What about it," I said tightly. I stayed rooted to my spot.

Norm looked at me for several heartbeats, pleading silently. I did not soften to him. "Sit down, Annie. Please," he murmured. He was running one fingertip softly back and forth over the pillow fabric.

I stood my ground for one more moment, before I huffed and stalked over to the couch. I sat down heavily on the opposite arm from Norm with my back ramrod straight and my knees pressed together.

It occurred to me that since we'd known each other, Norm had never seen me genuinely angry—a small part of me wondered if that was normal, if it was par for the course for a couple to stumble into a lifetime without first sinking their teeth into the flesh of a real argument.

"I volunteered for the trial," Norm said carefully.

I stared at him. My hands began to shake.

When I didn't say anything, Norm continued: "McCabe approved me. But I wanted to let you know before I accepted."

My throat worked twice around a dry, hollow gulp of air. This wasn't exciting anymore. Parsing the reality of a worst-case scenario was easier when it wasn't one of us being considered, when it wasn't *him*.

I opened my mouth once to speak, then again when my words failed the first time—"Did you think to tell me?" My voice wavered, but I kept it firmly to heel. "To consider me at any point, before you'd already made up your mind?"

Norm watched me sideways, his gaze fevered and cervine. "I'm telling you now," he said.

I couldn't sit still. I pressed my fingers to my forehead, shutting my eyes, and started to pace. "I can't begin to tell you how—just how *stupid* this is, Norman. Risking your life? How dare you?"

Norm shoved the pillow back down onto the couch and stood up as well, his hands on his hips. "How *dare I*? Who are you to tell me what I can and can't do, professionally?"

"I'm your *wife*!" I shouted, whirling to face him. "Does that mean *anything* to you!"

"Of course it does!" Norm cried. "But it has nothing to do with me making choices for our project!"

I narrowed my eyes, leaning close as though Norm was some sort of equation I might read more clearly by drawing nearer. "*Our* project. Do you hear yourself, Norman? None of this would be possible without me. *None* of it."

Norm tried to take my hand in both of his, but I ripped it away. His face fell. "Annie," he said carefully, "you know they'll never let me fly. This is my only shot."

That heart of his, always skipping beats, holding him a painful nearly-there away from his dreams. My nostrils flared. "You don't even know what could happen," I shot back. "What if your heart gives out, what if they're keeping you out of a voyage for a reason?"

Norm's mouth tightened. "Since when did you let the unknown get the best of you?"

I threw my hands out in front of me. "Since none of the cats ever came back!"

Norm cracked a laugh. We had run four tests for sentient passage with a cabal of stray cats Gene had charmed into the Center with liberal helpings of tuna fish. None of them had come back after being placed on the anomaly. "That's horseshit and you know it. I'm not a fucking cat, Annie, I can stay in one place."

"Well, excuse me for not wanting you to take a risk on something with limits we haven't been able to record for *any living thing*."

"We know it's location-based, for Chrissake!" Norm gestured sharply from side to side with both hands, as though cordoning off bits of space. "Thing goes in, thing comes back. Six minutes. You can't tell a cat to stay put. I am not a *fucking cat*."

"And how do you know that's the reason they weren't coming back? What if . . . if they're *dying*, getting lost along the way!"

"The scientific method!" Norm shouted. He looked as though he hardly knew me. My heart dropped. "Just look at the—the *hundreds* of tests we've run before the cats! Jesus, Annie, since when did logic quit holding water for you?"

I gestured sharply with my left hand, pressing my ring hard against my knuckle with my thumb as I shook it at Norm. "Since I hitched my future to yours!"

"And how does that change anything!"

"Because I'm *scared*, Norm!" I cried, breaking into a hideous sob. "I'm fucking TERRIFIED!"

Norm stared at me. In the silence that persisted as I scrambled to quit bawling and collect myself, the refrigerator buzzed to life quietly in the kitchen.

I crammed a lungful of air into my tightening rib cage and tried again; "I'm *terrified*. My world is—it's so small, Norman. If I lose you, then *I'm* all I have left. I can't do that. I can't lose anyone else. I *can't*. I can't be alone!"

Norm's fists were still clenched and his jaw flexed with frustration, but his eyes had softened. He stared at me in my hot-cheeked misery for another long stretch of silence before he swiped his hand down his mouth. "We're being careful, Annie. We're testing this thing; we know how it works. I don't know what else to tell you."

"But we can't control it. It's distilled chaos." I ripped off my glasses and mashed my fingertips into my eyes to swipe away the tears. I shook my head.

Norm moved slowly to close the space between us. He smoothed his hands slowly down my arms, shoulder to wrist, before holding my fingers loosely in his. This time, I let him. "None of this has ever been about control," he murmured.

I tossed my head and avoided his gaze. "Fine. Discovery, conquest, whatever you want to call it—"

"It's about *proof*," Norm said gently. "We're not sending someone to discover what we can already see. We're sending someone out there to prove we can, and then see what else we can do with it. Now call me selfish, but can you blame me for wanting to have some hand in it, too? *You* found it. *You* studied it. Let me contribute something meaningful, too. Please."

The rounded edge of my ring dug into my palm, and as I loosened the clenching through every finger I thought of my father—proving what was beneath the visible; proving what, exactly, mankind was capable of.

A shallow shiver crept through me. Norm was right. I had no control over what the Center would ultimately do with the anomaly any more than I could control his decision to see what lay on the other side of it.

I shook my head. "Alright. Fine. Whatever you want. I can't stop you."

Norm pulled me hard into a fierce embrace. I stared with an unfocused and watery gaze over his shoulder at the tiny Christmas tree we had decorated together in our precious handfuls of hours outside of work, glittering with strands of tinsel. Above it, the clock shaved away at time by one unseeable slice a second.

There, that was it, the thing I was most desperate to hold on to and cherish with Norm, whether it was spent bent over experiments or stealing handfuls of minutes each morning in the bedsheets: time.

Norm pulled back and took a breath to say something before he stopped himself. He kissed me instead, his arms still wrapped tightly around me, and held on as though I was the one planning to risk everything.

I shut my eyes and gave over to him as I silently pleaded with myself to have this one moment with him set free from my fear of losing him. Just one moment. Just for now.

"Come to bed," I relented against the corner of Norm's lips when we separated. I didn't want to keep talking circles around the same undefined horrors. I wanted to lose myself in the parts of him I loved best—his heart, his breath, his heat—to run away into him the way I had learned with Evelyn. When love terrified me, pleasure was the safest place to hide.

Norm nodded, resting our foreheads together as he held fast to the back of my neck. "Okay," he murmured.

I turned, my hand in his, and took him into my room.

I drew Norm down onto the covers after me. He melted against me, hands to my thighs and mouth to my collar, and as I looped my arms around his shoulders, I bid my mind to quit racing.

Please, I begged to nothing, to everything, to the stars themselves. *Please*.

I chanted it as I lowered myself astride Norm's hips and he memorized every edge of me.

"Please!" I gasped when my nerves sparked just so, my skirt rucked to my waist and my hands gripping him close, closer, closest.

The light that burst behind my eyes as I dissolved was made of sharp fractals, endless and white. I couldn't see from where they began or where they would end. *Please*.

And time spun ever onward, deaf and unceasing.

1962–KELLER AND EVELYN'S STUDIO IN TOBIN HILL

San Antonio, Texas

With my last exam done, I found the wind of achievement beneath my wings and my brain gone to pea soup from all the studying and calcu- lating and formula-making during finals. All I had left to do was wait for my grades to post before I could usher myself onto the world's door- step with two degrees in hand.

The quad stretching around me was not enough freedom from the lecture halls. I was exhausted and nearly asleep on my feet, but poten- tial buzzed in my fingertips. The thought had hit me two nights ago in the middle of reviewing rotation matrices, bent over my desk with my nose nearly touching the paper, when I looked over and saw the Sher- man Morgan book I still hadn't returned to Professor Laitz: *NASA*.

Could I really do it?

My gut twisted itself up around memories of the papers that had snagged in the rosebushes at Apodaca.

The Manned Space Center. Houston, Texas.

Annie H. Fisk.

Einstein, Dirac, Sherman Morgan, Booth.

It was insanity, but the aberration I had seen in my own backyard burned coal-bright in my cognition.

Now that I was well and truly through with my coursework, the burbling maybes of everything that awaited made the top of my skull feel like it might just pop off at any moment—but there was one person I could always trust to clear my head.

Evelyn would be at work in the studio space she shared with Keller at this hour. I boarded the bus to North Main, where their airy warehouse on the border between the city and the suburbs sat on the lively side of the avenue like a sideways punctuation mark.

Evelyn had given me a key after she signed onto the lease with Keller. *You're just as much a tenant as I am by now*, she had insisted.

I knocked before unlocking the door, behind which a loud crashing of classical music was erupting from the radio. Evelyn was here alone then—Keller worked in silence and made Evelyn take her radio outside when she needed her noise.

"Evelyn?" My voice slapped against the rafters. I dropped my purse by the door and headed down the wide, empty foyer toward a wall of west-facing windows slotted high up against the soaring ceiling. She didn't respond, but the music persisted—something bold, all brass, marching itself through the air. Aimless giddiness was making my heart race at a similar tempo.

I rounded the corner to find Evelyn tall and steady before a massive canvas that took up the entire bottom half of the studio wall. She had a flat paintbrush held in both hands with a brilliant indigo sousing its bristles, and as she dragged it in a straight, solemn line she used her entire body to guide it in one great stripe—slowly, steadily, carving a horizon.

She was still at work on her *Artemis* series, a parade of pieces in Prussian blue with drybrush detailing like rain clouds opening over the distance in a desert sky.

"Hey," I called over the music when she reached the edge and lowered the brush. She turned to face me with a grin, swiping at her forehead with the back of one wrist. Keller didn't turn on the window units for cooling until June.

"Hey! You're early."

I glanced at my watch and shrugged. "Last exam was thermodynamics. Didn't take very long."

Evelyn rolled her eyes as she replaced the brush in its soaking bucket and came over to kiss me hello. I shut my eyes, savoring it despite the brevity.

"The list of people who consider thermodynamics *easy* is probably very short," Evelyn said when she pulled back, her hands in the pockets of her smock. Her hair was up in two low pigtails and her feathered bangs were pinned back from her face. She smiled at me as though she had been waiting for me all day.

"I'm done," I said, holding out my hands, "officially."

Evelyn came forward to take me by the back of the head and kiss me again, and the cool dollop of paint transferring from the tip of her nose to mine made me flinch and laugh against her lips.

Evelyn had finished all her own coursework the semester before. We had spent the interim between her graduation and mine daydreaming about what we would do when I was finished, both of us reaching to see what it might look like for us to face the future together. She wanted to go West, out into the desert, seize those O'Keeffe dreams. Up until now, I had been happy to play along and drum up visions of a little house in the middle of nowhere and a sky that never stopped.

But the truth of the matter was that daydreaming was all I was doing. I would never be able to make sense of my own ambition if I let Evelyn steer the ship. It was too easy to give in and let her be the happy one.

As Evelyn stepped away to hang up her smock, I thumbed the paint from my nose and drew a deep breath.

"I'm going to move to Houston."

Evelyn looked over at me and frowned. The radio was still blaring. "Pardon?" she said, her brows twisting.

I stepped over to the radio and switched it off. In the silence, nothing but the mutter of the street outside persisted.

The unfinished canvas between us sat impassive and massive. I turned to face Evelyn again, resolution lodged and scraping like a peach pit behind my breastbone. "I'm moving to Houston."

Several things flickered through Evelyn's face at once—surprise, excitement, disappointment, everything blurring together as though she had drybrushed her own face. She did not move from her spot across the room from me.

"What's in Houston?" she said gently after a long moment.

"NASA."

Evelyn's shoulders sagged. She nodded to herself, not quite bitterly but with a calculated distance. "NASA," she repeated. A colorless laugh jetted from her. "I shouldn't be surprised, right?"

My insides looped around in a complicated knot as I followed her eyes to the couch—where Evelyn had point-blank called me her girlfriend in the rare company of others who would understand. The community she had made for herself, always finding her people. She was amazing to me. Always had been.

"It's—not very far away," I tried, twisting my fingers together. Evelyn put her hands on her hips and leaned sideways, looking at me with her eyes bright and her jaw tight.

"It's kinda far away, Annie," she said.

I gestured in the air. "It's what, three? Four hours from here? My parents wrote letters across the Atlantic for two years when my dad was getting his master's. People have done more with less."

I caught my breath, realizing my voice had gotten a touch louder than I had meant for it to and Evelyn was giving me a stiff sort of patient look.

"I don't want to do more with less," she murmured. Shaking her head, she glanced down at her feet and let her head hang there. "I was going to ask you to move with me. I bought land in Marfa, out West."

My stomach bottomed out and dropped straight to my feet. "Oh."

Evelyn looked back up and averted her eyes to the corner of the ceiling with a wry twitch of her eyebrows. "Yeah. *Oh.*"

I stared at her, dyed in a dusty shaft of sun coming in through the skylight. If the way I moved through life was a chest of drawers, open and shut, Evelyn was a palette of paints: vague categories with everything blended at its edges, one vibrant wash of color and sound.

We were not the same, which was a lot of why we fit so well together. But there was so little I could do to preempt her, which ground against me like pebbles poured in the very mechanism that made me tick.

Maybe it was better to part then, before my gears could grind.

I didn't want to leave her, but this was what I *had* to do.

"It's like," I finally blurted, pausing to make sure I had my words set. "There's something drawing me there. I have to go, Ev. It's inevitable."

Evelyn lifted the cigarette from behind her ear and struck it with the lighter from her back pocket. She looked at me as she smoked and didn't blink for a long time. I couldn't bring myself to tell her the deeper truth: *I found a note addressed to me from seven years in the future. I've never belonged anywhere in my life, but I might belong there. Does any of this make sense?*

"I wouldn't believe that Beat bullshit if it was coming from anyone but you," she finally murmured.

"Yeah, that's me," I said dryly, gesturing down at myself, "Annie the Beat. Itching to work for the government."

We shared a brittle, deflated laugh, but the resignation in Evelyn's stare still struck me right to my core. "I'm sorry," I said.

Evelyn's thick, sandy brows creased. "For what?"

I shrugged. "For not—I don't know, for not seeing this coming. I don't do well with unexpected things. You know that."

"Well, you might want to practice," Evelyn bit out. She exhaled tightly, one arm crossed over her chest. "Life is one big mess of quick decisions. What do you think this whole space race will be? Predictable? Not a chance."

I scowled. "That's different."

Evelyn made a face. "How?"

She was right. She was always right. Evelyn Moore led with her heart and moved more easily through life than I ever had leading with my head, which was exactly why I loved her.

I *loved* her.

I flapped a hand at the empty floor between us as Evelyn's canvas loomed, bisected in deep blue—here or there? Stay or go? Say it or hold it in? I swallowed. "You . . . said you wanted me to move in, but I don't even know for sure if you love me yet. What do I do with that?" I blurted, all of my nerves leaping as I pushed the mirror away from myself.

Evelyn's coyote laugh flew through the studio's high ceilings like a spooked bird. She looked incredulously at me for a moment that stunned me still. "What do you *do* with that?" she said. Flabbergast puffed up between each word. Evelyn extinguished her cigarette with a hissing crunch into an ashtray propped on top of the now-silent radio. "Annie, what the fuck are you talking about?"

The edges of my ears burned an abashed pink. "Well, I'm sorry if I—"

Evelyn took a step forward and I snapped my mouth shut as I met her glare. With her voice strong and even as the lush lines of her body, she pointed at the floor. "I've loved you," she said, "since the day I sat down in that lecture hall and realized I was *terrified* of making an idiot of myself. You ever wonder why it took me three fucking weeks to talk to you?"

"You had a question about ellipses," I insisted. Evelyn smiled sardonically and came closer to hold my face.

"You were so dialed in," Evelyn said, her palms warm on my cheeks, "and all I wanted to do was ask what made you tick."

Evelyn nodded her chin at the far side of the studio, where a series of her smaller canvases were waiting for a gallery showing next month themed around constellations. A lump was beginning to form at the base of my throat. "All of this," Evelyn continued, "the stars, the moon, the sky, Annie, you make it make *sense*. If I've forgotten to say it out loud, that's only because I've been saying it to myself this whole time. I figured you were one of those gals who didn't really do . . . feelings, I don't know. But I *do* know I love you. Probably a little too much."

I had no words left in my noisy thoughts. I reached up and held her by both wrists to kiss her quiet in lieu of a proper reply.

I loved her right back. I loved her down to the bedrock of this building and up to where the atmosphere held the planet in an embrace.

But I couldn't say it back. We were already leaving each other. It wasn't worth it—that was what I told myself. It just wasn't worth the squeeze.

"What can I say?" I whispered against her cheek. "I'm rotten with subtext."

Evelyn shook her head and tipped her face up to kiss me between the eyebrows. "You and this beautiful brain. Always needing your proof."

She looked at me with the subtlest need, a yearn behind her eyes that I caught but did not—*could* not—follow. I set my back teeth. The warm amber shine of Evelyn's gaze searched my face. "You're gonna go then, huh?"

I blinked quickly to keep the threat of traitorous tears at bay. My fingers tightened on her wrists as I nodded. "Yeah. Can we still write letters?"

"Of course we can still write letters. You have a place in Houston yet?"

"No."

"Well, you have to be sure you call me so I can give you my address before I head out. I'm here through the end of the year."

I leaned in to kiss her again and she responded with a quiet desperation, a softly clinging apology.

"I want to stay friends," I whispered.

"We'll stay friends, Red. Two gals I know in the classics department, Mitzy and Elaine? They dated for two years before breaking it off. They still house-sit for each other all the time."

"Okay," I said, nodded, dragging her back to me. "That's good. I want that."

Evelyn hummed. "Might be kind of a schlep to house-sit for you," she teased lightly as she traced my bottom lip with the flat of her thumb.

"D'you want to go get dinner?" I asked when her hand roamed slowly down my waist. "Or—something?"

"I'd rather something," Evelyn said. Our legs knocked together as she began walking us toward the pull-curtain that sectioned her bedroom off from the rest of the studio.

I let myself be led. "When's Keller back?"

"Tomorrow," Evelyn said as her mouth hunted down my neck to my shirt collar. I shut my eyes as she reached up and threw back the curtain before lifting me by the waist onto the secondhand yellow chaise against the wall.

I looked at her, my knees parted, my skirt already skewed by Evelyn's expeditious hand, and was struck by the thought that Evelyn hid from things that scared her in the safety of my body, our bodies together. The idea of me leaving San Antonio had frightened her.

"Hey," I murmured as Evelyn knelt before me and shrugged my knees up onto her shoulders with slow, steady purpose.

"Hey," she said right back. I combed one hand into her hair.

I love you, I rehearsed at the back of my mind. *I love you.*

But the sash of it stuck to the sill.

Evelyn slid one hand up to gently hike the hem of my skirt. I stared at her down the plane of my belly, my blouse mussed. "Keep looking at me," I said, as Evelyn's fingers roved gently along the tops of my stockings.

With a kiss to my hip bone, Evelyn nodded and did not take her eyes off me. "Okay."

And we ran from ourselves there, with the studio quiet and her canvas unfinished and my future open like a cracked egg before me.

I looked at her and I loved her so hard I couldn't even blink. But to say it was to lose her—and so I only gasped Evelyn's name with her tongue intent on me. Her stare never broke. *I dare you*, it said with every beat, *I dare you, I dare you, I dare you.*

1968—THE MANNED SPACECRAFT CENTER, ART McCABE'S OFFICE
Houston, Texas

The door was ajar, but still I knocked twice against its edge. "Sir?" I called through the gap in the jamb, and watched as McCabe glanced up from the papers sprawled across his desk. A pair of very small reading glasses were balanced on his nose.

"Come in."

I stepped inside and shut the door behind me. "About the trial, sir, I—"

McCabe cut me off with a low, heavy sigh. I stared at him, all of me stilled, as he removed the glasses and tucked them into his breast pocket under his jacket. "Decision's been made, Fisk. I don't know what to tell you."

I worked my jaw for several seconds as we shared an unblinking look. *Damn you*, roiled the storm in my chest, *damn him and damn you*.

"Tell me you're willing to reconsider. Please." My voice cracked. I didn't acknowledge it.

McCabe pursed his mouth and folded his hands on top of the sheets and notes and memos collaging his desk. "You know about that heart thing of his, don't you?"

"Of course."

"Then you know how badly this poor kid has wanted to go on a voyage since he understood which direction was up, and how much this means to him *and* the project. It's hard enough to find qualified astros for all our other shit."

Something low in me groaned like a buckling hull. I swallowed and cleared my throat. "It's dangerous," I insisted. McCabe raised an eyebrow.

"Of course it's dangerous."

My face flared pink. "Let me go instead."

Both McCabe's brows shot up. I scowled at him.

"Don't give me that look," I spat miserably, "you heard me. Sir."

"Oh, I heard you. If I so much as *float* the idea of sending a woman on one of our missions, I'll get a lecture from my general about how there isn't any budget for sanitary belts outside of atmosphere."

"I hardly think that—"

"Fisk." McCabe bid me to still and listen with a look. I shut my mouth. "What did I say when you two brought me the first proposal?"

I breathed steadily through my nose, my teeth ground together. "That what we do is proving to the rest of the world we're not to be fucked with."

McCabe grunted assent. He sat back in his chair and smoothed his tie, glancing down at his desk. He thought for a moment, the gears turning behind his eyes.

"There's a seminar the astronauts' wives go through," he said gently. "'Your family and the lunar mission,' that whole . . . dog and pony show. It's mostly fluff. There's an educational portion on tape for the children and everything, we hired animators from cartoon shows. We dump as much information and hope on them as possible, so that if their daddy doesn't come back, they're not left—wondering, angry. It's emotional insurance."

I vised my jaw, my back teeth aching. I watched McCabe, unblinking. "So you're keeping me ground-side because I'm, what, someone's wife?"

"I didn't *say that*," McCabe said with a firm jut to his jaw. "I'm not insulting your intelligence by suggesting we give you the same song and dance. All I'm saying is that I know it isn't easy to watch these decisions get made."

"It isn't easy not to even be consulted from the first."

McCabe raised two hands. "Hale assured me he'd gotten the okay from you. I don't make any claims of conspiring. He's a big boy; he can face his own music." He watched me for a moment, his unflinching officer's gaze hard as steel. "You have to understand, Fisk, this is difficult *because* I'm trusting you to take this on the chin. I'm not going to pander to you."

The backs of my eyes prickled. I rallied every measure of gumption in my body and held in those goddamn tears.

"If I can be candid," I said, "I never expected it to get to this point."

An exhausted, genial tide behind McCabe's eyes ebbed the hard lines of his brow. "That makes two of us."

I thought of my bargain. If progress was sacrifice, then I really did have to put my money where my mouth was.

I had to let Norman go.

"Yeah." I swallowed and rubbed at my forehead as I glanced away. "I—yeah. I guess. Okay."

McCabe stood and made his way to the bar cart beside his bookshelf across the office. "For what it's worth," he said over the soft rattle of a bottle and glasses, "you're about the only thing I've ever seen that puts more stars in Hale's eyes than launch vectors."

I sniffed a resigned and bitter laugh as McCabe poured two shallow draughts of gin. "I'd call launch vectors a lot easier to wrangle than women."

McCabe offered me one of the glasses. He clinked his rim against mine and sipped it down in one go before the lightest hint of an ironic smile took up at the edge of his mouth. "Without women, we'd all still be tits up in the gulf."

I tossed back the drink, bright and vernal through my mouth. "So when do you think we'll have tits up among the stars?"

McCabe chuckled. He turned the cup in his hand and watched the shallow bend of the light moving along the fluted etching of the glass. "Maybe someday. Let's make sure we can get up there first, then we can start planning for the good stuff."

Regarding me evenly, McCabe's gaze swam with sympathy. I wondered if he knew what it was like, to feel like there were two hearts in your chest: one for the work, and one for the living. If he knew the ache when they began beating out of sync.

"Go home, Annie," he murmured. "It's almost Christmas."

✳

1948—THE APODACA HOUSE, THE BACK GARDEN
Santa Fe, New Mexico

The day the man came from nowhere, Annie should have known something was different. The air felt thicker than usual by the roses, greasy with a sharp and metallic smell, as she played quietly on her own.

One moment Annie was examining a tube of lipstick that must have been Mother's at the root of the bushes—and then the next, a man in a strange white suit appeared as if he had simply blinked into being.

He was tall, with long legs piled in a cluttered, sideways pose against the garden wall. He had a dark helmet on that covered his entire head and reflected the outward bend of the sky like a mirror, fish-eyed and vast. A scraped-out, tinny gasp came from inside the helmet. Annie frowned and put down the lipstick.

"Who are you?"

The man turned the visor to face her as his shoulders jumped, as though he hadn't noticed Annie sitting here.

"I—" he stammered and stopped. The bulky white suit had buttons and funny shapes all over it, and he was gripping his left side with his right hand; his arm vised across his body like a shield. It sounded like he was panting, thirsty, and wrung out. He made a tight, sudden sound. "Oh my God."

The gardening hose was coiled on the other end of the flower beds, where the peonies had only bloomed once. "Here," Annie said, taking it up and offering the man the spigot end, "do you want a drink?"

Was he even human? Did he even have a mouth? He had two arms, two legs, and a head—and he seemed to know how to speak and breathe. The man shook his head. Fear began fluttering in Annie's chest.

"Could you, ah, remind me where we are?" the man asked. Annie glanced around for any signs of Mother or Daddy back from their drive to Albuquerque for Daddy's monthly appointments there, but the backyard was empty. They were alone.

"This is Apodaca Street," Annie recited, "number three. Santa Fe, New Mexico."

A pale sound fluttered through the helmet. It took a moment for Annie to realize he was laughing. "Yeah. I guess it is. This is—your house, huh?"

Annie sat down and, making sure her skirt was over her knees as she'd been taught was becoming of a young lady, crossed her legs to sit on the gravel beside the strange man. "Yes. Are you also from Santa Fe?" she asked.

"Oh, I'm from far away," the man said. The helmet turned, as though he was casting his gaze around the yard. "Very—far away."

Maybe the visor was his eyeball, one singular viewpoint like the cyclops from the story about the man and his ship, crossing ocean after ocean to get home. The man in the white suit managed to wrest off one of his chunky gloves and checked a gold wristwatch, squinting at its face. He had human hands. Annie stared at his wrist, the peppering of fair hair there along the back of his arm. "Is your watch okay?" she asked. Its hands had stopped.

The man gave a wheezy sound and shifted carefully. "I think," he panted, "it might be broken."

"Did somebody give it to you? My friend Diana wears a watch, she got it from her mother."

"Yeah." A sticky, swallowing sound came from inside the helmet. Annie stared at her curved reflection on its surface, marveling at the way her glasses morphed oblong in its shine. The man coughed. Maybe he had a cold; Annie had just gotten over a cold two weeks ago. Mother made her special soup to help her feel better. She held out her wrist so the man could see her own watch. "My daddy gave me mine."

"Did he?" The big visor shifted. "Wow. That's a . . . a real beauty. Your daddy has good taste."

Annie smiled and tipped her head. Her reflection looked back at her in the dark mirror of the man's helmet. "Are you from the moon?"

The man shifted and made another sound of pain. Maybe he'd hit an asteroid—Annie had just learned about those in science class.

He kept his hand pressed tight to his side and slowly, slowly leaned more evenly against the brick behind him. He tipped his visor up at the sky and breathed hard. Annie watched him, unblinking.

"From the moon," he said eventually, his breath shallow. A little huff of laughter scraped out from him. "That would sure be something, wouldn't it?"

Annie stayed quiet, simply watching him. He checked his watch again and looked down at Annie with a faraway sort of appraisal. "I'm sorry," he panted, "I'm being awfully rude. I'm—a little out of sorts."

"That's okay." Annie looked at him, absorbed by the sight. She thought for a moment before asking softly, "Are you hurt?"

The man drew a labored breath to respond. "I think so," he said, a hint of mirth still managing to dance under his words. "Don't worry, though, darlin'. It's nothing."

With his free hand, the bare one with the wristwatch, he reached up to pry at the bottom of the helmet visor. "Could you—hell, can you help with this?" He paused to catch his breath. "There's a switch. Thing. See if you can find it. If there's anything there."

Annie leaned forward and felt along the visor until she found what seemed like a latch. She pressed it, and the visor slid open.

He was perfectly human, if a little pale and sweaty. A pair of glasses that looked like Daddy's were slightly askew on the bridge of his nose. He gave Annie a lopsided smile, as he leaned his head back against the bricks. His eyes were all pink and filled with tears.

"Thanks." His voice was much more pleasant without the fuzzy box making it sound alien. One of those tears shivered down his cheek. "Just—wanted to see if the sky was as blue as I've been told."

"It's my favorite color," Annie agreed gently. The man smiled again, more subtle and a little wobbly, and shut his eyes.

"Yeah. Mine, too."

He had long eyelashes. Annie reached out and straightened his glasses for him, and his eyelids cracked open to rove his bright-green gaze over to her. Her heartbeat hummed for an instant before the sensation flitted away, petals on the wind. "Are you sad?" she asked carefully.

The man sniffed once and shook his head. "No, nothing like that. I'm happy. These are good tears."

When she looked down, Annie saw the second hand of the man's watch struggling to tick, as though the guts were stuck—she had taken Daddy's apart once to see what would happen, and then had to sheepishly ask him to help her repair it again when it wouldn't start.

"Hope I didn't spook you," the man said, his eyes still closed. His voice was very gentle. Annie shook her head as she slipped her hand into his. It just felt like the right thing to do.

They sat in silence for a little while. "Do you want a souvenir?" she whispered after a moment.

"I'd love that," he whispered back.

Perhaps this man came from the same place as Diana? The thought was comforting, that Annie's friend might know this man from nowhere.

She picked the prettiest, fullest rose head on the bush nearest her. The man took it gently in his bare hand when Annie passed it to him. His fingers were shaking.

"I'm Annie," she told him. "I hope you get home safe."

The man pressed the rose to his chest. "I hope so, too."

A sparrow burst from the roof of the house. Annie looked over as it soared into the sky, shouting a brief spray of song.

When she turned back to the man, he was gone. All that remained were the roses, brushing quietly together with the soft breeze that carried the dusty smell of aspens.

1969—THE MANNED SPACECRAFT CENTER, THE PROGRAMMING SUITE
Houston, Texas

The human trial for Aion was officially scheduled for six months to the day before the lunar launch. The nook behind my heart where I kept my fury, my regret, my terror was overfull—and yet I kept it at bay. I did not think of Apollo 1, or the tragedy of being subsumed by the work of progress. It was a new year, after all. Anything was possible.

Our tailoring team at NASA had a prototype lunar suit for Norm put together. Eleanor, the department head, called it the perfect trial run, helmet and boots and all. Pride and fear warred something awful in my gut as I watched from across the racks while Norm did his checks with his helmet under his elbow like one of the astronauts before their practice modules. Today must have felt like every holiday at once for him, the very top of the mountain.

To keep unexpected variables at bay, the other programmers had gotten the day off. But it felt lately that every day was its own unexpected variable. The most surprising thing would have been the expected happening right when it was supposed to without any surprises.

I'd worn the Project Y pin again, a desperate reach toward good luck. Norm had whistled low as I pinned it on that morning and came up to kiss me behind my left ear. He met my gaze in the mirror and cooed, *Big day today.*

I had wormed my way out of his hug, my heart bursting at its seams with too many emotions to be so close to him. When his face fell ever so slightly, I patched it over with a kiss to his cheek. *Sorry. I'm nervous.*

So am I, Norm relented, holding me close and planting a soft, earnest kiss on my mouth. *Ain't no sorry.*

But where my nerves had ratcheted up to live-wire heat burning through my gut, Norm's had evidently given way to adrenal glee—his laugh arced like thrown sunlight as I looked over to see McCabe clapping him on the shoulder through the bulky suit.

My heart ached with hairline fractures. I dreaded the faint ringing of portent.

McCabe ran his safety checks before calling me over to time the test from beside Gene's camera—as though this was any other run, as though we still had Bessie set up over the tile, as though my world itself wasn't hanging here in the balance.

My knees went to water as I made my way over and leaned against Norm.

"What do you think?" he said, posing dramatically. Norm looked the full part, his boyhood fantasies fulfilled. I had never seen him look so pleased with himself. Nobody deserved to have his dreams come true like this more than him.

"Very official," I said. My throat vised tight as banded iron.

Norm searched my face briefly and leaned in with a gentle kiss— too brief, too light, not nearly enough of him to brand the sensation as deep into my brain as I wanted to.

"Hey," he murmured, nudging my chin up to make me face him in full. Something in me listed at the potent thought that I would never get to look at him like this again. "It'll be great. This is what we're here for."

I managed to swallow the dread around my voice box. "This is what we're here for," I repeated, and sick of holding myself back, I threw my arms around him and squeezed.

"I love you," I said against his shoulder. Norm's embrace tightened in kind.

"It'll be great," he insisted, and kissed me once more. "Love you more, darlin'."

I sniffled against his mouth and held tight to the tears, kept them in check. "I love you," I said again, just because I could: *I love you, I love you, I love you.*

Love in the time of discovery: desperate and messy and too little too late. At least I had finally said it.

One of the flight controllers ushered Norm to the tile just shy of the anomaly's edge. I wiped my eyes and cleared my throat.

Gene nodded at me. We were rolling.

"Aion Test C-11," I announced around the thick clutch of my tears, "Norman Hale for human trial one. Gene Sutton on camera, Annie Fisk on timer. T-minus ten, nine, eight . . ."

As I counted down, a heavy fist tightened around my heart. My father's voice rose up in my head, speaking the numbers along with me as though my only worry was turning in a completed sheet of calculations to my teacher.

Seven. Six. Five. Four.

Three.

Two.

One.

I shifted the notepad in my hand to ready my thumb on the stopwatch, and the edge of it caught my pin.

I watched as time seemed to freeze; the clasp gave out and the pin broke free, sailing onto the floor and skittering into the anomaly's center.

No.

"NORMAN!"

I cried out to stop him, but he was already mid-stride, both feet in the active zone.

The corners of my eyes buzzed. The pin disappeared. On its own, my thumb clicked down to start the timer.

The last I saw of Norman's face was an inquisitive sort of openness in the shaft of fluorescent light carving through his visor, looking at me the same way he'd looked at the moon that first night we met.

And then he was gone, and all hell broke loose.

"What the fuck was that, Fisk?" McCabe barked.

I whirled to face him, shaking my head.

"It—simultaneous passage!" I clamored. "You were there, Art, you—every other time this happened, either nothing came back or whatever did was fucked, it—"

I stopped myself with my sleeve between my teeth, my breath coming quickly as my pulse began to tighten. This was my fault. After all of the trepidation, all of the nameless fear, it was *my fucking fault*.

"Jesus Christ," McCabe hissed. He whirled to face the medics, two at the end of the power banks as a safety protocol looking panicked and stricken. "Stand by!" he shouted. The computer bank was tomb-silent.

Tik-tik-tik-tik-tik-tik-tik. The stopwatch sang a frenetic song, my heartbeat twice its speed as I trembled all over and stared hard at the anomaly space.

Come on, I begged the pin-drop stillness as tears tripped madly down my cheeks, *come on, Norman.* I sniffled hard and swiped at them with the back of my hand and did not look away.

Three minutes passed.

Four.

Five minutes.

My face burned, my pulse pelting at a painful sprint. I wondered if this was what it was like to look out into infinity, the eye of everything open wide and unblinking.

Five minutes and fifty-seven seconds. Fifty-eight. Fifty-nine—

With a crack, making us jump and several of us shout out loud, a light flashed from the empty tile. The space had never made so much as a peep before. I dropped my notes and the watch without stopping it, lunging to cover my middle as though the anomaly had reared up and bitten me.

When I looked up, Norm was in a pile on the floor with his visor open and one glove off.

"Get him to medical!" McCabe ordered, his voice cracking, one hand knit into his hair. I squeezed my way in between the two paramedics as they dragged Norm from the anomaly bounds. My heart spilled over to find his eyes fighting to stay open.

"Norman. *Norm.*" I took up his one bare fist in both of mine, all of me shaking. "Norm, it's Annie. Can you hear me?"

He groaned. A sharp grimace puckered his face. The corners of his mouth and the seams between his teeth were traced with bubbling, bright red. My stomach dropped. "Norm." I clutched his hand to my chest as the paramedics wrestled a stretcher beneath his body.

"Annie," he wheezed. Misery billowed up in me. His fingers flexed weakly under mine. "Hey there, Annie."

A rushing culmination of some sharp-toothed, distant memory curdled through my heart. He was dying.

"What did you see?" I whispered, leaning my head down through his open visor to touch our foreheads together one last time. His eyes were distant, fading, but full of hope. His throat worked around a labored breath.

"I found you," he whispered, barely audible as his breath ghosted against my cheek. "Hello, world."

A soft prickling dug into my thumb, and I pulled away to find him peeling open his fist under my grip.

A late-summer rose, pale-pink and soft as dawn.

The paramedics lifted him away. His body was slack, heavy with absence. Unthinkingly, I tore off one petal and worked it between my trembling fingers to a floral paste as I stared at the floor where Norm had lain.

The smell of roses would never be comforting again. My mother's garden—the garden, he had *seen it.*

I had told him I loved him, and now he was dead.

I loved him. I did, more than anything.

I clung to the rose and pressed it to my chest as I doubled over and wailed into my knees.

My body heaved with grief's ugly, spinal pitch. Fresh, although I'd mourned before—the sharp angles punching straight through to the center of me, where it could gut me from back to front.

"*Cut it*, Sutton," I heard McCabe hiss, but I couldn't care that the camera was still rolling in the first place or that my watch was still running on the floor.

The very thread that pulled me here, inexorably, was the same that tore Norm away.

In the place where we were striving to push the boundaries of our planet, where we were dragging between our gritted teeth the very nature of human exploration out among the stars, my own world shrank even further.

Hello, world.

All I had left was me.

06:00

---✦---

1969—GLENWOOD CEMETERY

Houston, Texas

I went to pieces.

The programmers and the navigation team held me together with many tender hands, and I didn't know enough words in any language to tell them how much that meant. Through the endless to-do list of severing myself from Norman's death, the weight of it, I drummed up every ounce of strength I had ever had and just kept going.

I packed up and sold his townhouse. I gave the Barracuda to one of the other navigators and kept the Rambler for myself. I telegrammed Norman's brothers at their bases to let them know he had died.

One was stationed in West Berlin, and the other so remote on an aircraft carrier in the Pacific that I was gently told by the operator the message would take a matter of *weeks* to get to him. A combination of quiet cruelty, time, and distance.

A very sweet and near-immediate reply came from the brother in Berlin, effusive and gentle: that he was so sorry, that he would try to find me next time he was stateside—and of *course* Normie hitched himself to a gal at NASA, of course he would be so lucky to find his other half amid all his numbers; of course it was that goddamn heart of his, the biggest heart of all, that saw him out in the end.

I had told them the short version of events, the same version Mc-Cabe had in his own report. I didn't think they would take it seriously if I had tried with any measure of the truth.

The days washed together in the mill-wheel slog of closing out a life. It would have been more difficult had we not already been married, but still—the weight of it all but crushed me. I was a rinsed-out facsimile of myself for days, and then there was a funeral to see to. The others were singing a hymn, all of them. There were so many people here who had loved Norm in their own way. The casket stared up at me from the hole in the ground. I couldn't have felt less like singing if I tried.

To be sure, it was as warm as a funeral could be. Norm would have been pleased with the turnout; a real party crammed around one plot. *You'll wake the dead!* he might have teased us had he been here, too, sauntering up fashionably late to his own farewell.

I couldn't help but imagine picking myself apart atom by atom until all I was, all I had ever been, was nothing but a pile of fine atomic dust. Whenever I shut my eyes, my mind ran wild through its own halls—I saw Norm's dead eyes, felt the slackened grip of his hand on my wrist, guessed at the phantom violence of dimensional shards ruining him from the inside.

They had to have done an autopsy. I couldn't quit wondering what they found. The thought of my father's pin in a biohazard bag, encrusted with those glittering spikes, made the backs of my eyes throb.

I hadn't managed a good night's sleep in days. As the rest of our—*my* colleagues, only one of us had them now—as the rest of *my* colleagues left for the wake one of the navigators had arranged at Sal's, I stood over the fresh grave and wondered if they could dig any deeper here than they could in the Santa Fe desert.

I had visited my father's gravestone only once after Mother and I watched him get buried—alone, sad, quiet, and bitter, and private. The clearest memory I had of my father was his headstone: *Sanford William Fisk. Father, Husband, Innovator.*

Norm's epitaph was a little simpler. Granite, just his name, but I had sprung for the tidy detail of a waxing crescent moon beneath his life span: *1935–1969.*

God, but that was nothing. Thirty-four years in the entire arc of the universe, a blip.

"He was young, wasn't he?"

I turned to see an old woman with an austere pile of fair hair pinned neatly on top of her head. She wore a purple linen dress and a very fine silk hat to match, with a large pair of sunglasses perched on a handsome, hawkish nose. Her mouth was pursed in thought and painted coral. I swallowed and sniffled down the sorrow plugged up at the back of my mouth. "He was," I grated out.

"How did you know him?"

"He was my husband."

The woman clicked her tongue gently. "Poor thing. Can't have been married long?"

I shook my head. "No, ma'am. Just over two months."

With a compassionate sigh, the woman regarded the headstone. I looked at it along with her. *Norman Robert Hale.*

"What a small world," she hummed. "My late husband's name was Robert."

A young woman in a blue shirtdress and a nurse's cap gave me a soft, sympathetic smile as she came up to the older woman's side. "Addie-Mae, the car is here."

"The car?" The older woman's brow creased a little tartly. "What for? All the way out here?"

"Well, it's here to take us home. Are you ready to go home?"

"Oh. Yes, I think that would be nice."

Squeezing my arm in parting, the nurse guided the older woman by the elbow with a gentle hand.

She turned to face me again and removed her sunglasses. Looking at me directly through the pale winter sun, her eyes were the keen green I had only ever seen in one other gaze. "You're such a pretty thing, so take it from an old gal like me," she offered in parting. "Don't let this blow send you to the edge of the range for good. I don't know much these days, but if he was a good man, he wouldn't want you to be lonely."

My chest caught. Tears sprinted to my eyes anew, blurring her and her nurse against the tidy rise and fall of the hills and Spanish moss hanging heavily from the trees. I nodded messily and hid my face in my handkerchief. "Thank you," I managed around the formless shape of a sob.

Norm's mother and her nurse made their careful way back to the road. I cried and cried and cried until my lungs burned.

I reached into my purse with trembling hands. Carefully, I lifted out the now-dried rose Norm had brought back through the anomaly. I went to my knees in the Houston dirt. It smelled of life splitting open and the tilled turn of time.

"I love you," I whispered, once more for the keeping.

Maybe Norman was persisting somewhere, some splinter of him left hurtling through the veins between the dimensions. It was a comforting thought. Perhaps that was where he could have been happiest: returned to the very processes he studied, guiding everything from here on out with the twisting of the cosmic winds.

I let the rose flutter down among the fresher ones we had thrown onto the casket. I drew my thumb once more over his name on the headstone.

And when there was nothing more to offer, no other loose ends to cinch up, I stood and dusted off my knees. I wiped my nose and I walked to the car that would take me to Sal's.

I would sit at the head of the table with the rickety legs. Gene would bring me a very stiff drink and pat my shoulder with that gentle way of his. I would cry and laugh and sing and remember Norm as we toasted him over and over again, refusing to forget him and the ways he touched our lives.

And when it came time for Sal to start shutting the place down around us as night ripened, Betty Eagan would offer to drive me home even though she had never done that before, and let me weep in her passenger's seat without saying anything sideways about it.

1969—THE MANNED SPACECRAFT CENTER, ART McCABE'S OFFICE
Houston, Texas

Another Tuesday. Time would not stand still, not even after taking everything good from me.

A very grave-looking sheaf of paperwork glared up at me from McCabe's desk.

I stared, unseeing, as a low rumble of fury began chewing at the back of my neck. My margins were still raw, jagged, all of me touchy as an exposed nerve. "What the hell is this, Art?"

McCabe sighed and rubbed his forehead with his fore and middle fingers. "A bilateral non-disclosure agreement. Sutton and the rest of the programming team already signed."

I flipped through the sheets, my eyes blurring at the legalese. I reached the last page and riffled again, then once more. "This has nothing do to with the launch, does it? This i—"

"The only concrete fact here," McCabe said carefully, "is that a navigator died on our property six months before launch. The higher-ups don't want it getting out to spook anyone. There are more eyes on us now than ever."

I pawed back to the second page, and finally found it: *The approved trial, heretofore known as AION . . .* I stepped back from the desk and put a hand to my forehead, giving a dry cough of disbelief and shaking my head. "Nobody else knows about the trial. Oh my God, you told them it was, what, a heart attack?"

McCabe's mouth pinched fiercely. "There was medical record enough to make it believable."

"Unbelievable *gall*." I raked my hand into my hair instead and began pacing. I shot a disgusted look at McCabe. "At least respect *me* enough for the truth. Why the hell are they shutting it down?"

"We have to draw lines in the sand with how far we're willing to go with this shit, Fisk. It went too far."

"Too far!" I scoffed. "Art, we're going to the fucking *moon*."

McCabe set his jaw and glared at me. "The hardest part of this job is knowing when to tell your ambition to heel. It's *too far*, Annie. I'm sorry."

"Fuck you," I spat. I started pacing again as McCabe's face twisted with fury. He jabbed a finger at the closed office door, out toward the programming suite.

"I'm trying to *help you!* You think it's easy to pretend I didn't see? That I didn't get the—the goddamn back of my *skull* blown off by witnessing what you two did back there?"

My gut dropped. I rounded on him. "Art. Tell me you didn't destroy the reports."

He clenched his jaw hard. "I didn't destroy them. They're vaulted."

"Jesus Christ." Another manic trip of laughter leapt out from between my teeth. I prowled like a caged thing. "*Vaulted.* That was our work, Art. That's—it was the last thing he touched; what do you mean it's getting *vaulted*?"

"It isn't my call."

"You're a fucking director, what here isn't your call?"

"Just sign the papers, Fisk. We can figure out later how—"

"If there's any figuring to do," I insisted, my voice risen to tremble and crack, "we can do it *now*."

"One of my navigators is dead!" McCabe shouted. "I can't afford to have that shit hanging over any of our heads right now! There's too much at stake!"

He held his ground and stared me down. He put one large hand on his hip and looked down at the floor before he swiped at his mouth, clearly reining in his emotion.

"It isn't personal. It *isn't*," he said after a long stretch of silence. His voice broke, catching hard on the low ridge of his throat. "I keep . . . trying to quit thinking that if I'd made Hale take one more second to think before jumping at the chance, maybe he could have lived and been able to watch what he helped accomplish. We could have—done something with Aion. I don't know. But I can't let this failure cause another."

I stared at him. Tears tripped down my cheeks in the flutter of my lashes blinking quickly. "If we're trying to blame anyone here, Art, it's not you and it wasn't the anomaly. Point at me if you really need to."

"It wasn't any of us." He drew his hand down his face again and sniffed once, glancing for a sticky moment up at the ceiling. "Wasn't that the whole mystery of the thing? Randomness, that old mess? We still have a chance at reaching the moon, Annie. Men have already died to get us there. This sort of work doesn't come without costs; I know you know that."

He was right. I wrested my kerchief from my skirt pocket and dabbed under my eyes before casting a long look at the stack of papers, crumpling the little linen square. The stillness of the office fluttered across my face like the whisper of a shroud.

"Right. You're right."

I snatched a pen up from McCabe's desk and flipped to the last page, where I scratched my name onto the line and slapped the folder shut. I looked for a long moment at the *CLASSIFIED* stamp on its cover before I put the pen down. "Maybe this is a sign," I said, halfway to myself.

"Of what? Don't tell me you're superstitious about the landing."

"No." I turned to face McCabe and sighed. "Maybe it's time for me to move on."

He watched me, unblinking, from across the length of his desk. We stood on the same side, both of us leaning heavily onto an edge.

"Where would you go?" he finally asked. I shrugged one shoulder and looked at the washed-out bleed of the horizon through McCabe's window.

"I don't know. Try to find home again, maybe."

"At least stay through the launch."

The gentle bargaining softened me somewhat. My mouth twitched at one side. "I might just be bad luck, Art. I don't think me staying would make much difference."

McCabe's chin buckled just a little. "You make a big difference, Fisk."

He held out a hand. I took it, a solid clasp, and forced myself to hold his stare as my own face crumpled for a moment. I schooled my tears down and focused on the shape of Art's hand firm in mine. "That's kind of you."

McCabe gave me an inscrutable look. "Regardless. You take care of yourself, okay?"

I knew that was his way of approving my quiet disappearance, whenever I wanted to make it. I nodded. "You too, Art."

I went home early. Nobody questioned it.

✦ ✦ ✦

Halfway down the stretch of the freeway that carried me to the home I had so recently begun packing to move in with Norm, the Nash's engine began to turn over worryingly. *Shit.*

The car stalled with a lurch. I set my teeth and began steering it carefully as the wheel juddered across four lanes, sparse for the midday ease of traffic.

When it stopped, I sat and listened to pebbles cooling on the engine for several long beats of absence. I tipped my head back against the headrest and squeezed my eyes shut.

My gut heaved with a vengeance.

I threw on my hazard lights before clamoring over the passenger's seat and fumbling the door open on the shoulder side. I leaned over the warmth radiating up from the road and vomited onto the asphalt.

When it was done, I wrestled the glove box open and pawed a fistful of leftover napkins I found there along the corners of my mouth. Around the sour taste on my tongue, a deep and roiling knowledge took root in me. I pulled the door shut again and sank low along the bench seat.

My hand roved down to splay across my belly. I dug my fingertips into the fabric of my dress, twisting and pulling, as though if only I was able to reach in and touch it, I could shield what was growing there.

Wasn't it bizarre, how life could spring up in spite of itself? How wastelands laid bare by disaster could, given time and the privilege of natural happenstance, return to something fitting for continuance?

Something very small had begun bringing itself to purpose through the frantic division of cells in my body—one last piece of Norm, reaching back to me through the dark, and I would have to find a way to love it without losing myself in the process.

1969—THE MANNED SPACECRAFT CENTER, THE PROGRAMMING SUITE
Houston, Texas

Writing my code and getting myself from one day to the next were the only things that mattered, nothing but the present. The past was a shambles, and the future was so uncertain I couldn't bear to think of it.

So I didn't. I didn't think.

I didn't think of my mother, how it might have been for her to carry me as I was carrying Norm's baby.

I didn't think of my father, whatever had plagued his mind during my childhood and dragged him down into the dread that took him in the end.

I didn't think of the life inside me, that undefined presence, a quantum defiance, and how many ways I might fail as the person responsible to raise a life from the tabula rasa of unasked-for birth. I was just a courier.

I didn't think. I simply existed.

If I didn't slow down, I didn't have to process it. I didn't have to relive the failure of it all over and over again.

After Aion was vaulted, I carried into the Center with me each day a battery of Norm-isms like armor: his watch around my wrist despite the fact that it'd quit running, his spare bottle of cologne dabbed at the creases of my elbows and the hollows of my ears. I stacked his books on my bookshelves. I saved his notes and filed them with my own. When that blackboard was finally delivered, I wheeled it down to Gibbs's office and gave it to him to use instead.

I found myself awake some nights, my right thumb turning the ring I still wore around my knuckle as I stared up at the ceiling, wondering at all the various might-have-beens we could have had together if time had relented and let me keep him.

Summer rolled itself forward into July, heat stuck to itself like a waxy snowball, and the Apollo mission mounted.

And then it was the sixteenth, and the crux of history waited ajar just outside our atmosphere. The Center stopped in its tracks.

We all milled, funneling into or as close to the mission control pit as we could get without being obvious—ambling through the hall, lingering in the break room, loitering up and down the corridors that led to and from the trenches. If we couldn't be privy to the minute-to-minute of mission control inside, we could certainly touch the energy at its edges.

Ros had the television set clicked on at eight o'clock sharp that morning and hadn't quit pacing since, there and back across the suite. I turned my ring around and around on my finger. My coffee was going cold beside me as I stared at my blank transport, input blinking, pretending at productivity. We were all in the same ship. Betty was knitting at her desk. One of the newer hires, Gale, seemed to be reading the same passage of the Assembly guide over and over again.

I glanced at the clock on my desk, beside the photo of Norman I'd taken with his camera on one of the first late-night Aion tests. He was smiling as he leaned jauntily on one of the power racks—*Look professo-*

rial, I had coached him from behind the viewfinder, *like I'm taking your dust jacket photo.*

Past Gale's desk toward the back of the racks was a sheet of thick plastic and a measure of caution tape blocking off the far section of the power banks. It made the fans hum with a different timbre. I still couldn't so much as glance at the end of the room without wanting to crawl out of my own skin.

"I'll go see if they have the color set on in logistics," I said, easing my chair back from my desk. A walk to the far end of the building would do my sore ankles some good.

As I approached logistics, a quick set of jogging heels came careening down the hallway. "T-minus two minutes!" a high voice called, snatched away into the ceiling tiles as she passed.

I stopped outside the lounge near the cargo bay. It was quiet down here for once, which made the going easier. My nerves were bright, open-ended things today.

A clutter of junior staff was already circled up on the floor. I looked inside right as one of them lit a cigarette. They froze and stared at me like a mob of baby deer.

"I just wanted a color set," I said, sidling in along the back wall. "Don't mind me."

One of the girls grinned at me as I eased down into a sit on the couch at the back of the room. She looked to be a typist who was apparently attending the Fran Greene school of toeing the regulation line with the height of her platform shoes. I gave her a thin smile. "The color," she said, "makes it feel more real, huh?"

She and the other girls stole glances at me with a subtle sort of curiosity. I wondered if it was my belly, or the rumor mill, or my unannounced invasion into what was obviously a juniors-only event. I was the odd one out here, a free radical.

The timer at the bottom of the screen ticked down into mere seconds to go. The camera frame was squared on the rocket and its spindly scaffolding arm. The crew was already inside. What must that have felt like, to hold the dreams of so many people in their hands? To not fear what might await past the invisible membrane of our atmosphere and the gravity holding us all together?

I wondered for the first time, with a shallow plunging in my gut, what my father must have felt exactly twenty-four years ago to the day, the early morning of the Trinity test.

Did he have any sense of what the future would hold for him, or of what he had helped build?

In another twenty-four years, would we discover I and everyone else at the Center had carved our names into an ark, or a tomb?

Three.

Two.

One.

Liftoff.

The engines fired.

The rocket cleared the tower.

Seemingly from the very bones of the building celebration erupted, cheering and shouting, as the rocket plunged into the sky like a god's pointer finger — upward amid the sear of the summer sun, declamatory and audacious.

We had done it. They were soaring.

The junior staff erupted with celebration, cheering and hugging and even full-tilt necking. I couldn't sit still. I hefted myself back to my feet and slipped away unmissed.

The hum of excitement persisted through the Center's halls like the low rumble of planetary turning, turning, ever turning. Every single operative I passed was giddy with victory — the liquor carts were already rolling out and the bottles cracking open. I remained on the fringes. Most of the building had filtered out into the hallways in a mad crush of joy and wild abandon at a job well done.

A starry-eyed woman passed me a half-glass of champagne outside of the secretarial pool. I quaffed it and handed the empty back with another brittle smile.

I wished I could celebrate. I wished I could care more deeply. We were going to the *fucking moon*, and here I was numb at my edges.

I made my way back to the programming suite. It was empty now for the magnetic pull of celebration closer to the heart of things near mission control. Everyone's desks were left mid-distraction — Gale's manual open on the same page it had been this morning, Betty's knitting needles abandoned on her chair without her casting off. I peered around and sat again at my desk, slowly and alone.

Despite the broadcast, it was like believing a dream upon waking to think the crew was finally on their way even after so much care and preparation.

I rolled my chair back and stared hard at the cordoned-off anomaly. *You have to love, jellybean.*

The fabric of my dress whispered warm under the palm I put to my belly as though I could feel the swift little heartbeat coming through my skin.

I opened a blank text file on my transport and set my fingers to the keys. My hands were tingling.

Whenever you are, this is for you.

I typed the letter out as accurately as I could recall. When it printed steadily from the matrix printer across the room, I watched it emerge inch by inch and accepted the itch of déjà vu prickling across my brain.

I left the sheet unsigned and folded it in three. I took the slide ruler with me from the far side of my desk and picked my careful way past the taped-off plastic sheet to approach the anomaly.

A dragging resistance in my chest stopped me short of walking straight into it. My eyes welled up as I saw it again for the first time since Norm died—a perfectly blank spot of space-time taunting me with its stillness.

"I'm so sorry," I whispered. I watched it for a long moment before lowering myself down beside it, curling my knees up under me to sit as though beside the den of something delicate and afraid.

Perhaps that was our first mistake: believing we could poke at the nest of something that just wanted to exist in peace without getting stung. But could it truly be a mistake? And if not a mistake, then what had we learned? What was gained by such fathomless potential cut short, such loss?

Maybe the results of our findings could be many things at once, in fractals: in leaving it undefined, Aion was everything and nothing at all.

"I don't blame you," I said to the empty tile. "Everything is chance. Chaos. All of creation is particles colliding by accident. That's the big secret, isn't it? Everything is just an accident. Even the good stuff."

I ran my thumb along the slide rule and fidgeted with the edge of the letter in my hand. Roving my nail over and over the six-centimeter mark on the wood, I smiled wryly to myself. "I guess we happened to pay enough attention to make some of our own luck for a while, even just a bit."

The impassive hum of the computers soothed me. Emotion came thick at the bottom of my throat. I swallowed it away. "Thank you," I told it, my voice very small, "for letting me see you. I love you. Take care of him for me, okay?"

I slipped off my ring and put it on the end of the rule, shifting steadily onto my knees. I dropped the little silver loop onto the tile and blinked as it disappeared, and then counted two seconds before sending the letter through as well.

Anchored. Gone. Right where it needed to be.

The minutes ticked past as I crouched there and stared at the ground, daring either trinket to return. My hand felt infinitely lighter without the ring. I wasn't sure if I would ever learn to get used to it.

When the sixth minute passed and neither the ring nor the letter reappeared, peace washed across the nerves strung through me like a slow current washing footprints from the shoreline.

I sidled my oblong body back out through the racks and returned to my desk. In strange solace, I sat for a long time while the Center carried on without me. I stared into my computer screen with its waiting cursor still blinking softly. The chatter of the launch celebration pulled my mind back to that first party nearly three years ago—*So, Annie, secretary,* I heard Norm asking me, saw that sideways grin of his, *why do you want to go to the moon?*

And what of Armstrong, what of Aldrin; how small and manageable must every ounce of humanity seem from up there in the hurtling quiet, toward that new and alien surface, into the endless unknown? What of Norman's dreams of the stars—how much had we gotten correct about what lay beyond our planet, lonely and blue and singing into the vacuum?

I sat up and finished coding my last module before getting up to join the living.

I found Ros and Betty in the lounge packed to its seams and sat with them in the warmth of achievement.

"There you are!" Betty cried as she passed me a glass of sparkling apple cider—she was a Baptist who took her temperance very seriously, but the high flush of excitement on her face made it seem like it was the real stuff.

From across the room, I noticed Gene watching her fondly. I smiled into the lowball glass as I sipped and angled us toward him, so I could rope the two of them into a conversation that would give Gene the chance to hear Betty laughing that musical laugh of hers.

They looked as happy as we all deserved to feel today. I was warm with closure, firm in my own surety, finally feeling something other than guilt or sorrow, as though a leaden weight had been dragged up from my insides and flung into the gulf.

The afternoon wore on in a fast blaze, burning away quick as the thrusters pushing our men up into the atmosphere.

Evening came. I took my sweet time setting my desk as though I was going to come back tomorrow. As Betty tidied her station, I noticed Gene lingering in the doorway waiting to walk her to her car.

I sat in the silence of the programming suite when it was only me left. In the shallow throw of the soft fluorescent buzz of the safety lights, I slid an empty file box out from under my desk and began to fill it.

I thought of Apodaca while I worked, meticulous and slow in the bittersweet savor of departure. I thought of my father and I, drawn in bolder and bolder parallels—his work killing him, mine stealing my future. I sniffled raggedly and swiped at my nose with the back of my wrist as I opened the low desk drawer.

I reached into the back of it, deep and tucked away, and swiftly nestled the full file of my triplicate Aion notes into the bottom of my box.

Secretarial habits died hard.

With the desk empty, I sat back down in front of the computer transport and ran the local disc reset. It whirred and clicked, fans and processors kicking to speed, and gave a grainy beep when it was through.

I typed the *Hello, world!* command once more, just for old times' sake. The words glowed soft and green.

And then I collected the box of things I would keep, always, and left the Manned Space Center for the very last time.

1969—ANNIE FISK'S APARTMENT
Houston, Texas

Four days later, with the nation watching, the Apollo 11 crew landed safely on the surface of the moon around half-past three in the afternoon.

Now as the night carved onward, we waited for them to walk.

As I waited for the module to approach landing, I had gone through the Aion notes from start to finish just to see Norm's handwriting again; as though my memory could pull him closer, nearer to this monumental moment he helped bring to fruition.

I started crying when the module landing feed started up on the television. The surface of the moon scurried rubbly and alien in black-and-white beneath the belly of the lander. Curled up on my side on the floor, my hands wrapped around my belly, I imagined that if Norm was spooned beside me, he would also be bawling like a baby. The thought kept my tears coming like a faucet.

On the television, Cliff Charlesworth indicated a successful fixture of the broadcast camera. I knew every single engineer who so much as breathed on the module was now turning to his family all nodding with sleep saying, *Look, here we go, pay attention now.*

I watched as Armstrong practiced dismounting and getting back onto the ladder, floating, gravity there little more than a suggestion. *"The LM footpads are only depressed in the surface about one or two inches,"* he said, *"although the surface appears to be very, very fine grained, as you get close to it. It's almost like a powder."*

The moon looked, of all things, delicate. How untouched she was; how very in need of protection from humanity and everything we brought blustering with us.

I looked not at the shape of Armstrong as he came steadily down the ladder, but at the unmarked ground where his boots landed—the very first footprint in the fine-grained dust.

"That's one small step for a man," Armstrong proclaimed, two feet on solid ground, *"one giant leap for mankind."*

The baby stirred and pressed one tentative limb against the inside of my body.

My chest shuddered around a breath. "I did it," I breathed as I wrapped my arms around my middle. "I did it, Daddy. All the way to the moon."

I wished I could tell him in earnest. I wished I could hold his hand again. I felt very, very small.

I hugged myself and cried, and cried, and cried. If there was a limit to these tears, a bottom of my own well, I hadn't found it yet.

Beyond the television, into the kitchen, past the refrigerator, where I had hung an old crayon drawing of a family that shattered a long time ago, the sickle of the moon hung in her glowing rind.

You make it easy to find things worth painting out there. It's the truth.

I just like you, Fisk.

I looked away from the moon landing and lingered on the far shelf of my record cabinet, where a sheaf of letters bookended my Baez.

Would Evelyn even remember me? Our New Year's bet?

One thing I knew for certain: I needed my head emptied.

I staggered up onto my feet and shuffled to the records. The letters crunched gently in my hands when I drew them out, and I rummaged through the pile until I reached the one in which Evelyn detailed the gauntlet of getting a phone line set up in the middle of nowhere.

Sometimes, I read in her familiar handwriting as I teased the paper out from its carefully sliced envelope, *I sit outside and have to pinch myself to remember it's all real. It's beautiful here. You should let me know if you're ever on my side of the planet.*

The postscript was her phone number.

I sat on the couch and pulled the telephone over in front of me, regarding the rotary dial for a moment as Armstrong and Aldrin chattered and got the flag ready. I spread the letter out beside the handset.

All I had to do was dial her. The number didn't even leave the state—it was much closer than the moon. Anything was closer than the moon, even my uncertain future.

"One small step," I said under my breath, and snatched up the handset before I could lose my nerve.

As the dial tone trilled, I recalled how Evelyn and I had broken it off after the last night we spent together. She kissed me on the cheek and sent me on my way, friendly is as friendly does. I had returned to my dormitory from the studio in the gray guidance of dawn, smoked the half-pack of Salems Evelyn had left in my desk drawer, and cried my eyes pink as daylight burned and I spun my saddest Patsy Cline record.

The next morning, I made the one-way drive down to Houston.

I didn't regret it. How could I have regretted it? I was happy here, or at least I had been. I had been let free to grow up, to do everything I had ever dreamed of doing.

I wondered if Evelyn felt similarly.

The line crackled, beeped, and then the receiver clicked on: "Evie Moore."

My tongue stuck to the roof of my mouth as her unmistakable voice came through the line. I shut my eyes and leaned my forehead hard against my knuckles, relief sousing me at the same time as a depthless ache cleaved between my ribs.

The soft hiss of a cigarette draw, a pause. "Hello?" she said, and I scrambled to clear my throat.

"Evelyn?" I said, breathless. "Hi. It's—Annie. Annie Fisk."

A stunned silence scored the soft noise of the line, simmering with potential. "Annie Fisk, as I live and breathe. You have anything to do with the news right now?"

I couldn't help the grin that fought its way onto my face, desperate and allayed. "Yeah," I gasped, my voice wet. I ground the edge of my fist against my top lip as another bout of tears began building in my eyes. On the television screen, they had planted the flag. "I did."

Another slow draw whispered up from Evelyn's end. In a delayed double, I could hear the radio on Evelyn's end of the phone chattering with the same feed coming through my television. She was probably painting while she listened. "Congratulations," she murmured, earnest as the night was dark.

I took off my glasses and scraped a hand down my face. "Figured I'd call to remind you," I said. "If you're still holding me to that bet, you won."

Evelyn chuckled softly. My heart flexed hard in my chest. "Well, I'll be damned. You're right, we're still five months in the clear. You owe me, Fisk." She paused. "If you still want to."

I pressed a flat hand to my mouth, and let consolation wash over me. I did not have to be alone.

The only certain thing is uncertainty. Your ante against it must be love.

"Just name the place," I finally said into the receiver, laughing a little with blind relief, "and I'll be there. I need my head emptied."

"Yeah?" There was a grin in her voice. "Been a little while. Tough to write letters when you're ferrying people out of atmosphere, huh?"

"Sorry," I said. Her smile was still infectious, even across the phone line. "Although I don't have much of an excuse, I wasn't even the one steering the lander."

Evelyn made a smug sound and drew another mouthful of smoke. "Ain't no sorry."

We talked for nearly an hour as the lunar walk carried on from the television set. She told me about her paintings, all the work she'd done in the last seven years, all the different people she had been. I told her about NASA and the launch. I didn't tell her about Norm, or the baby, or even the anomaly. Over the phone didn't feel like the right place for those truths. But I told her I had seen amazing things, and how I wished she could have seen them, too.

Midnight turned itself over into stillness. The news coverage had long since switched to talking heads, a march of politicians and anchors giving their two cents on the ground America had just broken. I gave a wide yawn, and Evelyn chuckled that low, throaty laugh of hers.

"You know," she said, "you're welcome to come stay for a while if you'd like. It sounds like you could use a rest, and you could tell me about those amazing things."

"You think? Are you sure?"

"Of course. West Texas isn't quite O'Keeffe country, but it's near enough. I like it. You might, too."

"Well, hell," I said, sniffling shallowly, tipping my head back against the arm of the couch, "I'll take what I can get."

Evelyn gave me her address and told me to come by whenever I wanted. "If you get there while I'm out," she said with a smile in her voice, "the key is under the blue rock."

We wished each other a good night and hung up. My pulse was pounding. I turned my face into my collar and imagined the smell of her perfume; I wondered if she still wore the same one.

I drew my knees up onto the sofa as far as they could go given the baby's growing bulk and stared at the moon through the kitchen window. If I looked for long enough, I might have been able to see the fresh footprints on the surface.

1969—INTERSTATE 10, APPROACHING MARFA
West Texas

It was quick work to pack up the hatchback the next day with a suitcase of clothes, a box of a few other comfort-sundries, and notes I wouldn't want to go without for too long. Evelyn said I was welcome for as long as I wanted, but I had a feeling I was going to be keenly aware of being a guest in her home and told myself I would only stay for two weeks.

The drive was long and dusty, the radio cutting into the alleys between stations for stretched-out spells of silence, but some peaceful desert silence was exactly what I needed. Diners and freight stops along the way kept my body from complaining when the baby got all squished against my bladder, and every stranger I came across harbored a specific and patient kindness for the pregnant woman who looked like she needed the world's longest vacation.

My nerves ran hotter than the road that stretched before and behind me the entire way, empty and baking in the sun. Now, I'd hit the last mile-marker before the exit Evelyn had dictated to me while I scratched her directions onto the back of my Aion notes folder. I pulled up beside it with the engine idling and the radio buzzing with static.

My heartbeat thundered. I drew a breath as deep as I could and held it for several seconds with my knuckles vised around the wheel, frantically trying to drum up some fucking courage.

Evelyn wanted me there. She had invited me. I hadn't seen her in years, but she wouldn't have told me to come if she didn't want to see me, too.

The baby twisted softly. A nudge, a little elbow or the edge of a fist, prodded right under my diaphragm.

"Fine," I muttered. I yanked the gearshift and steered wide back onto the highway. The front axle lurched gently over a pit in the asphalt, and the radio skittered into clarity as I pulled ahead.

When I took the exit, the baby turned again. The desert opened before me, and I drove into its heart on the delicate pathway of parallel tire treads like a ray pointing into infinity.

I rolled to a stop in front of Evelyn's house. It was a smudge of clean adobe and fresh timbers that sharpened into coziness as I drew near. Sparkling threads of sculpture hanging from her porch winked sharp as laughter in the sunlight.

It looked immediately more like home than the Apodaca house ever had.

I hefted my suitcase from the hatchback and lugged it through the cut gravel beds of rangy cacti that led to the front porch. I paused at the foot of the porch steps and sat on the top edge of my suitcase to peer at the yard.

It was so quiet here.

And all of the rocks were blue.

I didn't know where to start, but I caught my breath before standing up again and beginning to toe at stone after stone in the hopes one of them had a key underneath it.

"Damn it, Evelyn," I muttered to myself after the first five minutes. Sweat prickled on my skin in the dry heat. I needed a shower and a fucking nap.

The grumble of a truck drew in from the main road and turned closer. Standing with a hand propped against the bend of my lower back, I swiped my hair from my forehead. I watched an old rust-spotted white Chevy trundle toward the house and tightened my fist around the latest rock I had stooped to pick up and check.

My heart leapt into my throat. Evelyn was behind the wheel. The windows were down, and the radio was blaring a wail of opera music. When the engine cut, the silence slammed back down. Evelyn swung down from the driver's seat and walked around the back of the truck.

She'd kept her hair short, trimmed into a modish style that just skirted her chin with a short set of bangs framing a face even sweeter than I had hazarded to remember properly. She still painted her eyes heavy on the bottom, and her nails were short and clear-lacquered, but her clothes were more relaxed and paint-spattered than even her last couple semesters at school. Her carriage looked proud as ever, observational tension in her body where she stood at the long end of the driveway with her hands on her hips. I watched her eyes flicker down to my belly, my bare left hand, back to my face—eyes, nose, lips, eyes.

"Annie," she murmured, a little breathless. "Figured that might have been you from the road. How was the drive?"

"All of your rocks are blue," I blurted. Evelyn tilted her head and squinted a little in the sun.

"How's that?"

"All your rocks are blue. I can't find the key."

I gestured with the stone in my hand at the piles and piles of others and promptly burst into tears.

Evelyn came forward with her arms outstretched and gathered me to her, lulling me gently. I tucked my face into her shoulder, where she guided it to rest as I cried. Arrival, the sensation of returning to somewhere I had never even been before, dropped hard as a stone through me. Rippling outward, the still pool of my apprehension broke; the high key of unbearable stress finally released with a faint snap like a small and brittle bone.

She didn't know the whole of it, the rambling thread that had brought me back to her, but Evelyn had loved me once. That was enough.

The familiarity of her smell came to me with fresh touches—sandalwood and woodsmoke, the brisk scent of her menthols again instead of clove, the lightest hint of paint and the notes of her shampoo. I reached up to cling to her shoulders as Evelyn cradled me close and rocked me gently back and forth.

"I missed you," I wailed between wet hiccups, "I really, really missed you—I swear I did!"

She shushed into my hair, all of her warm. "It's okay, Annie. I missed you, too."

It wasn't only that I missed her, but that I missed the Annie I had been when I knew her. I wanted nothing more than to reach back to myself from what felt like a lifetime ago, untouched by fresher grief, and tell her how much I had tried to protect her.

When I'd spent my tears on Evelyn's shoulder, she brought me up the front walk and in through the storm door on a creaking hinge. She led me, steady with an arm around my shoulders and my suitcase in her other hand. The shallow front hall opened up into a little sitting room, with a window that gave a view of the sprawling landscape and her kitchen to the left. A comfortable-looking studio sat beyond the brightly patterned sofas and afghan blankets arranged in the low light of the afternoon, and a tidy bedroom with its door sitting half-open waited at the other end.

"This is nice," I offered, my nose still fugged.

"Designed it myself. Local folks helped build it," Evelyn said from the kitchen, where she poured me a tall glass of water. I drank it standing, all in one go when she brought it out. As she eyed my belly again, I put a self-conscious hand to it. "There's a doctor back in town," she said. "Ten, fifteen minutes down the main road." She led me to one of the plush-cushioned armchairs just across the rug.

"I had a husband," I blurted as I lowered myself into the chair. My hand was still flat on my body, as though I might guard the growing baby from all of life's strange ugliness. "He helped get us to the moon. He's dead."

"Jesus. How?" Evelyn watched me calmly from beside the chair, her arms crossed. "Was he an astronaut?"

"No. I'm sorry, Ev," I said, biting down on a sharp swell of emotion. "I'm—not ready to explain, not yet. It's too fresh. But I do want you to know. I *want* to tell you."

Evelyn nodded. She sat down on the floor beside my chair, her long legs stretched out before her, and held my hand. "We've got time."

She was right. We did.

The fact of it hit me sharp as iron: We had time.

"His baby?" Evelyn asked gently. Her wrist rested against my belly, warm and present. I willed my sorrow to give way to comfort.

"Yeah."

We sat still with our hands clasped for a long time, relearning each other's pulse and the way we looked. Evelyn chewed on the corner of her bottom lip and let out a slow, low breath through her nose.

"I wasn't sure if . . ." Evelyn's voice was light before it trailed away like one of the dust motes dancing in the pour of sun through a skylight between the ceiling's timbers. She paused and took a gentle breath. "Well. I don't want to suppose, but if you aren't keen on women anymore, if you're just looking for hospitality, I can do that, I only figured y—"

I gripped my fingers around her hand and held it fiercely against me, her blood running rabbit-quick between the fine bones.

The baby kicked again, and the tiny edge of its quiet fussing bumped softly against the back of Evelyn's hand.

Hello, world.

Evelyn's throat bobbed as she swallowed. She nodded gently to herself, staring for a long moment at the place where the baby had nudged her.

Eventually she came up on her knees to face me, smoothing her free hand over my brow—she pushed my hair behind my ear and leaned over to kiss me just above the stem of my glasses. "For future reference," she murmured, "all those other rocks are teal. The only one that's actually blue is beside the crow statue."

"Oh—*fuck* you," I said, exhausted and raw but still jaggedly humored. "You could have just told me it was next to the crow statue."

"I should have, Red. You're right."

I clutched her hand to my face and shut my eyes, reveling in the weight of her gaze on me again. "I'll need some time," I said again, the jumping in my chest snagging my voice to make it hitch, "but I'm here."

"Never left," Evelyn whispered, and her lips came again, soft and slow, to the edge of my forehead. "Think you broke my orbit, Fisk."

"Planets can't fall out of orbit," I said automatically. I sniffled and shook my head. "Sorry."

"No," Evelyn said, the soft curve of her lips turning up in a smile, "give me the facts; I missed this."

I leaned into her and let my eyes fall shut. "Orbital resonance is most likely to pull a body out of its path if it falls into step with another, but even then, it wouldn't be noticeable for at least a millennium. Nothing short of a sun collapsing can break an orbit entirely."

Evelyn made a considering sound, her lips still pressed to my skin. "Who's to say the sun didn't dim for a while without you?"

I tightened my grip on her arm and reveled in the feeling of being close to her again. The universe was infinite and my world was so, so small, but Evelyn's home could be its center in the unfathomable ocean.

"That was corny," I whispered.

"Yeah, but I think you liked it."

An irrefutable truth then, brighter than any sun I could fathom: I would not be alone.

1969—DOWNTOWN
Marfa, Texas

In Marfa, I could feel again. I could breathe. The sky went on forever, and goddamn, could I *breathe*.

I had forgotten how easily Evelyn pulled open those endless drawers inside me. Evelyn could dye sides of me with colors I never expected could fit—her Prussian blues, her endless canvases, all of it freed me.

On the third morning I woke up beside her, I watched from the kitchen table as Evelyn prepared her first hand-rolled cigarette of the day with all the care and attention of an intricate ritual. Right then and there I announced over the rim of my coffee cup that I wasn't planning on leaving anytime soon. I sent for the rest of my things from the Houston walk-up that same afternoon.

A weight in me lifted with each day I spent in the quiet sprawl. I had grown comfortable in those narrow places that now felt so far away— the knothole of my Houston home, the drop ceilings of the Center, the dizzying attenuation of my work in its spiraling thread toward the im- possible. Stooped, hunched around myself, I had thought there was comfort in growing small.

And I was growing no smaller these days.

I was relearning, slowly, to stand up straighter. Spread out. Take up space.

"Well, Mrs. Fisk," Dr. Kirsch said as he stood back from the stirrups and peeled off his gloves, "baby seems perfectly happy. How have you been feeling?"

Fucking boundless. "Lately? Good." I blinked a few times and cleared my throat, aiming a belated sketch of a smile up at him. "I feel great, lately. Thanks."

Dr. Kirsch nodded to himself and made a few tidy marks on a chart. He shuffled the papers inside the folder back together and gave me a neighborly smile. "Out on Cenizo . . ." He tapped twice on the page, where Evelyn's address sat alongside my name. "You're a friend of Evelyn Moore's, aren't you?"

"I am, yes." *Friend* could be perfectly benign, and I had the additional bulwark of carrying a baby to deflect any lancing of questions. I steeled myself for a bitter sort of *bless-your-heart* recognition of that flimsiness, but Dr. Kirsch simply grinned at me.

"Those paintings of hers sure are something, aren't they?"

Surprised relief skittered through the branches of my chest. I nodded and shimmied my feet down out of the stirrups. "They really are."

I left the doctor's office in half a daze. The sun here looked down just as intensely as it did in Houston, but the brittle desert air woke my body up with familiarity and made it easier to ignore the heat. The list Evelyn had written for me of the new paints she needed was tucked into the sun visor above the driver's seat. I stared at it as I parked in front of the general store on my way home.

Home.

It was at once strange and perfectly, paradoxically normal to think of Marfa as home. When the scrawny kid behind the counter helped me load an armful of fresh canvases into the trunk of the car, he asked me to tell Ms. Moore that Kenny said the new drybrush technique she told him about was working beautifully. The fact of Evelyn taking someone under her wing by virtue of wanting to share a beautiful thing moved me so deeply that I had to lean on the truck for a moment and blame the baby for knocking me winded.

Evelyn was a collector of strays. She was someone who could make a motherland out of nowhere by simply cracking open her heart and saying, *Look here, see me, the whole truth of me.*

A scrap of paper pinned to the storm door screen when I got back to the house and up the porch said simply *Groceries* ♡ *–Ev.* I left the canvases in the hatchback for Evelyn to unload when she got home and immediately went for the phone as I set the box of paints down on the kitchen table.

I paused when I caught a glimpse of Evelyn's latest painting through the open studio door. Her eye for the sky had matured stunningly over these years spent apart, distilling into a delicate shape language made acute with its aching simplicity. It made me want to peer back into the past and see if everything I knew now would make it look different; the same array of my own stars twinkling with yet-unfound brilliance.

Evelyn had a push-button phone. I dialed quickly, flubbing the order of the number for the Marfa exchange and having to hang up once to do it again.

As the line rang, I coiled the phone cord around my fingers in an aimless pattern. When the operator picked up, my throat caught strangely.

"San Antonio, St. Christopher. Prof–Dr. Edward Laitz, please."

"The college," the operator asked, the snap of her chewing gum audible over the line, "or the high school?"

"The college."

"One moment."

My back had been protesting since the afternoon. As the connection buzzed and clicked, I lowered myself steadily into a seat on the linoleum against the wall.

"Hello?"

I frowned. A woman's voice. "Hello, this is Anne Fisk. I'm a former student of Ed's. Uh, Dr. Laitz. Is he in?"

The pause that came was even more swollen than my belly. A stone dropped hard into my gut.

I knew this feeling.

Why did I know this feeling?

"I'm—so sorry," the woman stammered. My mouth hung open. Only a shallow puff of breath left me. She explained . . . something. A stroke. A few errant blood vessels, not terribly long ago. Another tragic act of chance. My mind reeled to catch up.

"Oh," I finally breathed. "Oh, I'm so sorry."

Had he lived to see the moon landing? God, I hoped so.

The woman apologized, and I apologized again right back. A hall of mirrors, throwing the same useless refrain back and back and back and forth: *I'm sorry. I'm so sorry. I'm so, so sorry.*

We said goodbye. The handset went to dial tone. I clutched it hard in both hands, my arms lax to hang useless between my spread knees.

From beyond my diaphragm, the baby kicked. It was getting wigglier lately, eager to be born. A spigot somewhere deep inside me cracked, the straw meeting the camel's back.

I thought I had cried in a regular enough stream since the day Norm died that it had emptied my reserves. Once, it was the smell of coffee beans reminding me of him standing in the kitchen preparing the morning's pot in nothing but those hideous orange boxer shorts he always saved until he was nearly out of clean clothes. This was like the opening gambit of a summer storm, the sudden clap of a deluge that smelled like hot tin. I had thought I was finally through with the exhaustion of remembering how deeply I could be wounded by life happening.

My face crumpled. Vision blurring, phone still chirping its tinny dial tone, my throat leapt around a sob that burst out alone into the empty kitchen.

Everyone I loved would leave. I could never let myself forget that. What, then, of Evelyn? What of my *child*?

I clutched my belly and leaned my head back against the cabinets behind me as I wept quietly to myself. What could this mean for the poor thing growing inside me, the one who would inherit this loss? How could I do that?

How many spiraling lifetimes of guilt and regret was I going to pass on to someone who asked for none of it but would have to learn to balance all of it?

It wasn't fair. None of it was fair. "It's not *fair*," I whispered, pressing a hand to my heart as I swallowed a hiccupping breath.

But fairness was an illusion. Bad things happened to good people all the time. There were those who needed me to love them in spite of the risk, and I had to be brave enough to do it or crumble into nothing but my own very fine dust.

You will stumble and wander, but I promise you will find your way.

I was right. I had been right the whole time.

I managed to quit the tears and catch my breath against the cabinets. The phone handset was dangling from its coiled noose to hang limp against the floor. I slid my hands soothingly down the mound of my belly, making a low lulling sound in my throat as I went.

"It's okay," I rasped. "We're gonna be okay."

I pulled myself together: the phone back to the receiver, my glasses straightened, my hair combed through with my fingers. I hoisted myself back up to my feet, tottering, and splashed my palms with cold water to dash them brisk against my red, tear-hot cheeks.

The front door sighed open. "Annie?"

I sniffled. I dragged the back of my wrist across my nose. "In here."

Evelyn's footsteps stopped in the kitchen archway, both her arms full of grocery sacks. She looked at me for a moment and frowned slightly. "You okay? How's the baby?"

"I'm fine. Baby's fine, everything is—all's well. Healthy as a horse."

Evelyn set the groceries on the counter. "Sure hope it's not a horse."

I made like I had only been tidying the sink and the surrounding counters. We moved around each other in silence as she got the bread put away in its box on the counter; the apples into the crisper; the milk tucked into the refrigerator door.

She gave me a sideways look when she noticed me standing there watching her. "You sure you're okay? Seems like y—"

"I love you."

Every line of Evelyn's body froze in the open mouth of the fridge, the light buzzing softly from inside. Ramrod, stunned, she stared at me without so much as a blink.

I sniffled, tossing out a nervous shrug. "I never told you. And that was . . . shitty; it was really awful of me. To not tell you." I shook my head shallowly. "I should have told you."

Evelyn shut the refrigerator very slowly and leaned a hip sideways on it. The drawing from the Apodaca kitchen was fixed to the far side of it, held on with the chunky Albuquerque magnet beside a Polaroid photo of Evelyn posing on her empty plot of land before the house was built.

"I think I knew, mostly." Evelyn crossed her arms and nodded at the middle distance. "You didn't say it, but you . . . said it. Without saying it."

I chuckled. "You're a hell of a lot more patient than I am. That sounds exhausting."

"You? Exhausting?"

I gave her a look across the kitchen, exasperated with a bracing gar-nish of affection. Evelyn smiled sideways at me. I worried the tip of my tongue along the bitten edge of my lower lip. "Professor Laitz died," I murmured.

Evelyn's expression crumbled into minor, manageable regret. "Hell, Red. Was he sick?"

"A stroke."

"Fuck. He was great. He adored you."

Evelyn didn't give any pale apologies or try to steer me away from the fact of people leaving; it was a fact, and it was awful, but it was al-ways going to happen regardless of how I felt about it.

You loved people, and then they left, and the hurt of losing them someday was as deep as the privilege of knowing them was wide—but if you never told anyone what they meant to you along the way, the regret would bury all that beauty in its own ashes.

I really should have told Evelyn sooner. I crossed the shallow kitchen and took her hand as she unfolded her arms.

"I love you," I said again, this time a whisper shaved down to its marrow. Evelyn's knuckles were lightly chapped when I brought them to my lips.

"Yeah?" She ran her thumb over my lip. "Sounds nice, when you put it like that."

She kissed me then, and again, I belonged; again, I came home.

I loved her. I loved her. I still and always loved her.

1970—THE CENIZO HOUSE, POSTPARTUM
Marfa, Texas

I had the baby in early September, when the evening wind went crisp and the desert took on a dull hardening as summer took its first ceding steps back. I hesitated to name her, but she was perfect. The spit of Norm, all big green eyes and a wide little mouth; I would stare at her for hours as though I might find him moving in her nascent depths.

"I want to tell you about him," I said to Evelyn one night, staring at the baby as she stared up at me as though I held the answer to every secret in her tiny little universe. "Her daddy."

All three of us were lying on the ocean of a bed we shared made from two box springs pushed together. Evelyn watched me carefully. "Are you sure?"

"Yeah."

"Okay. What was his name?"

"Norman."

"What was he like?"

I swept a wisp of the baby's hair from her forehead and smiled as she burbled at me. "He was amazing."

I told her about everything—the simulation notes, the programming, the anomaly in the racks, our experiments, Norm's leap of faith. Evelyn held my hand the whole time, watching me intently, as the night stretched long above my story.

When I was done, Evelyn kissed me on the forehead and got up to pour us a pair of drinks. I listened to her fussing with the bottles and watched my baby, feeling flimsy and wrung out.

"There's bound to be other places," I said when Evelyn came back in and set my glass on the nightstand. She sipped from hers and sat back on the edge of the bed, tracing the tiny unfinished bones of the baby's hand.

"Other places for what?"

"The anomalies. It can't just be the one."

Evelyn's thumb stuttered. "Are you going to keep chasing them?" she asked.

The automatic *yes* sat frozen on my tongue. I stared at the shape of her hand around my daughter's and wondered if she would want to be a mother, too, if I asked her.

"I won't chase them," I said instead, "but I'll keep looking for them. I have to. It's the least I can do."

So I never quit studying.

If anything, now that I had nothing but time, pursuing the anomalies became the majority of how I decorated my hours. I would keep the baby on my hip when I could stand to hold her—or when looking at her made my heart hurt too deeply, I would lay her down in the crib Evelyn had built and sit on the floor beside it with my notes spread out around me. There with a little stuffed star in the crib for company, and the baby would flail her fists and coo to herself as I pored over text after journal after cross-referenced pile of notes.

She was a good baby. She only cried about half the time.

Scattered stacks of journals I ordered from academic presses filled the corner of the main room I'd made into my own. Ed's daughter mailed me several boxes of his books. Sheafs of paper sporting the NASA letterhead burst from stacks of my smuggled file folders, with old notes and coordinate calculations still made from Norm's hand in the margins of the pages.

Norm's stopped watch was a comfortable weight on my wrist as I pored over page after page of Aion transcripts and tried to puzzle out some rhyme or reason to where another anomaly might crop up.

Evelyn distrusted my fixation but kept judiciously quiet about it for the most part. As I struggled to understand how motherhood fit itself around me, she lived with patience and filled in my gaps. She took over looking after the baby when I couldn't handle the colic that sheared my heart like the slow pass of a razor.

"I'm going to ruin her," I moaned one night after feeding the baby for the third time in four hours. Evelyn rubbed my back in soothing circles.

"You're not going to ruin her, Red."

"How do you know?"

"Because you love her."

"I can't quit *worrying* about her. I don't know if I love her."

I flopped my face sideways to frown at Evelyn. She smirked at me. I frowned harder. "That's love," she insisted, and kissed me until I couldn't remember why I was upset in the first place.

Pockets of peace found us happy, through her efforts. We would sprawl out on the rug in the sitting room with the baby between us, babbling joyful nonsense and playing with her toes. One night, she had Evelyn's finger wrapped hard in one fierce fist as she stared at me with her green, green eyes. I wondered what she thought of me, this creature who bore her into the wide and cosmic joke of living. I wondered if she already loved me.

"She needs a name," Evelyn murmured. "Can't just call her 'baby' forever."

I hummed, noncommittal. "I'll figure something out. I can't think of anything that fits."

I'd called her Jane on the birth certificate at the hospital, simply because they wouldn't let us go home without signing it—there was no rain check for Social Security. At least I'd held up the matrilineal tradition: her middle name was Anne.

I found not affection in me when I looked at my daughter but a hollow sense of obligation. I was now bound to someone more permanently than even marriage had done, and if I didn't feel outright annoyance when taking care of her kept me from my research, there was always a slow simmer of regret.

But what could I regret? Having the child in the first place? The baby was not a mistake; that I knew like the thump of my own heartbeat. I would protect her with my own life twelve times over. But there was no way to make the room for her that she deserved with that sealed box still taking up every spare space in me. I didn't know what I was going to do.

I found that answer late one night in early summer, bent in half over my notes.

The hypothesis about precise gaps between quasars causing dimensional holes had become my fully fledged theory. The gaps shifted with the lunar cycles; those same properties of gravity that guided ocean tides would push and pull the temporal output from an entrance in the present. An anomaly that might have taken a passenger twenty years into the past at the beginning of the month might only have led to five years ago by the end of it.

It was a cycle—ebb and flow, stretch and give. Time was not a fixed line, where something discarded from the present was gone forever. It was imperfectly cyclical. An ellipse.

I still had no evidence for how the anomaly at the Center had its other mouth at the Apodaca house, but I could draw conclusions as to why. I cross-referenced distances and altitudes and average air pressures. I combed news reports of disappearances, strange happenings, declassified sightings, and interviews from all over the country. But even with a few too-sharp coincidences pinpointed, nothing gave me more insight than calculating the periodic orbital placement of the moon.

She pulled, and time pushed. It was right there.

My pulse was heavy in my ears as I calculated the angle of that night's moon. I triple-checked the coordinates of the Cenizo house, which were pinned to the wall above my desk for quick reference.

The baby began to cry in her crib, tight little fussing sounds from behind the bedroom door, where Evelyn had gone to sleep ahead of me.

Another anomaly waited ten miles east, to the decimal, of exactly where I was sitting.

If I didn't seize the chance now, it could disappear. The mouth might have moved, this edge of the lattice pulled somehow by some variable I hadn't yet thought to chase down. It was now, or a what-if forever.

I snatched up the map and Norm's watch. Evelyn's fluffy blue robe was hanging on the back of the sofa, and I threw it around my shoulders as I hurried to the door. I scrawled a hasty note, which I wedged in the jamb: *Out. Back soon. —A.*

If I was wrong, I would be there and back in half an hour with my tail between my legs. If I was right, I'd only be six minutes more.

I grabbed the keys to the truck, jogged down the lane to hoist myself into the front seat, and revved the engine to life over the still of the night like a bird bursting from a bush.

As I hurtled down the highway, apprehension sang through me. I was on the cusp of time, and it was all that mattered—not myself, not Evelyn, not even my daughter.

The moon was ready to show me something, and she would not wait.

◆　◆　◆

By the time I stopped a long way off the road, glancing down periodically and squinting at the positioner unit Evelyn had helped me mount on the dashboard a few months back so I could track coordinates, the dump of adrenaline had evened into static behind my eyes. The desert was still, its silence broken only by the distant *skrush*ing of cars along the highway far, far against the hills.

I left the truck idling with its headlights on. In the middle of the twin cones of light sat an anomaly space. I knew it immediately like an old friend, a gap in the roadside brush, and got out to stand beside it and feel the pull again.

A perfect ring of absolutely nothing sat silently on the dirt, about a foot across. Insects playing in a wide radius, flitting barely there through the headlight shafts, seemed to avoid it on instinct.

My hands were shaking. I gripped Norm's watch until the edges dug into my palms. I couldn't tell what scared me more—the fact I knew I was going to go through, or the fact I wasn't afraid of going.

What was there to see, or touch, or even find on the other end of time? What would I risk ruining with my meddling, my trespassing? Reason banged its fists against impenetrable glass through which I could hear it railing, but I refused to listen. A righteous compulsion rattled at my throat like chains against the ground.

I didn't even think before I stepped into the space. By the time my second foot met the dirt, I was flying.

Immense motion slid past me. Air rushed at my ears in a silent slipstream of phantom sensation. I stayed fixed to one place, or at least it *felt* as though I stayed fixed to one place. I should have been afraid. White and blue spangled over my vision, a madness of light thrown in long lances like the sun filtering through billowing sheets hung out to dry. Memories dragged and combed against the crags of my brain, all of them at once; eternity pulled at the fine hairs on my arms and the back of my neck, every moment compounded down into a single breath.

Amniotic suspension propelled this strange, sideways-rightways-allways hurtling. Reality bent around me, ahead of me, and behind me in two fish-eye spirals like water sluicing away down a drain.

This was it. The mouth of the other end rose up before me. The orb of it swelled in a hyperspherical warp, flattening like a shivering raindrop caught on a windshield; wider, wider, wider still, and then—

A head rush pitched through me and made me swoon. I managed not to stumble, squeezed my eyes shut—and held myself very still as it stopped at once.

Ground beneath my feet. Atmosphere in the air. I took a deep lungful of it and tasted sweet mountain springtime.

When I opened my eyes, I was in the garden.

The backyard was empty, but not with disrepair or the hollowness that had met me when I had cleared it out ten years ago. The Apodaca house was brand-new: the soil hadn't yet been packed into the beds; the ivies were only just starting to crawl, whiplike and young; the porch furniture was nowhere to be found, perhaps not yet even purchased. The slice of the den I could see through the glass sliding door was sparse, un-lived-in, and my heart leapt in my chest to guess at the when of it all. Did anyone live here yet? Had my parents even moved in?

As I turned to the bare wall behind me that would soon be a backstop to riotous roses, I felt a frantic ticking in my fist and peeled open my fingers.

Norm's watch had begun running. The second hand chipped its way along the face, *tiktiktiktik*, as though it had never quit to begin with.

From the moon, I heard Norman musing from somewhere deep at the back of my mind. *That would sure be something, wouldn't it?*

My chest vised hard and made me stagger back as my pulse kicked up several notches at once. I had seen him there. I'd met him, as a girl. I had—his face swam up from the back of my mind like a head-on collision, his visor open and his face tipped up to the blue, blue sky; so wondrous, and I had—I—

I slouched back against the wall and pressed my hand to my sternum as my breath went tight. From deep inside me the box gave a great lurching, as though time itself had finally gotten its fingers around the lid and *pulled*.

In one great rush, my very seams tore as one.

I remembered everything.

Every afternoon I spent here as a girl returned to me in wild scraps—curiosity, comfort, happiness; and then from another angle, time folding in on itself, I saw the flip side of it: the emptiness, the solitude, the harrowing persistence of guilt.

It was messy, it was terrifying, it was red, red, red—unstoppable. *It sticks to everything it touches. You can never wash it away*, my father's soft voice rattled like a shout through my body.

I saw him dead, sprawled across his desk. I saw him smoothing my hair back from my head as he smiled at me over the kitchen table. I saw him.

I *saw* him.

It wasn't unhappiness that had killed him but *guilt*, and in running from what I hadn't understood I had accidentally closed the loop and done the same.

I was him and he was me. If I couldn't keep from losing myself in my own work—the man I had enchanted and loved and then killed, the answers left obscured, the potential of Aion dead in the water—I would succumb and my daughter would be doomed to the same cycle.

My *daughter.*

I was flirting with my own demise. If the anomalies held more sway over my heart than my own child, I could never give her what she deserved. I was plagued to run the same circles I tried so hard to evade, a wormhole of my own making feeding pain back into itself.

My obsession, my fixation, was too large to control. I had to let my daughter decide what she needed me to be.

I had to trust her. I had to trust that I could love her. I had to let her—

The door to the den slid open. I gasped and scrambled behind the bend in the wall, and from behind the brick I strained my ears to listen. I looked down at the watch—one minute remained.

A low humming floated from the middle of the empty yard, a warm song without words. The root of my brain lit up with comfort at the tune I had forgotten. I listened for a precious handful of seconds.

My mother was singing a lullaby.

I stole a glance around the corner of the wall. Cradled in her arms, smiling up at her just as brightly as Mother was smiling back down, was a baby swaddled and happy. Me.

My mother wore a contented ease so unguarded that I hardly recognized her. Youth shone from her every edge while she bounced me softly in place, singing to me and looking at me like I'd helped hang the moon itself.

I looked down at the watch—twenty seconds.

Seizing time by its neck, greedy to be seen, I stepped out from around the wall and re-placed myself on the anomaly spot.

"Helen," I said clearly.

My mother looked up, shocked, clutching my infant self to her chest. Her eyes met mine with a clash of selfsame blue, sharp and protective.

"Who . . . ?" she asked, but the question died in her throat as she stared. Against her shoulder, I made a fussy sound of curiosity. She loosened her grip ever so slightly. The light behind her pupils flared; the cogs of her mind at work.

Something very deep inside her pushed at dawning recognition against reality; I could see it. I swallowed and counted the seconds ticking down against the meat of my palm — *ten, nine, eight . . .*

"I miss you so much," I said, my throat breaking around the words. "None of this was your fault."

Three. Two.

One.

And passage whisked me away again.

The desert rushed back up to meet me. I gasped as my knees gave out and I fell to the dirt, scrambling away from the clearing. When I was far enough away that I didn't see the shape of Norm in a heap on the Center floor, I flopped onto my back and stared up at the sky.

What lingered in me was not a pin in my gut or the horror of regret. My inner ear rang with love, the lullaby, the sound of the past reaching into my future with long fingers that begged and begged and begged to be touched.

My mother had seen me for what I would become, for better or for worse.

None of this was your fault, I heard her murmur on the cemetery road; in the den that night the summer before I left for good.

So she would remember. She would recognize me. And that would have to be enough — far better late than never.

Lights danced in strange, boozy whorls at the lip of the horizon where the stars gave way to the mountains. *God*, how risky. How awful. How fucking terrible would it have been if I couldn't get back through?

I watched the lights and let a disbelieving chuckle burble up from my depths. It swelled, building and building until I was laughing breathlessly at the sky.

I took a moment to collect myself. For several long minutes, I stared at the anomaly in the pour of my headlights. I couldn't tell for how long exactly. The watch had stopped again.

I had time. For once in my life, I finally believed that I had time.

✦   ✦   ✦

The porch light was on when I coasted into the driveway. Evelyn slipped out onto the steps with the baby sleeping heavily in one arm as I came around the bed of the truck and loped up to her, my mind running at six-speed.

"I found your note. Where were you?" Evelyn whispered. The baby snuffled dreamily against her shoulder, the picture of peace—I took Evelyn by both sides of the face and kissed her, greeting and apology at once. She stared at me when I pulled back.

"Out," I said, half breathless. We juggled the baby carefully into my arms. I kissed Evelyn again. "I have a name for her."

Evelyn's eyebrows went up. "You went looking for a name in the middle of nowhere at two in the morning?"

I loved her. I loved both of them: Evelyn Florence Moore, and this helpless little thing in my arms. I wanted to shout it to the endless sprawl of the desert.

I cradled the baby to my chest as my mother had done all those years ago, inhaling the soft smell of her. I pressed my lips to the crown of her head and nodded. "Diana."

Evelyn made a soft sound before reaching out to smooth the flax-floss hair on the top of Diana's head. Her cheek against my chest was smushing her face a little bit. The edge of her button nose bent gently sideways, her mouth gently suckling in her sleep.

"Diana. I like it."

"So do I."

My last missing piece finally flew home to roost. It nested easily in the wreckage of the box deep inside of me that would never close again, its hinges cracked open and overflowing with memories.

1978—ROUTE 90, APPROACHING
THE MARFA ANOMALY
West Texas

It was Diana's eighth birthday, and I had promised her something amazing.

I had finally brought the Marfa anomaly into the light after years of searching, testing, digging, and an ever-rotating battery of hypotheses. Evelyn kept telling me I should submit my findings somewhere, but who would take them seriously? The Houston anomaly had bitten NASA's hand already, and I had no intention of being laughed out of every other scientific authority in the country. The knowledge was mine to keep as I saw fit until it was time to pass it all on, my best and only heirloom.

Diana grew into a carbon copy of Norm. She had only the barest touches of my complexion, her father's template through and through—his dimpled chin, his tall nose, the way she crinkled her eyebrows when she was baffled by something. She was brilliant. The only piece I could claim was her dogged curiosity.

Her interest in what Mama was doing with her numbers and her maps and the sheets and sheets of calculations deepened with every passing year. When she was five years old, she came along with Evelyn for the first time to watch me test the anomaly out past Route 90.

"Mama," she said, resolute as her father, looking up at me with her cheeks flushed pink and her little jaw set, "can people do that, too?"

My heart soared. I hadn't gone through again. Once was enough. I had closed my loop, but Diana's was only just beginning.

I shared a look with Evelyn, and she nodded.

"Someday," I promised, smoothing flyaway hairs back from her face.

I watched my daughter grow and shift into the rangy bundle of imagination and energy I so dearly loved, and soon the day came that she matched the memories I could finally recall—the good mingled in my head with the bad, as it always should have been. Evelyn knew how to take care of me when the bads sometimes got a little heavy, and I was slowly learning how to weather those days alongside her.

That empty box hung around in my depths like nothing but decoration anymore, not unlike one of the glittering scrap sculptures on the porch—Keller sent a few each year, his experiments with new welding and twisting techniques, accompanied by letters or postcards from all the places he and Fede caroused around the world to see.

I tended Diana's hunger for knowledge and waited until I was sure it was exactly the right time.

She picked her favorite clothes that morning and told Evelyn how she wanted her hair done after we ate birthday pancakes. My heart was fit to burst as I watched her become the girl whose friendship had sustained me when loneliness was all I knew. I thought of my mother with her newborn in the garden; I thought of the precocious little Annie who would see herself so thoroughly in her own child.

"Evie says you're a genius, Mom," Diana announced from the passenger's seat of the truck as we trundled down the highway, her chin lifted to see over the dash. She had started calling me *Mom* instead of *Mama* earlier that year. Evelyn thought it was a hoot.

Diana had a protective hand laid over my book of notes on the bench seat, with my stopwatch tied to its spiral spine. Her own little cocktail bracelet watch ticked away with its bright-red second hand on her wrist, a birthday gift from Evelyn.

"Does she?" I hummed. Diana nodded in my periphery.

"What does that mean?" she asked. I glanced at her, meeting her inquisitive stare through the glasses she'd been prescribed two years back.

"It means I don't let normal tell me who's boss," I said, and when she grinned at me, I found traces of Norm doing the same in her puckish face.

Diana led the way to where she knew the inlet waited, the gap on the ground that she called *the 'nomaly*. "Hurry up!" she called back to me. I rested a hand on her head when I reached her and ruffled her hair, just a little.

"I'm right here, jellybean." I knelt down and met her eyes, level and serious. "Now tell me what you'll do to go there and come back."

Diana took a deep breath and ticked off each rule on her little fingers: "Cross my arms over my chest and don't let go until the air stops swimming. Make sure I stay in one place in the garden when I get there. Never go inside the house, don't talk to the grown-ups, and when the minute hand is almost counted to six, get ready to leave again."

"Very good," I said. "And what do you say if someone asks where you came from?"

"I'm from very far away, just visiting."

I nodded at her and kissed her on the forehead. "Perfect."

I led her to the edge of the anomaly space, her hand held tight in mine. "Ready?" I asked. She nodded once—beside her I imagined a shimmering vision of Norm in his spacesuit, ready for the journey of his lifetime.

I stared my own fear straight down its endless event horizon and let go of Diana's hand.

"Go ahead," I said, my voice thick. I couldn't watch her go as the air warped and made me blink.

When I opened my eyes again to find her gone, I started the stopwatch.

I remembered what it had been like to see her there in the backyard, a friend when I had needed one most. I swiped away the tears from my lashes and drew a deep breath with my entire body for what felt like the first time in years.

The anomalies gave and the anomalies took, but ultimately I had spurred the unexpected itself to bend against its own horizon and finally turn back to nuzzle at my hand with something like tenderness.

The desert breeze kissed me softly at every edge as the stopwatch churned along. I shut my eyes. "Thank you," I whispered to the emptiness, and time combed its fingers through my hair in sweet response.

The stopwatch reached its tail end—*seven, six, five, four, three, two, one.*

My daughter stood before me with wonder in her eyes.

"I did it!" she cried, rushing at me as I knelt with my arms open and gathered her into a tight hug. The lump in my throat gave way to tears as I held her close, smelling the faintest trace of roses.

"I'm so proud of you, baby," I said when I pulled back to kiss her noisily on the cheek. "I missed you."

"*Missed* me?" Diana squirmed and giggled. "It was only six minutes, that's what you always say."

"Oh, it feels different when you're older." I sniffled and dabbed at the corners of my eyes with the shoulder of my T-shirt.

A furrow leapt up between Diana's eyebrows. "Are you sad?"

I shook my head and smoothed her hair back from her forehead before running a thumb down the plaited ridge of one of her braids. I had been so enchanted by her hair as a kid. "I'm happy," I said, "these are good tears."

Assuaged, Diana opened her little fist to me. "Look what I got," she whispered ineffectually, as though her gift could spook and break apart.

My heart soared to see the spring-new pink rose waiting there in Diana's palm. I took it up gingerly and turned it by the stem to examine every little petal of this delicate passenger across time and space.

"I met a girl," Diana said, her voice conspiratorial. She was wide eyed when I looked up at her again. "She was dressed a little funny, and she said her name was Annie, just like you."

I smiled. "Was she fun?"

"I want to go back and play again!" Diana cried as excitement finally got the best of her and she jumped in place just to vent it. I chuckled and brushed away the last of my tears clinging to my lashes.

"Later," I promised her. I sniffed and nodded at her. "But now we should go home and tell Evie."

"Evie should come, too! And you!" Diana cried as I took her hand again and began leading her back to the truck.

"Oh, no," I said, "the anomaly is yours now. Evie has lots of other stuff to do, and I've already visited."

"You have?"

Diana fixed me with an awestruck look when I lifted her into the passenger's seat and set my notes on the seat beside her. Again I saw Norm in her insistence, her boldness, her unflagging brilliance.

"It's a special place, and you've got a friend there now." I swooped a finger against the tip of her nose, the way I had since she was just a baby. "A reason to keep visiting."

Diana swelled with pride and importance. "Can we get ice cream?" she asked. I kissed her again on one round cheek.

"Of course we can, jellybean."

The plastic plant with its parabolic bisection of time-teeth jiggled a little from its place tacked to the dashboard as I swung into the driver's seat. I keyed the rumbling engine. The photo of Norm in the power racks clipped to the inside of the sun visor smiled down on us.

As we pulled back onto the highway, I watched the anomaly shrink away in my rearview. Unassuming, empty, quiet as the desert around it, the past would no longer take from me. It would give and give and give, buoying us onward into our future.

Acknowledgments

---　✳　---

I wrote the first version of this book in somewhat of a fugue state in about a month. In that very early version, it centered around letters addressed to Galileo (things have, of course, changed since then). There is no entirely perfect time at which to write a book, but something out there helped ensure the bones of this story were birthed intact. It may be backward to invoke the muse *after* the story is over, but let's call it modern practice: to whomever you are guiding me from your silver screen at the back of my mind, thank you.

My agent, Chris Bucci, has had an unkillable passion for my stories from our first meeting, and I can never thank him enough for how deeply he believes in me (but here's me trying—thank you!!!!!). To the editorial powerhouse of the brilliant Kate Dresser and Tarini Sipahimalani, to Sally Kim, and to the rest of my publication team at Putnam: your confidence and guidance have been world-class. Working with you has been a gift and one hell of a bright spot the whole way through. Thank you for everything.

Acknowledgments

To Suzanne Ohlmann for your wisdom; to Rose Sutherland, Janna Noelle, and Katie Crabb for your time (ha!), authorly thoughts, and balmy levity; and to my Cantina crew: thank you for everything. Thank you as well to everyone who has shared very kind words about Annie's journey, and the things I have hopefully succeeded in saying with it.

I would be remiss not to recognize Dr. Maurice Wright, Dr. Adam Vidiksis, and Dr. Steven Kreinberg in their direct responsibility for making me fall in love with the language of computers, the music they can make, and the person I can be when I just keep looking. Your lessons persist in every word I write, even if I'm not always singing them.

I have mined and plumbed a mountain of transcripts and transmissions from the NASA archives to ensure I've presented the organization and their projects here as accurately as possible and with all due respect. To the archivists and organizers keeping those databases running, thank you for your care over the history behind us.

To my family, who has always been there: Karen and Rolf, Kristina, Diane and Larry, Amy and Rome, and Leslie and Sandy—thank you for loving me and giving me the space to dream. I love you more than there are words to say, all the way up to the moon and back. And to Luke: thank you for believing I could do it, and all your years of support.

Thank you to the artists whose work sat with me as this book came to life, particularly Jessica Pratt, Linda Perhacs, and Amos Roddy for the music; E. K. Weaver for the lessons on love in the mundane, as well as the touchstone "ain't no sorry"; Kathe Koja for the early encouragement and the aplomb with which you blur the borders of fiction; and Anne Carson for the peace amid the noise.

And finally to you, my readers, you travelers through this grand and twisting wormhole of life: thank you for picking up this book, for taking the hand of a girl with fear in her chest, and trusting that I would let her be okay. Thank you for your attention, your care, and your support. I'll find you in the next one :)